THE MAIN SUSPECT

"There's something obviously still bothering you. You've laid out lots of theories, but you don't sound convinced about any of them. From what you've said, besides Grace, you've got lots of possible suspects for Harlan and Chief Gerard to look at. Right?"

"In a sense." Sarah held up her fingers as she ticked them off. "They should consider anyone who was on the floor when Grace and I got there. That would be Wanda, Franklin, Chef Bernardi, Fern, Nancy, Dr. Williams, and the people who waited to be interviewed in their offices who I don't even know. The same holds true on the tenure issue, because most of the faculty is working its way toward tenure."

Sarah put her hands back on the table. "I don't think I have enough fingers to count everyone. When I add in family, there's Wanda, but also Wanda's biological mom, Dr. Martin's new wife, Lynn, and Kait. There might also be someone at the retirement home who has a connection to Dr. Martin that I haven't discovered yet. Someone mentioned that because of Kait, they considered Dr. Martin to be part of the Sunshine Retirement Home family."

"That's a long list of potential suspects. Surely Harlan can find enough motivation for most of them to raise doubt if Grace is arrested or tried. What's really bothering you? What's going on in your head?"

"I have to admit that if I were Chief Gerard and I was committed to following the money and the blood, Grace would be my primary suspect too . . ."

Books by Debra H. Goldstein

ONE TASTE TOO MANY

TWO BITES TOO MANY

THREE TREATS TOO MANY

FOUR CUTS TOO MANY

Published by Kensington Publishing Corp.

FOUR CUTS TOO MANY

Debra H. Goldstein

www.kensingtonbooks.com

KENSINGTON BOOKS are published by

Kensington Publishing Corp.
119 West 40th Street
New York, NY 10018

First Printing: June 2021
ISBN-13: 978-1-4967-3221-7
ISBN-10: 1-4967-3221-9

ISBN-13: 978-1-4967-3222-4 (ebook)
ISBN-10: 1-4967-3222-7 (ebook)

10 9 8 7 6 5 4 3 2 1

Printed in the United States of America

In memory of April Autrey Deal
In appreciation of Fran Godchaux

Acknowledgments

A random sentence or phrase is usually the springboard for my writing. Sometimes, words don't flow. For weeks, although I knew what *Four Cuts Too Many* was going to be about, I couldn't find my way into the book. Frustrated, I looked forward to a long-planned beach weekend with two friends, April Deal and Fran Godchaux.

People debate beach or mountains, but the beach is my haven. Looking at water relaxes me. Many of my best writings were done at the beach. I was positive once we arrived, I'd find my magic sentence.

I didn't.

Two days into the weekend, I was still staring at sand, white capped waves, and a blank page. April joined me on the condo's balcony and, as we watched a beautiful sundown, we began to talk about the knives, cooking, and murders my protagonist, Sarah Blair, would encounter. When April laughingly mentioned a rhyme that she'd jumped rope to as a child, "Went upstairs to get my knife. Made a mistake and stabbed my wife," I had my opening.

The remainder of the weekend was perfect. My writing went well, and April, Fran, and I walked, laughed, ate, and relaxed. Two weeks after we returned home, April unexpectantly died. This book, which she helped trigger into being, is dedicated to her memory.

The other dedication is to Fran Godchaux in appreciation for her always being there. At different times, she's been my sounding board, beta reader, proofreader, sister from another mother, and true friend. A dedication can't nearly express my appreciation and gratitude, so I repeat it here.

There are several other people I must acknowledge for helping make *Four Cuts Too Many* more than an initial rhyme. Susan Mason helped me understand various knives and cuts and was kind enough to refrain from chuckling at my lack of culinary knowledge. Lee Godchaux was a master beta reader. Barb Goffman and Lourdes Venard read and edited early versions—pointing out the holes and inconsistencies I needed to address. My agent, Dawn Dowdle, once again helped make *Four Cuts Too Many* a better book. My sincere thanks to each of them.

Finally, a nod and hug for my husband, Joel, who, during the stay-at-home stage of the pandemic, put up with my cooking and the time I devoted to Sarah's adventures.

CHAPTER 1

Went upstairs to get my knife. Made a mistake and stabbed my wife. Sarah Blair hadn't thought about that horribly worded jump rope rhyme in twenty years. What was worse, she realized, was that most of the jumping rhymes her mother taught Sarah and her twin sister, Emily, had been violent. Sarah doubted the idea of sending children out to play in rhythm to Lizzie Borden's axe and whacks would be considered politically correct today, but landing on them at the right moment certainly was fun then.

As she waited on the wood bench in front of Carleton Junior Community College's culinary arts building for Grace Winston to finish teaching her knife skills class, Sarah let her mind wander to some of the other rhymes and scary fairy tales her mother read the twins. It was better exercise than repeatedly checking the time.

Sarah wished Grace would hurry. She sent her a quick text and waited. Benches hewn from oak trees might be interesting to the eye, but this one certainly wasn't comfortable. Plus, she was getting hot from sitting outside in the bright sun for the twenty minutes since Grace's class should have ended.

Still no message on her phone. She leaned against the back of the bench, trying to find a comfortable spot. When Grace, Chef Emily's sous-chef, announced to Emily and Sarah she'd been hired as an adjunct by CJCC to teach a knife skills class, Sarah hadn't believed her. Considering Sarah's knife drawer was filled with the black plastic ones that came with her takeout dinners, she couldn't fathom there were enough knives and cutting methods for a semester-long class.

Scoffing at her ignorance, Emily and Grace had taken Sarah into the Southwind Pub's kitchen and enlightened her on the art of the knife by deftly demonstrating various cuts. By the time they finished, Sarah still couldn't tell the difference between dicing, mincing, or cuts with fancy names like julienne, *brunoise*, or chiffonade, but she'd been properly impressed by their knife skills. It gave Sarah a better idea of how they used them when preparing food at the two restaurants, Southwind and the Southwind Pub, Emily and her boyfriend, Chef Marcus, co-owned.

She wondered if Grace had changed her mind about their meeting. She hoped not. After all, Sarah was here now, instead of at work, because of Grace's urgent whisper to her yesterday during a celebration held at the white-tableclothed Southwind restaurant. "Please, can we meet tomorrow somewhere away from the restaurants to talk?"

Sarah had quickly agreed for two reasons. First, it

seemed that whatever Grace wanted to talk about was important, but secretive, because Grace obviously wanted to ensure Emily and Marcus didn't hear what she had to say. Apparently, Grace didn't equate Sarah as being an equal partner in Southwind because her interest was only tied to the building's ownership.

The other reason, which she knew Grace was unaware of, was that during yesterday's celebration, Sarah saw Grace slip out of Southwind's front door, cross Main Street, and walk up the sidewalk to Jane's Place. Sarah's antenna for trouble had instantly shot up. Not only was Jane's Place Southwind's chief competitor in Wheaton, Alabama, but its scheming owner, Jane Clark, was Sarah and Emily's biggest nemesis, personally and professionally.

Where was Grace?

Hopefully Grace was okay and simply hadn't seen Sarah's text. Sarah stared at the building's front door, wishing Grace to come through it. Nothing. Apparently, wishing couldn't speed up her future any more than Sarah could change her past.

Almost two years ago, at age twenty-eight, instead of marking her tenth anniversary, Sarah got divorced because Jane, or "the bimbo" as Sarah preferred to refer to her, broke up Sarah's marriage to Bill Blair. Surprised and shattered, Sarah began a receptionist/secretarial job in Harlan Endicott's law firm and regrouped with the only thing she got out of the divorce: RahRah, her Siamese cat. Now, feeling more secure and because Harlan had prodded her, she'd recently begun thinking about her future.

Although Sarah wasn't ready to give up her daytime job, nor did she know what she exactly wanted to study, she'd decided to go after the college degree she'd turned away from to marry Bill. She thought a night class or two at the community college would be an easy way to shake off the rust she'd gathered by not being a student since her high school graduation. Sarah decided to give Grace five more minutes before running by the admissions office to pick up a current class catalog before she went to work.

"Hey, Sarah!"

Sarah raised her head and looked in the direction her name was being shouted from. Grace was bounding down the building's front steps.

Stopping in front of Sarah, Grace struggled to catch her breath. "I'm so glad you're still here. I was afraid you were going to leave!"

Sarah stared at her. Grace was a mess. Unlike how everything about Grace was usually crisp and clean, random strands of her curled Afro escaped from her hairnet, and she'd traded her standard impeccably white chef's jacket for a red-and-white–speckled apron. Looking more closely at the apron, it dawned on Sarah its red stains didn't follow a pattern. They were random dots and splotches.

"You're covered in blood!"

Grace looked at the places on her apron where Sarah pointed but didn't say anything.

Not sure why Grace wasn't answering her, Sarah prodded her. "Are you okay?"

"Oh, a knife went awry this morning. I somehow cut myself." Grace held up her hand so Sarah could see it was bandaged.

The center of the clumsy bandage was darkening. "Grace, you're bleeding!"

Grace stared at her hand, as if seeing it for the first time. "I thought it had stopped."

"Apparently not." Avoiding the arm with the bandaged hand, Sarah grabbed Grace's other arm. As she pulled Grace onto the bench, she scanned the arm she held to make sure that none of the color or lines associated with Grace's farm-to-table sleeve tattoo were from another wound. They weren't.

Sarah picked up her purse and rummaged in it until she pulled out two large Band-Aids. "Hold out your hand, palm up."

While Grace simply stared at her weeping hand, Sarah tore open the Band-Aids and repeated her command.

This time, Grace obeyed.

Sarah bent over Grace's hand and carefully criss-crossed the two Band-Aids to cover the existing bandage. Finished, she shoved the discarded bandage backings into the pocket of her pants. "Keep pressure on your palm. Hopefully, that will stop the bleeding."

Grace kept her face turned toward her hand but didn't immediately move. Finally, she placed her good hand over the injured one and pressed against the bandage.

"Grace, what happened?"

Without letting go of her hand, Grace met Sarah's gaze. "Dr. Douglas Martin. He's what happened."

"Who's Dr. Douglas Martin? And why did he cut your hand?"

Grace blinked and again glanced at her hand. "Dr. Martin didn't cut my hand. I did. He made me do it."

"How?"

Grace wasn't the type of person who'd hurt herself because someone told her to. There had to be more to this story.

"Dr. Martin is the new interim chairman of the culinary program. If it gives you a better idea about him,

Malevolent Monster is what the faculty calls him behind his back. He's known for surprise visits and scathing critiques. This morning, he made one of his unexpected visits to my classroom. He shook my students and me up so much, my hand got sliced."

Knowing she'd get the rest of the details in a moment, Sarah honed in on Dr. Martin's nickname. "Malevolent Monster?"

"Yes. Some people think he's evil."

"Why?" Evil wasn't a word Sarah imagined was used often in a college setting to describe a member of the faculty, especially one in a management position. In Sarah's mind, calling someone evil was quite a pronouncement.

Instead of answering, Grace checked her bandage as she eased off from applying pressure to her hand. Apparently satisfied with whatever she saw, she looked at Sarah. "Like I said, he enjoys making surprise visits."

Sarah tilted her body to be closer to Grace. "How does that make him evil? Don't most department chairs visit classrooms?"

"They do, but remember Dr. Martin is only the interim chairman. The hospitality chairman, Dr. Williams, and other faculty members who evaluate or give teachers constructive criticism do it in a gentle manner. That's not Dr. Martin's style. He consistently makes scenes or rides roughshod over staff and students."

"And he visited your classroom today?"

"Yes, to my surprise. I figured, because I'm only an adjunct, he'd ignore me or wouldn't drop into my classroom until later in the term." Grace again turned her attention to her bandage. She picked at the side of one of Sarah's added bandage strips, where it was curling up.

Watching her, Sarah wished Grace would leave her

hand alone. Sarah was relieved to see the stain no longer was spreading. "From what you're saying, I don't understand why you and the other faculty members think he's evil."

"It's because of the deliberate state of turmoil he's creating. Teachers and students don't know what to expect, except that someone or all of them are going to be humiliated. That's why they've nicknamed him the Malevolent Monster."

Sarah sat back, reflecting on Grace's comments. "Sounds like he's into control and power plays."

"Exactly. He's the culinary program's interim chair, but he makes no bones that he is the heir anointed to move up the food chain as the college expands the culinary and hospitality programs into a full-fledged department. He's making everyone in his area jump through hoops for fear he won't bring them along with him."

Sarah furrowed her brow as she pointed at Grace's bandaged hand. "But your main job is at Southwind. This is only a side gig. Why would you let him bother you so much that you cut yourself?"

Grace peered to the sides and behind the bench before bending toward Sarah. In a low voice, she hurriedly said, "I was distracted when the Malevolent Monster went after one of my students. His behavior to the student was uncalled for."

Sarah crossed her arms and made herself give Grace time to continue her story. She knew mere distraction wouldn't have resulted in a cut like this one.

"You remember how Emily and I explained to you that my knife skills class is an introductory course that covers all types of knives and possible knife cuts?"

Sarah nodded.

"Most of my students are in a culinary-related degree program, but I also have a lot of students who are majoring in non-culinary topics."

Sarah knew she would never sign up for a knives class. It would be the last elective she'd ever consider. "Why would a non-culinary student take a course about knives?"

"A few think it will be an easy class that fits into their schedules. Two told me they are in the criminal justice program and believe it will help in their future work to understand the ins and outs of knives."

Sarah muffled a chuckle. "Sounds like they want to know where to put a knife in and out of."

Grace didn't react to Sarah's corny joke. "Anyway, because this was just the second class of the semester, I was giving an overview of the different knives we'll be using by holding up a knife, having different students identify the type of knife it is, and then having that student help me demonstrate its use by cutting up different types of cheese."

"That sounds fairly simple."

"It was an easy lesson plan until Dr. Martin interrupted my class just after I'd called one of my students, Franklin, to the front of the room. Before I could say anything, Dr. Martin faced off in front of Franklin, grabbed two knives, waved them in the air, and asked him which one Franklin thought could do more damage."

"Wasn't it obvious?"

"Not to Franklin. He's one of those criminal justice kids I mentioned. I'm convinced he really signed up because of a girl. He's made sure to sit at the same prep table with her both times. Anyway, when Dr. Martin held up a small deboning knife and a giant bread slicing knife,

Franklin stared at them for so long you could almost feel the other students praying the correct answer to him."

"Did he pick the right knife?"

"Of course not. He went with size and picked the bread knife. The class let out a collective sigh as Dr. Martin dramatically thrust the diminutive knife, one strong enough to separate meat from bones, toward him. I doubt Dr. Martin's jab would have reached him, but Franklin got rattled and instinctively reached for the blade of the knife as it came toward him."

"Not a good idea?"

"Not by a long shot. Deboning knives may be slim and small, but they're super-sharp. Knowing exactly how wicked that kind of knife is, I put my hand out to prevent Franklin from grabbing the blade. I knocked his arm hard enough to keep him from touching the blade, but I caused Franklin to bump into Dr. Martin's outstretched hand. Dr. Martin lost his grip on the knife and it flew up in the air."

"And you caught the knife?"

Grace shook her head. "No. That wouldn't have been smart. I was just hoping it wouldn't hit any of us. When it clanked on the floor, I thought we'd been lucky. Apparently, though, it hit me. The blade was so sharp it sliced my hand quickly and deeply before I felt any pain or saw blood."

"Now I understand why you said Dr. Martin was the one at fault."

Grace grimaced and raised her hand. "He didn't even acknowledge I was hurt. He was too busy screaming."

"At the student or you?"

Grace made a face and tilted her head away from Sarah. "At the situation. When my hand deflected the knife's fall, the blade nicked Dr. Martin."

Imagining the scene in her mind, Sarah tried not to laugh but couldn't contain herself. It seemed like a comedy of errors that would make a good TV farce. In between giggles, she managed to say, "The case of the rogue knife?" As her mind raced through more possible titles, Sarah lost it again. When she got control of herself, she asked if he'd been injured badly too.

Grace held up her good hand, as if to motion Sarah to stop, but gave up and began laughing too. "He was barely cut, but you wouldn't have known it from the way he carried on. Apparently, the drop of his spilled blood fanned his anger at Franklin even more."

Swallowing, Sarah stopped laughing. "That's terrible."

"It was. Dr. Martin dabbed his arm with the first thing he could reach, while he continued screaming viciously at Franklin, who was apologizing profusely. In the meantime, because my hand was now bleeding so freely, some of the other students were helping me."

"What about Dr. Martin? Surely, by then, he could see you needed medical attention?"

"I have no idea if Dr. Martin noticed my hand or the students helping me. Either something in the hallway caught his eye or he realized how out of control he was, because he abruptly stopped screaming and stomped out of the room."

"Without even trying to help you? What was so important he could possibly have ignored how badly you were bleeding?"

"I don't know." Grace waved her hand. "Another student, Wanda, stepped forward and applied pressure with a towel, while a third ran to get our full first aid kit. When she got back with the kit, I dismissed class while Wanda bandaged my hand. You can imagine how fast most of the students fled the classroom. I doubt it was a full minute before Franklin and Wanda were the only ones left with me. They offered to help me clean up the room, but I told them it wasn't necessary. I wanted to get down to meet you, so I said I'd take care of everything myself later."

"You should have taken them up on their offer." From the cut's position, Sarah couldn't help wondering if the wound was going to interfere with Grace's prep work at Southwind.

"I should have. The minute they left, before I had a chance to leave, Dr. Martin came back."

Sarah leaned forward. "Do you think he was waiting in the hallway for the students to leave?"

"I don't think so. Surely, if the students ran into him, I'd have heard them talking. What I can tell you is that today I learned his nickname is well deserved. He spent the next fifteen minutes chastising me about my ability to control my students and my personal life. He told me he couldn't see how he was going to be able to let me continue instructing this class, as I obviously lacked the experience and qualities necessary to teach in his program."

"But . . . well . . ." Sarah tripped over her words before getting the right ones out. "It was an accident. After all, he got cut too. Why did he get so bent out of shape over an accident?"

"I have no idea. I'll tell you this: He ranted and raved so loudly, I'm sure everyone on the floor heard him." Grace stared at her feet. "And I'm sure they heard me too. I couldn't help myself. I was so mad at what he said, I could have strangled him. Instead, I let him have it with both barrels."

"You did?"

Grace met Sarah's gaze. "Yes. I know he's my boss and I should have kept my mouth shut, but I didn't. Instead, I told him he was out of line and neither the students nor I deserved this kind of treatment from him. I also yelled something like if he kept behaving this way, he shouldn't be surprised if someone didn't punch him out—or worse."

"After you sounded off, what did Dr. Martin do?"

Grace looked at the ground. "I don't know. I left him there sputtering while I walked out of my classroom and came to meet you."

"You what?"

"We both needed to cool off, so I left."

Sarah stared at Grace, speechless.

"I'm so embarrassed." Grace shook her head, causing more wisps of hair to escape her hairnet. "I was so proud of being invited back to teach at my alma mater, despite only having six months of practical experience since I earned my degree, but now, I probably no longer have a job."

"Don't think like that. Remember the nickname you said the faculty has for Dr. Martin. There's got to be evidence of a pattern of this type of behavior that you can take before a board at the college. I'm sure Harlan will help you. In fact, if anyone has something to worry about, it's Dr. Martin. From what you've said, not only has he riled everyone up through verbal abuse, he's put students in danger. Like you said, someone might go further than mere words next time."

Grace brushed back a stray hair falling into her eye. Her hand touched her hairnet. She pulled it off. "Why didn't you tell me I was still wearing this?"

"I thought it added to your campus ambience."

Grace flicked the hairnet at Sarah, making sure it didn't touch her. "Ugh! Anyway, that's why I'm late. I'm so glad you waited."

"I told you I would." Sarah didn't think it was worth mentioning she had thought about leaving.

"Do you mind coming back inside and talking to me while I put things away? Even if Dr. Martin fires me, I want to leave my room in order."

"Well, you know how I feel about kitchens, even teaching . . ." Because Grace obviously wasn't on the same wavelength as her humor today, Sarah changed her tack. "No problem, as long as I don't have to do anything that resembles cooking."

"It's a deal. While I put things in order, you can nibble the cheese the students and I cut before I hurt my hand. Don't worry, none of that is tainted."

Grace stood, as did Sarah. With a slight bow and sweep of her arm, Sarah motioned Grace to go before her up the building's front marble steps.

Inside the main entrance, Grace took a quick turn to the right, stopping in front of a stairwell door. "My classroom is on the third floor, nearer the stairwell than the elevator."

"Lead away."

Grace pulled open the door and started up the stairs.

Sarah followed, immediately unable to quite keep up with Grace's pace. For someone who thought she was in pretty good shape, Sarah realized she didn't do stairs very often and should probably add it to her exercise program, if she ever created one. She decided it might slow Grace down a step or two if she asked her to explain the real reason Grace requested this meeting. "Why don't you tell me what's on your mind besides Dr. Martin?"

"Isn't that enough?"

"That wasn't why you asked to speak to me alone, yesterday."

Grace laughed. "It's Jane, but my concerns from yesterday may not be as major as they seemed then."

Even knowing the topic would be Jane, Sarah struggled to keep her voice civil. "Did she make you another offer?"

Grace rounded the first landing with Sarah at her heels. "Yes, but . . ."

Sarah stopped on the step below the landing. "Are you going to become her executive chef?"

"Oh, no. I turned that down. It was something else Jane wanted me involved in that I wanted to discuss with you."

Relieved but confused, Sarah joined Grace on the landing. "What was it?"

Grace resumed climbing the stairs. "Like I said, it seemed like a big problem yesterday, but, after the events of today, what I wanted to talk to you about is probably moot."

Grace yanked open the door to the third floor. The door rapped against the wall. Sarah slid by it before it slammed shut again. Immediately, she became aware of a buzzing sound in the hallway. Ahead of her, Grace strode purposely toward a doorway in front of which several people were crowded. What Sarah had thought was a buzz was the sound of their chattering voices.

She instinctively quickened her step to catch up to Grace who, seemingly oblivious to the people in the hall, made a beeline for what Sarah presumed was Grace's classroom. Before Sarah could work her way around the other onlookers and catch up to Grace, she saw Grace's path into the classroom blocked by a young man clad in gray cargo pants and a long-sleeved blue collared shirt. Reaching Grace's side, Sarah observed the shirt had the college's insignia on the sleeve of his right arm, the one he held stretched across the open doorway, effectively blocking Grace from entering the classroom.

"Franklin, what's going on in my classroom?"

The young man lowered his eyes, but not his arm. Realizing this might be the student Grace had just told her about, Sarah stared at him, trying to see if she recognized him. She didn't. She felt certain that if she'd ever seen him around the Southwind Pub or the higher-end Southwind restaurant, she would have remembered his almost crew cut and six-pack ab look.

"I'm sorry, Ms. Winston. There's been a problem. No one can go in or out until the campus police and paramedics arrive."

Grace tried again to go around him, but, holding his body like a rigid board, he cut her off.

"The police? The paramedics? I don't understand, Franklin. What's going on?"

Rather than trying to skirt Franklin, Sarah positioned herself to peer over his arm through the open door. Nothing seemed out of the ordinary by the doorway, but when she looked toward the front of the room, she saw knives and cheese haphazardly strewn on the floor in the open space between two large metal preparation tables. A man's body was sprawled spread-eagled over the edge of one of the tables. From the way his arms and head lay, he could have been asleep, but a thin line of blood running down his neck from where a short, pearl-handled knife rested next to him made her doubt that possibility.

Sarah gagged and covered her mouth with her hand.

When Grace turned toward her, Sarah pointed inside the room. She watched as Grace followed the angle of her finger. Although Sarah couldn't see Grace's face, the gulping sound she made let Sarah know Grace had observed the same scenario.

Grace's words, "It's Dr. Martin!" confirmed it.

CHAPTER 2

Grace shoved Franklin. "Get out of the way! He's hurt. I need to help him."

Franklin held her back. "I'm sorry, Ms. Winston, he's beyond help."

Grace shifted her gaze between Dr. Martin and Franklin. "You don't understand. He was fine. When I last saw him, he was fine."

"I'm sure he was, ma'am." Franklin's tone sounded comforting, but Sarah noted he kept his arm positioned as a makeshift guardrail. When he nodded toward an auburn-haired woman standing a few feet from the classroom door, Sarah shifted her attention to her.

The young woman, like the rest of them, appeared upset, but her mood only seemed to intensify her vivid green eyes, pale skin, and the light sprinkling of freckles that ran across her nose. From her jeans and Carleton T-shirt, she looked like a student. Franklin's next comment supported her belief.

"Wanda and I came back to make sure you were okay, and we found him like this. I checked, but there was nothing we could do, so I immediately called the campus police. They should be here any moment. We came out here to wait for them." Franklin paused, fighting his own emotions.

Sarah used the time it took him to regain his composure to view the other people standing in the hall before she focused back on him. From his next words, she gathered he'd observed her looking around.

"Except for the two teaching classrooms on this end of the hall, everything else is faculty offices. Most of these people came out of their offices into the hallway when Wanda screamed. I told them I'd called the campus police and paramedics. I also explained they needed to keep out of the crime scene but could stay in the hall or go back into their offices, as long as they were available when the police arrived."

Sarah was surprised the crowd, most of whom had now moved away from the door to the classroom, had listened to a student. "How did you manage to keep them confined to this floor?"

"I explained I'm a campus police intern with the authority to preserve this crime scene. Although I was sorry if anyone was inconvenienced, they needed to stay put. Everyone except Dr. Williams agreed. Luckily, some of the other faculty members told him I was right and shamed him into staying."

Franklin pointed in the direction of the elevator. "As you can see, except for the small group still here in the hall, almost everyone else went back to their offices. If the two of you would like a little more breathing room while you wait, you might want to move down the hall closer to the elevator area."

Grace peered into the classroom again, this time touching Franklin's arm barrier, not trying to move beyond it. "We can't leave him alone like this. I know he's gone, but surely there's something we can do to put him in a more comfortable position."

Franklin placed his free arm around the much taller Grace. He spoke quietly to her. "Ms. Winston, the first thing they taught me in my internship is not to disrupt a crime scene. There's no question in my mind that this is a crime scene."

"But—"

He cut her off midsentence to tell her there were no *buts* in a situation like this. Franklin stiffened himself into such an upright position that, from Sarah's angle, his eyes almost appeared level to Grace's as he challenged her to disagree with him. Knowing Franklin was right, especially because Sarah knew there was no chance Dr. Martin was alive, she tugged Grace's sleeve. When Grace didn't respond, Sarah pulled harder.

Grace turned her head toward Sarah, but Sarah couldn't tell from the blankness in Grace's eyes if she was looking at her or beyond.

"Grace," Sarah said, fearful Grace was having a diabetic reaction. She was relieved when Grace became more responsive and allowed herself to be pulled down the hall.

There were four more people waiting in the hall. One man stood alone, near the elevator, which appeared to be the midpoint of the hall. The other three people were clustered together beyond the elevator, nearer to what, from what Franklin had said, were the faculty offices.

The man standing alone caught Sarah's attention. He could have been a stunt double for Oliver Hardy in the Laurel and Hardy movie reruns she'd watched with her grandfather when she was a child. Not only was he round, mini-mustached, and wearing the same kind of dark suit, button-down white shirt, and thin, dark tie Hardy always had on, but his face had the same exasperated look Hardy repeatedly gave Laurel's simpleminded way of looking at things.

From where Grace and she stood, Sarah observed him move closer to the wall between the two elevators. He kept his face turned toward the classroom end of the hall, but, with the tip of his elbow, he pushed the elevator's call button. There was no question in Sarah's mind that once the elevator arrived and its door opened, he would jump in and leave unless someone immediately intercepted him. As she debated whether she should step forward, one of the other women in the hall moved to quickly park herself in the man's personal space.

"Don't even think about it, Zach Williams."

Dr. Williams. He was the other program chair Grace had mentioned. Blushing, he dropped his hands to his sides. Thrilled that the middle-aged woman had intervened, Sarah stayed back, watching his gaze dart in all directions, except at his accuser. It was interesting to see how her bony physique filled the space between Dr. Williams and his planned elevator escape.

Because the woman wore an apron with the school's name embroidered on it like the one Grace had on, Sarah figured she must also be a culinary instructor. Sarah could see her apron lacked any of the speckling staining Grace's apron and it wasn't a perfect fit. It was far too short for her height.

"What do you mean, Nancy?"

Nancy laughed. "Give it up, Zach. I saw you punch the elevator button. You were going to sneak away."

"I was not!" Zach put his hand on his chest. "All I can think about is poor Doug. This is terrible. Simply terrible."

Sarah couldn't help but wonder if he thought what was terrible was what had happened to Dr. Martin or the bad publicity the college might get. Either way, she didn't find him any more believable than she bet Nancy did.

Watching him try to shuffle to create more distance between Nancy and himself, Sarah realized these two must have sparred before. She didn't know how those past battles had gone but, from the way Nancy kept digging her knife in, there wasn't any question in Sarah's mind who was going to win today's bout.

"Are you telling me the call button lit itself, Zach?"

He turned toward the lit button. "I may have bumped it. But you have to admit it is a waste of time for us to be standing here when there is so much we should be doing for Doug's family or to minimize the impact of this tragedy on the school and our students."

Having nailed his true motivation, Sarah waited for Nancy's next comment, but any further repertoire between the two was interrupted by the *ping* of the elevator's arrival. The doors opened. To Sarah's surprise, the car wasn't empty. Two men in khaki-green uniforms stepped out.

Even if Franklin hadn't immediately fawned over the older one, Sarah would have known from the stripes on his sleeve, the gun he carried, and the way he quickly assessed the scene that he ranked higher than his colleague. There was no question he was the campus police chief. With an almost imperceptible nod to his junior officer, he focused his attention on Franklin, who stood at military attention.

"I secured the scene for you, sir. All the possible witnesses are here in the hall."

"Good job." The campus chief patted Franklin's shoulder. "Now, if you'll stand down and step aside, we'll take it from here."

Sarah didn't watch Franklin move out of the doorway, because she was trying to make sure, as the junior officer separated the potential witnesses, she wasn't guided to a point too far from the classroom for her to observe what was going on. Happily, he positioned her between the first and second classrooms, just beyond a plaque hung on the wall. From where the junior officer left her, she turned her attention back to watching the campus police chief.

He stood in the doorway of Grace's room, methodically assessing the crime scene. Although he stayed outside the room, she had the distinct feeling he didn't miss a detail. Eventually, he turned back toward the hallway, pulled his phone from his pocket, and punched in several numbers.

Sarah heard him ask for Chief Gerard. After a moment of silence, she heard him share what had happened on campus. Finished with the call, he took the phone from his ear and punched what Sarah guessed was the *end* button. He barely looked up before Dr. Williams, who apparently, like Sarah, had been watching him make his call, got in his face.

"Officer." Dr. Williams looked at his watch. "I'm Dr. Zachary Williams, the head of the hotel-hospitality program. I not only have a very important meeting I need to be at momentarily, but, as the highest ranking academic here, I must inform Dr. Green, the school's president, and Dr. Martin's wife what has happened."

The campus chief waved his hand in the direction of the classroom where Dr. Martin lay. "I'm sorry, sir. This takes precedence over any other meeting or activity."

"That's ridiculous. It's not like you can't find us when you need us. Besides, it's already obvious who the guilty party is."

Sarah couldn't see if the chief rolled his eyes, but there was no question his honey-toned tongue would rather have been saying "Bless your heart" instead of "Now, Dr. Williams, I'm just doing my job connecting the dots. I don't remember circling anyone that jumped out to me as the guilty party."

"Are you kidding? Look at her. She's guilty as sin." He pointed at Grace. "Ask anyone standing here. We all heard them fighting not thirty minutes ago. I bet that's Dr. Martin's blood on her apron."

The campus police chief glanced in Grace's direction, but he didn't say anything as Dr. Williams continued his tirade.

"This is so obviously an open-and-shut case. Why don't you just arrest her and let the rest of us go? We've all got things to do."

"Now, Dr. Williams, you know I would let you go if I could, but I can't. If you'll go wait down the hall or in your office, it shouldn't be long before Chief Dwayne Gerard and his Wheaton police team get here and assume jurisdiction. I'm sure the chief will have some questions for you."

"Chief Gerard? But you're the head of the campus police and that's where this crime happened."

"Our campus police department handles almost everything on campus. And while we have the power to arrest and such, in an out of the ordinary case like this, we prefer to cede jurisdiction to the local authorities."

Despite what Sarah thought was a clear explanation, Dr. Williams continued to protest. While the campus police chief reiterated the jurisdictional issues of Dr. Martin's untimely death with a slight variation in his words, Sarah blocked him out and turned her attention to checking out the two people still waiting on the far side of the elevator, nearer the office side of the floor. Sarah was relieved to see their faces were familiar. She previously had met Chef Robert Bernardi and Fern Runskill.

Pastry chef Robert Bernardi was well-known in Wheaton for his wonderful desserts and for his now-closed bakery-café. Sarah had gotten to know him slightly when he had a pastry and baked goods stall near the Southwind booth at the Wheaton Food Expo. Although their acquaintance was passing, she had taken the opportunity to become good friends with quite a few of the delicious mini-treats he gave away. The memory of his iced chocolate brownie melting in her mouth made her swoon, as did his matinee idol looks, even now, six months later.

Sarah had no problem recognizing Fern Runskill. There was no one else Sarah knew with the same spiked hairstyle. On most women, the severely uneven side-length cuts, coupled with the gelled spikes topping her head, would have been a disaster; but, on Fern, it added to her mystique. Rail thin, with her signature uniform of black stiletto heels, tight black skirt, black or gray cape or poncho, and unique hairstyle, Fern had a look one didn't forget.

As imposing as Fern appeared, Sarah knew that wasn't an accurate assessment of her. Last year, when Sarah first worked up her courage to run by Carleton's admissions office for a catalog, she almost turned and left the office when she caught sight of Fern standing behind the counter. Thirty minutes later, Fern's laugh and genuine interest in Sarah put Sarah at ease.

Their paths had crossed periodically in town or at Southwind, but Sarah hadn't seen Fern since her recent move from admissions to fund development. Sarah had been hoping to visit Fern's new office for a few minutes this morning. She'd read in the paper the director of development had left the college for another position. She wondered if Fern would be in the mix for his job.

The murder and involvement of Chief Gerard and the local police force meant any visiting would need to wait for another day. The big question was how soon she'd get back to the office. She'd told Harlan she'd be late, but she'd thought she'd be in well before lunchtime. Now, she hoped she'd be back in time for the two o'clock meeting scheduled to discuss the next steps in making Wheaton's animal shelter a no-kill facility.

Unfortunately, in all her dealings with Chief Dwayne Gerard, there were two things always consistent. Chief Gerard often failed to develop crucial evidence because he jumped the gun trying to wrap things up quickly, and rushing him when he had it in his mind to do something was impossible. There was no doubt he would take his own sweet time taking the statements of everyone on the floor.

Her fear was whether Chief Gerard might assume, like Dr. Williams, that the obvious bloodstains on Grace's apron were enough evidence to solve this case without additional investigation. Considering Grace still seemed to be in a state of semi-shock at Dr. Martin's death, Sarah didn't know if Grace would shut down or if her instinctive catlike anti-police defense mechanism would be on display if Chief Gerard confronted her. Either probably wouldn't be to Grace's benefit in the long run. Glancing down the hallway to where Grace stood, Sarah feared she was too far away to run interference for Grace if it proved necessary. She weighed her options as to the best way to help Grace.

The sound of an elevator arriving sparked her decision as to what course of action to follow. As those in the hall looked or moved in the direction of the opening elevator doors to see if it was Chief Gerard, Sarah backed into the entryway of the second classroom and pulled her cell phone from her purse. Keeping her face turned away from everyone else, she started to dial the law office. She canceled the call when she realized—considering it was already midmorning— Harlan would probably have turned on the answering machine so he wouldn't be disturbed while he was working. Starting over, she punched in Harlan's private cell phone number. To the best of her recollection, Harlan didn't have any court appearances or client appointments this morning. She hoped, wherever he was, he'd hear his ringtone and would answer his phone.

He did.

When Sarah heard his voice, she was relieved. "Harlan, listen please. I can't talk but a moment. You need to come up to the third floor of CJCC's culinary arts building right now. I think Grace is going to need a good lawyer."

Chapter 3

Sarah hit *end* and looked up. The dynamics in the hall, especially its sound level, had diminished. It was as if everyone hushed in unison with the arrival of Police Chief Gerard and Wheaton's two other police officers: Officer Alvin Robinson and Dr. David Smith. Dr. Smith not only was on the Wheaton police force, but he was also its forensic specialist and the county coroner.

For a moment, even Dr. Williams was quiet as Chief Gerard and the campus police officers conferred. The silence didn't last. As soon as the younger campus police officer walked away, Dr. Williams verbally accosted Chief Gerard and the campus police chief. Dr. Williams loudly protested everyone's, especially his, detention. When he didn't seem to be making headway with his argument, he again repeated his accusations against Grace.

Sarah looked down the hall to where Grace stood,

knowing she had to have heard Dr. Williams's wild statements, but other than shaking her head, Grace wasn't reacting the way Sarah felt she should. As mad as Sarah was, she couldn't believe Grace wasn't stepping up and cutting Dr. Williams off. This wasn't the Grace that Sarah knew—which made her wish Harlan would get here sooner than later.

At least, it appeared Chief Gerard had had enough of Dr. Williams. With a flip of his hand, Chief Gerard signaled Officer Robinson to deal with Dr. Williams. Turning away from them, he told Dr. Smith to proceed with his investigation. Then he walked directly toward Sarah.

From the frown on his face, Sarah gathered he wasn't particularly pleased to see her.

Sarah pasted on a smile while shoving her cell phone, which was still in her hand, into her pocket. "Hello, Chief Gerard."

The chief skipped the pleasantries. "I'm surprised to see you here. Aren't you a bit out of your comfort zone?"

Realizing he wasn't talking about her presence at another murder, Sarah ignored his dig about her well-known fear of cooking. "Actually, the feeling is reciprocal. You're the last person I expected to see in the culinary arts building today."

He cocked his head in the direction of Grace's classroom. "And your presence here with Ms. Winston was arranged before or after the little incident in there?"

Sarah tilted her head and gave him her best Southern belle look. "Don't be silly. We made our plans yesterday, which predates what's happened here this morning."

"It would seem that way, unless it was premeditated, with you as Ms. Winston's cover."

The hairs on the back of her neck bristled, but she kept

her voice modulated. "Believe me, Chief Gerard, this was a total shock to Grace and me. We had no idea Dr. Martin was dead when we came upstairs. In fact," Sarah gratuitously offered, "the last time Grace saw him he was very much alive."

"I don't know why, but it seems like you have a propensity for being where bodies turn up."

Rather than responding to his sarcastic attitude by saying something she'd regret, Sarah pressed her lips together.

Chief Gerard looked behind him, in the direction of the classroom where Dr. Martin lay, before turning back to her. His frown was gone, but there was no sign of humor in his face. "Sarah, I'm sure I don't have to remind you to leave this matter to the proper authorities."

Sarah was about to sputter an answer when Chief Gerard touched the bill of his cap, turned on his heel, and walked away, with his back ramrod-straight. With her answer stuck on the tip of her tongue, Sarah watched him go.

Considering Chief Gerard's attitude and the state Grace was in, Sarah hoped Harlan would get here soon. It was obvious Dr. Williams, or perhaps the campus police, had planted more than a seed of doubt about Grace in Chief Gerard's brain. She didn't think Chief Gerard and Grace would be a good match without someone running interference between them.

When the chief reached an area just beyond the crime scene, he held up his hand and called for everyone's attention. A few more people joined those assembled in the hall. Everyone crowded closer to hear him. Sarah joined them, but she positioned herself outside Grace's classroom's door so she could see what Dr. Smith was doing.

He was walking the room from its outside edge to center, snapping pictures using the camera hung around his neck. When he neared Dr. Martin, he stopped and took several pictures of Dr. Martin's head and neck. She assumed he considered the small knife protruding from Dr. Martin's neck the murder weapon.

Sarah shivered. It was déjà vu. She'd seen him do the same thing when he took pictures of the corpse when her mother was accused of murder.

Chief Gerard's voice, raised to be heard throughout the hall, brought her attention back to him. "Listen up, everyone. While Dr. Smith finishes up, Officer Robinson and I are going to talk to each one of you. Once we get your statements, you'll be free to go."

There was some rumbling in the hallway, but Chief Gerard cut it off. "With two of us taking your statements, we shouldn't detain you too much longer. I know you've been waiting for quite a while already and I appreciate your continued cooperation."

Dr. Williams pressed himself forward. "If you insist on this farce, you must talk to me first. How many times do I need to tell you I'm the head of the hospitality program and have an obligation to inform the college's president about what happened, as well as break the news to Dr. Martin's poor wife, Lynn?"

The chief clamped his meaty hand on Dr. Williams's shoulder. "We'll get to you in due time, Dr. Williams. You don't have to worry. Campus police already informed the president and they're trying to locate Dr. Martin's wife. She doesn't seem to be home."

"You might try the Coffee Bar across the street in the new student center," Nancy, the woman who had stopped Dr. Williams's getaway attempt, interrupted. "Lynn was up here earlier this morning. When she isn't exercising or teaching a yoga class in that building, she often takes her computer and works there."

Chief Gerard whipped around toward Nancy. "You are?"

"Nancy Reynolds."

"And you saw Dr. Martin's wife up here this morning? When was that?"

"I don't remember the exact time. Lynn's up here so much, it's not predictable." She scratched her head. "Let me see. Oh yes, I remember. It was before I went for my coffee. I stopped to put my laptop and some other class materials in my office, and I heard voices. I looked out my doorway. Dr. Martin and his wife were standing in the hallway outside his office, which is next to mine. He seemed a little agitated and I heard him say something about being along shortly."

"But you don't remember the exact time you saw them?"

"Chief Gerard, I was in and out several times this morning." She stopped to think. "It probably was a little before nine."

"Was she often there when you got your coffee?"

"Sometimes. Seeing Dr. Martin's wife there or up here isn't anything out of the ordinary. Since Dr. Martin has been with the department, Lynn pops in at all different times as if she's checking up on what he's doing. What I can tell you is neither his being short with her, nor her hanging in the Coffee Bar is unusual. I can't put a more exact time on when I saw them outside his office this morning, but maybe Fern can. She was with them when I saw them."

Chief Gerard rolled his eyes in Fern's direction. To

Sarah, his expression was reminiscent of some of the exasperated looks he'd given her. Sarah wasn't sure if his exaggerated manner tied into some occurrence between Fern and Chief Gerard in the past, or if it was his reaction to another twist before his investigation was fully underway.

"You were up here today too?"

"Yes," Fern said.

To Sarah's surprise, Fern didn't volunteer any more information.

Seeming to accept her silent challenge, Chief Gerard probed further. "Do you remember when?"

Fern took a few steps closer to Chief Gerard, her stilettos clicking on the linoleum floor. "When Nancy saw me with the Martins, it was probably somewhere between eight-forty-five and nine."

"Your office is a floor down, right? What were you doing up here?"

"I brought Dr. Martin a donor list he needed."

"Do you usually make deliveries?"

Fern stiffened and stood erect in front of the more-corpulent police chief. "No, I don't, but when I deal with anyone, especially someone who may end up heading a department here at the college, I've found a little honey goes a long way. Haven't you?"

From the reddening of Chief Gerard's neck, Sarah wondered if Fern and he had crossed paths in the past. When he verbally ignored Fern's sarcasm and stuck to the topic he was concerned with, she was sure they had. "And Dr. Martin's wife was in his office with you too?"

"No. Well, physically yes, for a moment. She unexpectedly showed up. I was leaving when his wife came in, so right after he did some 'you remember' type introductions, he told her he'd need to catch up with her. Then he walked us both out of his office. That's probably when Nancy glimpsed us through her open office door."

Fern glanced in Nancy's direction. "It doesn't really matter, because there is no question I was up here and with the Martins while he was still alive. Nancy may not have seen me leave, but the Martins were still talking in the hall when I left the floor, so I'd put the time somewhere between eight-forty-five and nine."

Chief Gerard rubbed his neck. "What are you doing here now?"

"I was back on my own floor a little later, walking between the development and admissions offices, when I ran into Nancy, who asked me to come upstairs. She had a coffee cup from the Coffee Bar, if that helps clarify the time."

"You came back up here with her?"

"Not at that moment. I told her I needed to drop something at admissions but would come up right after that. When I arrived on the floor, I heard Grace and Dr. Martin yelling at each other."

"Were they in his office?"

"Oh, no. They were in her classroom."

"And you're sure it was them and that it was just the two of them?"

"No question. They were pretty loud, and their voices were quite distinct."

"Could you hear what they were yelling about?"

Fern hesitated. "Yes, but it really doesn't seem important."

The chief pressed his chest forward and thumped his suspenders. "Let me be the judge of that."

She swallowed before responding slowly. “They were arguing about whether she was fit to teach.”

“So it sounded as if she was upset because he was challenging her competency?”

Fern shook her head. She didn’t reply until Chief Gerard prompted her again.

“He might have talked about her teaching ability earlier. What I heard was more a reflection on the impact of her lifestyle on her ability to be in a classroom with students. At least, that’s what it sounded like to me.”

“Why don’t you clarify that for me? What exactly did you interpret his comments to mean?”

“I’m not positive, but I think he was talking about her personal relationship.”

Sarah wasn’t sure why Fern was pussyfooting around Chief Gerard’s questions. Grace didn’t make a big deal out of her relationship with Mandy, but she didn’t hide their relationship either. In fact, Sarah knew they’d attended a cocktail party at the president’s house before the term began, because Sarah worked a shift that night so Emily could cover for Grace in the kitchen.

She glanced in Grace’s direction, expecting her to react to what was being said, but Grace didn’t. Alarmed at what Grace might say if she did open her mouth, Sarah started to interrupt but paused when Chief Gerard raised his hand. “I’ll talk to you in a minute, Sarah.”

Focusing his attention back on Fern, he leaned slightly forward and lowered his voice. “Were you able to hear how Ms. Winston reacted to what he said?”

“My impression was she was furious. Grace talked loud and fast, so there was no mistaking what she said to him. She made it clear he was out of line and she wasn’t going to take that from him. That’s all I heard.”

Chief Gerard ran his hand across his chin. "It sounds like it was getting interesting, but you didn't stay and listen to more of what they were saying?"

"No, I didn't want to get involved with anything to do with Dr. Martin when he was on the warpath. Considering his reputation and that we'd probably need to work together on several projects, I didn't want to be in his line of fire when he left Grace's classroom. I went to Nancy's office and discovered Chef Bernardi was in there. That had to be a few minutes after nine. Right, Nancy?"

The other woman nodded.

The chief rubbed his neck, which Sarah observed was back to his normal pallor. "Folks, what with all of you coming and going, it must have been like Grand Central Station in this little hallway this morning."

His remark drew a few giggles. Chief Gerard's reiteration that Officer Robinson and he would take statements and move them along quickly was cut short by the return of the younger campus police officer. He went straight to his boss.

Although he spoke in a low voice, Sarah heard him clearly.

"I think I found something important."

Chapter 4

The unholy threesome of the two campus policemen and Chief Gerard had their heads together, discussing whatever it was the young officer had found. Sarah was immediately concerned when Chief Gerard went to the classroom door and interrupted Dr. Smith. "How close are you to finishing up here?"

"I've still got quite a bit to do."

"Well, mark where you are or whatever you do. I need you to go with this officer."

"But, Chief—"

Chief Gerard cut him off in a manner Sarah felt left no room for dispute. "Surely, if I keep the crime scene secure, you can break for a minute and then come back and use new gloves and booties to finish up."

Although Dr. Smith acquiesced, Sarah thought the thin-lipped straight line of his mouth, rather than his usual easy smile, indicated he wasn't thrilled with the situation. What scared her more was trying to figure out what could be so important for Chief Gerard to have Dr. Smith leave the corpse.

The answer to her question came swiftly. Not even five minutes passed before Dr. Smith and the officer returned. Besides using one hand to steady the camera slung around his neck, Dr. Smith now clutched a large plastic evidence bag in his other hand. As Dr. Smith passed Sarah, she saw something white visible through the clear plastic. She wasn't sure, but it appeared that it might be something made of cloth.

Dr. Smith brought the bag directly to Chief Gerard. Sarah craned her neck to get a better view. As Dr. Smith moved the bag so the chief could examine it from another angle, Sarah recognized the outline of a pocket with a thin red line of something written or stitched on it. To her dismay, it dawned on her that the style of the stitching was like the monogram her twin had created for everyone's white Southwind chef's jacket. Considering Grace was going to work right after Sarah and she met, Sarah feared the jacket belonged to Grace. She glanced toward where Grace was standing but realized that, from where she was, Grace couldn't see what Dr. Smith was holding.

Although Sarah couldn't be sure if it was Grace's jacket in the evidence bag, her prayer for Harlan to arrive grew more fervent when Chief Gerard signaled for Grace to join him and the campus security people.

Although Chief Gerard hadn't summoned her, Sarah took it upon herself to become part of their group. She stopped abruptly when Chief Gerard raised his hand and said, "Hold it there, Sarah. I only want to talk to Ms. Winston now."

Frustrated at being forced to keep her distance, Sarah opted to stay where she was because it was at least a little closer to Grace. Maybe, when he looked away, she could inch up because she still was too far from Grace to communicate even by making eye contact. The only good thing about where Sarah now stood was her ability to hear what was being said.

Chief Gerard sent Dr. Smith, who kept the evidence bag in his possession, back into the classroom to continue his forensic investigation. Once Dr. Smith left, Chief Gerard focused his attention on Grace. "Ms. Winston, did you have your Southwind jacket on campus with you this morning?"

Too far away to keep Grace from answering the chief's question, Sarah mentally pleaded for Grace to remain silent until Harlan arrived.

Grace didn't get Sarah's message. "Yes. Why?"

"Were you wearing it while you were teaching?"

"No. I had it with me for when I went to work, but I didn't want to get it dirty while I was teaching, so I wore one of the school's aprons."

"The college provides the faculty with aprons?"

"Not exactly. The last culinary arts director thought it would be nice for there to be some uniformity in what the staff wore in the classroom. He ordered a standard apron with the college's logo on the front and gave them out as holiday presents. The extra ones ended up in one of the storerooms. When I started teaching, Nancy showed me where they were. I took one to wear on the days I teach."

As Chief Gerard spoke more softly, Sarah leaned her head forward, not wanting to miss a word of their conversation.

"Tell me again, why did you have your Southwind jacket on campus?"

"I already told you."

Sarah was pleased Grace seemed more alert and involved, but she wished Grace would simply stop answering anything until Harlan arrived.

"Tell me again," Chief Gerard said.

Grace responded in an even tone, but her face looked exasperated. "I had my jacket with me because Sarah and I were meeting right after my class. By the time we finished visiting, I knew I'd have to go straight to work at Southwind. There wasn't going to be time for me to go home to pick up my whites. Why?"

Chief Gerard ignored her question. "Where is your jacket now?"

Grace pointed into her classroom. "In the chair near the desk. Here, I'll show you." Grace started toward the door of the classroom, but Chief Gerard, moving faster than Sarah thought him capable, managed to cut Grace off and grab her arm.

"You can't go in there until Dr. Smith finishes examining the scene."

Grace planted her feet slightly apart, put her hands on her hips, and jutted her chin toward Chief Gerard. "Then let Dr. Smith show you my jacket. I'm an adjunct. I don't have an office or even a locker. When I teach, I don't sit at the desk. In fact, the only time I'm near the front of the room is when I'm lecturing or demonstrating something. Otherwise, I'm in constant motion moving around the room, checking each student's work at his or her assigned prep table. That's why I use my desk chair for my stuff."

Chief Gerard peered into the classroom. "Are you talking about the rolling chair that's over there between the desk and the blackboard?"

"That's right. I'm sure anyone who teaches in this classroom does the same thing. With what we need to accomplish each session, there's rarely time to sit during class. Using the chair keeps my stuff off the floor and out of my way."

Sarah stared at Grace, wishing she'd stop talking.

Grace did, but only for a moment. When she resumed speaking in a muted voice, her words came more slowly, as if Grace were thinking aloud in a stream of consciousness. Sarah shook her head and stared at Grace, willing her to understand the impact anything she said could be used against her. Unfortunately, Sarah's telepathic effort to silence Grace was unsuccessful.

"The space at the front of the classroom was where Franklin and I were when he was trying to identify the different knives we were studying today."

"Different knives?"

"Yes. I was giving the students an overview of bread, boning, butcher, chef, paring, slicing, utility, and cheese knives. That's when Dr. Martin interrupted my lesson." She looked at her hand. "We both ended up being cut, and I got some of Dr. Martin's blood on my apron."

Sarah could have groaned when Grace pointed at the red stains on her apron, but, at least, something made Grace stop talking. Sarah could see what she interpreted as a look of blankness wash over Grace's face. She felt Grace might be reliving the moment in her head and hoped she would keep her thoughts there.

Again, no such luck. Almost as if repeating a bad dream, Grace continued in a monotone.

"Dr. Martin had the deboning knife in his hand. Franklin reached for it, blade first. Knowing how sharp a deboning knife is, I stuck my hand out to keep him from touching its blade. I bumped Franklin's hand or arm, but he hit Dr. Martin's arm. The knife got away from Dr. Martin and somehow sliced my hand and nicked Dr. Martin."

"You didn't know you and Dr. Martin had been injured?"

"No. I heard the knife hit the floor, but didn't realize I'd been cut because I didn't feel the pain or see the blood at first. I guess my body or mind went into some state of shock."

"And then?"

"I remember looking at my hand, watching it bleed. One of my students, Wanda, hurried to put pressure on it with a towel. I think that's when I became aware of a sound that was a cross between a high-pitched whine and a growl. It took me a moment to connect the noise to Dr. Martin. Once I did, I realized the sound was him letting out a yelp of pain and a string of four-letter words."

"He was injured too?"

"Yes, but not badly. The knife only nicked him."

"What makes you say that?"

"I couldn't see any blood oozing through whatever he held against his arm. From the tight clamping of his jaw, it seemed to me like he was putting all his efforts into controlling his temper."

"What was he holding? Could it have been something from your pile on the chair?"

Sarah didn't have to hear Wanda's interjection of "It was" for confirmation that the evidence bag contained Grace's Southwind jacket.

There was a loud intake of breath from Grace. Sarah

watched Grace glance to where Wanda still stood near Franklin. Wanda nodded.

Chief Gerard seemed happy to torture the moment out.

"Wanda, are you sure you saw Dr. Martin pick up Ms. Winston's jacket?"

"Yes, sir. I could tell from the way Ms. Winston seemed like she was stunned and the way her hand was bleeding that her wound was bad. The way the blood was pulsating, I was afraid she'd cut an artery or something. That's why I grabbed the towel and applied pressure. The pressure slowed the bleeding, but when Dr. Martin yelled, I automatically looked in his direction."

"And what did you see?"

Wanda glanced at her sweater. "I looked up just as he jerked his arm in our direction. Ms. Winston and I were close enough for a little of his blood to shake off." She pointed to a spot on her sweater. From where Sarah stood, she couldn't see anything more than the sweater itself.

"He was bleeding, but not badly. Although he managed to get some on both Ms. Winston and me when he flung his arm out, it was obvious to me from his movements and how angry he looked that he wasn't hurt badly."

Chief Gerard furrowed his brow. "Then why bother grabbing the jacket?"

Wanda shrugged. "I think it probably was a reflexive reaction. He certainly didn't need to put pressure on his wound for long to stop his bleeding, but he did do it for a moment. Then he stopped and glanced at his arm again."

"Did he lay the jacket back down?"

"Not that I saw. Once I realized he was okay, I was more concerned with Ms. Winston's hand. I heard Dr. Martin say something and leave the room, but I didn't watch if he took the jacket with him or not."

"Thank you," Chief Gerard said. "I think we can presume he had the jacket with him when he left, so, Ms. Winston . . ."

Unsure of where this conversation was going and knowing it shouldn't go any further without Harlan present, Sarah evaluated what she might use in the hallway to create a distraction. There wasn't much. She was too far away to pull the fire alarm and, even if she could, the repercussions of pulling the fire alarm in front of Chief Gerard were too great. Frustrated, she coughed.

That was it! Sarah coughed as loudly as she could. For good measure, she added a few gasps as if trying to catch her breath. It seemed like an eternity before Chief Gerard finally looked in her direction and asked if she was okay. Rather than responding quickly, she added to her dramatics while inching closer to where Grace stood.

Finally, Sarah slowed her coughing fit. "Sorry. Swallowed wrong. Water, please." She leaned against the wall to enhance the effect.

The chief dispatched Officer Robinson for water. Franklin, who had also come forward to help, took it upon himself to retrieve a chair for Sarah from the second classroom.

Officer Robinson returned with a cup of water first. He extended his hand with the cup to Sarah. Still leaning against the wall, she whispered her thanks to him but didn't immediately take the proffered cup. Instead, Sarah turned her head and coughed a few more times. Satisfied she couldn't milk the cough much more to buy time, Sarah tried to look somewhat faint as she sipped the water and let Franklin guide her to the chair he'd brought into the hallway.

Although the chief hadn't yet resumed his questioning, it was obvious from his body language it was only a matter of moments until he would. She weighed whether another coughing spell would work again but decided, while it might cause Officer Robinson to check on her, Chief Gerard was satisfied she'd live.

Just as Chief Gerard addressed Grace again, the elevator *ping*ed its arrival on the floor. When the doors opened, Sarah let out a sigh of relief. The cavalry was here.

CHAPTER 5

"Harlan Endicott, what are you doing here? I would think this building is a bit out of your normal stomping grounds for ambulance chasing."

Sarah wasn't sure if Chief Gerard's statement should be taken as rudeness or friendly ribbing. At their initial meeting last year, Harlan and then Officer Dwayne Gerard started out on opposite sides of a desk at the police station, but in the past six months there were times she could swear they had developed a bromance based upon the crimes she had solved.

"Now, Chief, you know my need to represent people has no bounds." Although his tone was light, Sarah noted Harlan, briefcase in hand, hadn't stopped walking down the hallway until he reached the place where Grace stood.

Chief Gerard glanced in Sarah's direction and made one of the faces she'd come to expect during their exchanges. "Especially if they have a connection to you-know-who."

To Sarah's dismay, Harlan didn't disagree with Chief Gerard. "Chief, when you're right, you're right."

"Well, from what I can tell, you don't have to be here. Sarah doesn't need a lawyer, today."

"I'm not here for Sarah. As you may recall, I began representing Ms. Winston years ago. I'm here to protect my client."

For a moment, Sarah wasn't sure what Harlan was referring to. Grace hadn't done anything with the firm since Sarah began her employment as Harlan's receptionist. Then she remembered the story Grace once shared with her about getting into a spot of trouble while running with the wrong crowd when Grace was a teenager.

Although innocent, Grace refused to rat out her buddies, even when they deserted her. Despite her refusal to cooperate, Grace's court-appointed attorney, Harlan, not only managed to clear her name but also convinced Sarah's ex-husband to underwrite a tuition scholarship for Grace to attend culinary school.

"Are you sure you're not ambulance chasing? Since I've been here, I didn't notice Ms. Winston calling anyone to talk, let alone establish a business relationship."

"Didn't need to. Our attorney-client relationship goes way back. Right, Grace?"

"Definitely," Grace said firmly. "Harlan has represented me for years. Also, you're right. We haven't had time to talk yet. I'd like to speak with my attorney now, please."

Sarah was thrilled to hear Grace stand up for her rights. That meant Grace was thinking more clearly. The question was how Grace's newly-found defiant attitude would sit with Chief Gerard. One thing was certain: Based upon how Chief Gerard and Harlan were staring each other down like two boxers before sparring, it wouldn't take long to find out.

"Come on, Dwayne. My client has every right to speak to me." Harlan stepped closer to Grace, but Sarah observed he didn't break eye contact with Chief Gerard.

For a moment, both stood erect, their gazes locked. Chief Gerard was the first to give. He threw his hands up in the air and pointed at Sarah. "Okay, why should this case be any different than the other ones you and Sarah have been involved with? You can talk with your client to your heart's content in that other classroom, but then I want to get Ms. Winston's statement."

Harlan took Grace by the arm and propelled her toward the second classroom. He didn't close the door, but it didn't matter. Grace and he talked so softly it was impossible for anyone else to overhear them.

Although Sarah would have loved to hear what they were saying, she didn't mind missing out this time. With Harlan, Grace was in good hands.

CHAPTER 6

Sarah jumped a mile when she heard her name. With her back to the hallway as she peered into the classroom where Harlan and Grace were talking, she hadn't heard Officer Robinson come up behind her.

She put her hand over her heart. "You scared me."

"Sorry. Usually stealth isn't one of my strong suits." He grinned.

Considering his size, Sarah couldn't disagree with him. In the months since he joined the Wheaton police force, the stories he shared about his football-playing days had made him quite popular with students at the various Wheaton schools he spent time in each week. Sarah also had been impressed with his even-temperedness in her dealings with him.

"If you wouldn't mind coming with me, please, I'd like to take your statement."

"But Harlan . . ."

"I believe he's busy with Ms. Winston right now."

"I don't mind waiting until they're finished."

"That could be quite a while. Chief Gerard plans to take Ms. Winston's statement next, and I'm sure Harlan will sit in on that. In the meantime, Chief Gerard asked me to take your statement. As you well know, taking everyone's statement is routine."

Although Sarah knew the process Officer Robinson described was the normal procedure in a case with witnesses, she was afraid she might say something that would incriminate Grace. Worse, what if she said something inconsistent with what Grace told Chief Gerard? She wished she could talk to Harlan for a moment, but, from what Officer Robinson indicated, that wasn't going to be possible for quite some time. She needed to make this decision on her own.

She was glad Officer Robinson, his stance marked by his feet spread apart, wasn't pressuring her to make a quick decision. He smiled and waited.

On one hand, she wasn't a suspect in any possible way in this case, so how could she justify not cooperating? Still, Sarah couldn't forget what happened with her mother and Emily when they said things without Harlan being with them when they gave statements. Still, she didn't think those instances would be something Officer Robinson would find an acceptable basis for a refusal, as he could as easily point out that, in both of those instances, everything had pointed to them being the killers. If he noted that wasn't something at issue in this case, she wouldn't be able to disagree with him.

Reflecting on the two other times Officer Robinson took her statement, she had to admit he'd always been gentle and fair with her. The scales seemed equally balanced. She decided to cooperate. "Where are we going?"

Officer Robinson pointed to the side of the hallway beyond the elevator. "Just down the hall. Once I interviewed Dr. Williams, he left in a hurry, but was kind enough to permit me to continue using his office to take statements."

Sarah followed him to Dr. Williams's office. When they reached the doorway, Officer Robinson stepped aside to let her enter first. She was surprised, considering Dr. Williams was the hospitality program chairman, at how tiny his office was. Its one window kept it from feeling like he'd been assigned a closet instead of an office.

There was a desk, credenza, and two chairs. Sarah didn't see any personal pictures or items. The top of the desk, except for a legal pad and pen, was as bare as the walls. A crumpled piece of paper in the open-wired wastebasket and several folders stacked on either end of the credenza were the only other things in the room. Not seeing a standalone computer in the space between the folders, Sarah assumed Dr. Williams used a laptop he either placed in the open area on the credenza or on his desk.

Without being prompted, Sarah sat in the guest chair. Officer Robinson squeezed his bulk into the chair between the desk and credenza. He picked up the pen and pulled the pad closer. His first questions, to which he marked her answers down on his legal pad, were much like the background ones he'd posed to her in the past.

Pausing, Officer Robinson leaned back. He flipped to the next clean page of his pad before positioning his pen to take notes again. "Now, I think you told Chief Gerard that Ms. Winston and you made plans yesterday to meet here on campus today?"

"That's right."

"Must have been something important that you took off work. You did, didn't you?"

Sarah wasn't quite sure how to answer him, but she remembered Harlan always was a stickler for the truth—but not for revealing more than necessary. "Grace had something important she wanted to talk to me about and, with her teaching and work schedule today, I thought it would be easier if I went into work a little late." She held up her arm with her watch. "I never expected to still be here."

Officer Robinson nodded. "I'll try to move this along. What did Grace want to talk to you about?"

"I don't know. We never got around to discussing it."

"At all?"

"When she came outside, my attention was focused on her injured hand. It was bleeding." She stopped and thought. "When we went up the steps to her classroom, I asked her what she wanted to talk about and she replied it had something to do with Jane, but that it was probably moot considering what had happened."

"You mean because Dr. Martin was killed?"

"Oh, no. When Grace and I were talking, we both thought he was alive."

"At least you did."

"That's not true. Grace had no idea, any more than I did, he'd been killed. She was as shocked as I was when we got upstairs and found out."

He let her comment go. "Even if she didn't tell you, do

you have any idea what it was about Jane she might have wanted to talk to you about?"

"Not really. The only thing I can think of is it might have had something to do with Jane's Place." Once the words slipped out of her mouth, Sarah wished she could take them back. The last thing she wanted to tell Officer Robinson was her guess was based on seeing Grace sneak across the street from Southwind to Jane's Place yesterday.

"What makes you think that?"

Sarah decided to gloss over the details. After all, she didn't really know what Grace wanted to tell her about Jane. With as serious an expression as she could muster, she looked directly at Officer Robinson. "What else could it be? You, of all people, know all the things that have gone on between Jane, Jane's Place, and her neighbors. Considering Jane and her schemes, I figured there must be a new something to do with Jane's Place that Grace wanted to tell me about."

Officer Robinson didn't press the issue. Because of the Wheaton police department's run-ins with Jane about Jane's Place, Sarah was sure his imagination was running rampant. He apparently decided that was enough questioning on that topic because he changed the subject.

"Did your conversation with Ms. Winston take place in her classroom?"

"No. Our plan was for me to wait on the bench in front of the culinary arts building for her to finish teaching her class. We were going to talk there or go over to the Coffee Bar. Our plans changed when she finally came outside and found me. She asked if I would go upstairs with her so she could clean up her classroom."

Officer Robinson drew a line on his paper, followed by

a circle. From upside down, it appeared to Sarah it was a straight line connecting some words in one of his notes to the empty circle. "You said you waited for her. How late was Ms. Winston?"

"About twenty minutes. I thought Grace would come right out when her class ended, but apparently, between getting her hand taken care of and a confrontation with Dr. Martin, she was delayed."

"What was their confrontation about?"

Sarah squirmed in her chair. "I think you need to get the details of that from Grace."

"Chief Gerard will. Personally, I'm interested in knowing her state of mind. Was she put together or agitated?"

"She was upset at keeping me waiting. Grace was also annoyed with Dr. Martin's behavior toward one of her students. I don't think she was any more agitated than you or I would have been in the same situation."

"Did you see any blood on her clothing?"

"There was some on her apron."

"Did she explain how it got there?"

"From the cut on her hand." Sarah shook her head and raised her hands in an *I don't know* motion. "Officer Robinson, Grace can tell you all about this much better than I can. I really don't have anything else to add."

Officer Robinson looked at the pages on which he'd made his notes. "Just a few more questions. You said Ms. Winston went back into the building to clean up her classroom. Why hadn't she done that already? Wouldn't that be the normal practice in a kitchen setting, even if it only is a prep classroom?"

"Like I told you, she was worried about whether I was still waiting. Consequently, rather than cleaning up immediately, she ran outside to see if I was still there. I was. After I realized her hand was bleeding, we focused on stopping it. Once we succeeded, she asked me to come upstairs while she put her room back in order from her lesson. It really wasn't a big deal until we got up to the third floor and discovered Dr. Martin was dead."

"Somehow, I think it was probably a big deal, at least to Dr. Martin, before the two of you got up there."

CHAPTER 7

On the way back to Harlan's office, after giving her statement, Sarah called her twin, Emily, and filled her in on why Grace was running late to work. Sarah figured Emily and maybe Chef Marcus might have to assume extra prep duties and she wasn't sure if Grace had been allowed to phone or text them. Glancing at her watch, Sarah realized how much of the morning had passed. She decided it would be better to stop by the carriage house and check on RahRah and Fluffy now, rather than leaving work again in forty-five minutes to come home to take care of her pets during her usual lunch hour.

By the time she finished turning the key in the front door's lock, Fluffy was whining on the other side of the door. When she opened the door, Fluffy was eagerly waiting for her.

Sarah dropped her keys into the blown-glass bowl she

kept on the wooden table by the front door before she bent and rubbed the top of Fluffy's head and behind her ears. The white fluffball of a dog lay down and rolled so her belly was exposed, begging for a little more love. Sarah gladly obliged her. "Did you miss me, girl?"

From the relaxed angle of Fluffy's ears, Sarah knew the answer without the need for a barked response. Less than a year ago, Fluffy had been an abandoned, frightened dog. Sarah's neighbor, Mr. Rogers, had managed to coax Fluffy into trusting people. Seeing Fluffy exhibiting this much joyful security was one of the reasons Sarah was so involved with Wheaton's animal shelter.

Her Saturday morning ritual—usually with Harlan—of walking dogs at the shelter was her way of sharing a little love with those dogs or cats who hadn't yet found forever homes. Knowing what happened to many unadopted animals throughout the country motivated her involvement with the group working to make Wheaton's shelter an official no-kill facility.

There already had been numerous planning meetings dividing up the tasks necessary to make their goal a reality. Harlan was handling the legal work pro bono. Two of the veterinarians, who cared for RahRah and Fluffy at the clinic across the street from Southwind and who took care of the shelter animals, were addressing any medical needs. Another committee, led by Sarah's on again-and-off-again boyfriend, Cliff Rogers, was analyzing the physical changes or additions the present shelter required. Because of Sarah's previous fundraiser success putting together YipYeow Day, she was working on the development and outreach-publicity committees. In her mind, and that of Phyllis, the shelter's recently hired director, part of the success of having a no-kill shelter was educating the public about ways to fund the facility and how to participate in adoption and fostering programs.

Thinking about the combined meeting of the two committees she served on scheduled for two in Harlan's office, Sarah glanced at her watch. It already was almost noon. She needed to check on RahRah, make sure both animals had enough food and water, and give Fluffy a quick walk so she could get back to the office and do some work before the committee members arrived. She only hoped Harlan and Grace would be finished with Chief Gerard in time for Harlan to be at the meeting.

"Come on, Fluffy, let's find RahRah. Obviously, I wasn't interesting enough for the king to move from wherever he is to give me a proper welcome."

Fluffy followed Sarah into the kitchen. The sun was streaming through the window, warming the exact spot where her Siamese cat preferred to lie, usually stretched out preening in the sunshine. RahRah wasn't there. "RahRah," she called.

No cat appeared. Sarah looked around the room. RahRah wasn't in his go-to-if-it-gets-too-warm-in-the-sun patch of linoleum under the table, nor was he anywhere near his litter box, emptied food bowl, or still almost-full water bowl. "Fluffy, do you know where RahRah is?"

The dog, who'd plopped herself down in RahRah's usual kitchen resting place, raised her head, but then laid it down again. Apparently, even though Fluffy usually followed RahRah wherever he went, today Fluffy seemed to happily be enjoying alone time.

Leaving Fluffy in the kitchen, Sarah went into her bedroom and loudly repeated RahRah's name while she looked for him.

RahRah wasn't in his cozy place under the bed nor

squeezed amid her shoes in the closet. As she checked her bathroom, which again didn't have a cat in it, Sarah began to panic. She couldn't count how many days and nights since her divorce she'd held RahRah tightly until a moment of fear or unrelenting tears passed. Sarah clenched her hands into tight fists, fighting the sensation the walls were closing in around her and she couldn't quite catch her breath. Not having her Siamese cat to hold made this moment different than when she was trying to get her life back on track.

A tinkling sound caught her ear. She walked down the hallway toward her living and dining rooms. It grew louder as she neared the front of the house.

Nothing seemed out of place in the living room, but as she entered the dining room, she could see the glasses hanging from the rack over the top of her small cabinet-bar swaying. Each time two collided, they made the tinkling sound. With his tail held high, RahRah was walking from one end of the bar to the other. Sarah caught RahRah before he could hit the glasses again, while making another pass across the bar.

"What are you doing up here?" She glanced around to see how RahRah had gotten up on the bar, as it was too high for him to have jumped without an intervening surface. A dining room chair sitting closer to the bar than the table provided a quick and obvious answer. With her foot, she pushed the chair back into its normal place.

"You're a pretty smart cat. How did you find the one chair that wasn't where it should be?"

RahRah snuggled against Sarah's chest as she carried him toward the kitchen.

"Are you trying to get back into my good graces? Do

you not want me to worry about you spending your day prowling the house looking for fun?"

Sarah could have sworn RahRah raised his little head above her arm and smiled at her. Intellectually, she knew that wasn't true, but she felt RahRah, in his own way, was a better communicator than many of the men she'd known. She gave RahRah a tight hug before putting him down on the kitchen floor. He immediately nudged Fluffy out of the RahRah spot in the sun.

A displaced Fluffy walked around in a circle before plopping herself in a shadier spot a few feet away from where RahRah lay. As Sarah checked to make sure each had enough water, she couldn't help but laugh watching the dynamics of their relationship. Still laughing, she glanced at where RahRah lay, unmoving. "You may be bossy, but you certainly are cuter than most of the men I've dated."

CHAPTER 8

Back at the office, Sarah was glad she'd opted to stop at home. Apparently, during the time before she called him to come help Grace, Harlan was extremely productive. Sarah was just finishing typing the brief, motion, and two letters he'd dictated when the door buzzer rang.

Sarah checked the monitor on her desk. Waving into the camera was Dr. Glenn Amos, the head of the veterinarian group located in the remodeled house that shared its parking area with Jane's Place, diagonally across Main Street from Southwind. His vet tech sister, Carole, was with him, as was her beloved three-legged dog, Buddy.

Truth be told, Sarah was especially happy to see Buddy. For the year before Carole adopted him, he'd been the first of the dogs Sarah walked each Saturday morning. Buddy was the perfect poster child for the topic of their meeting today. He held the record as being the longest sheltered dog in Wheaton before finding a forever home. Considering his infirmities, many shelters would never have kept him alive for the time it took to be adopted, but the Wheaton shelter staff had loved Buddy and knew there would be someone who would love him too.

Behind them, Sarah could see Phyllis coming up the path to the front door. With Harlan not here yet and Cliff not coming, she wondered, as she buzzed Buddy and the three of them in, who would run the meeting.

Hearing a key in the office's back door, her concern was alleviated. Harlan reached the front of the office at almost the same time the others were all in the waiting room area and Glenn was closing the door. Harlan pointed toward his office. "Please make yourselves comfortable in my office. Sarah and I will be there in a minute."

Sarah waited in her chair behind the partial wall that separated her space from the waiting room. Once the others were safely in his office, Harlan leaned over the wall.

Sarah looked at him. "Is Grace okay?"

"For the time being."

"Did Chief Gerard arrest her?"

"No, not yet, but I'm worried she doesn't realize how real that possibility is."

Sarah reached for the phone on her desk. "I can call her."

"That isn't necessary now. By the time Chief Gerard finished taking her statement and let her go, Grace's only concern, no matter how much I stressed the need for us to meet this afternoon, was rushing to the Southwind Pub. She was afraid Emily and Marcus would be mad because she promised her teaching wouldn't get in the way of her work assignments."

"Grace won't have any problem today. I gave Emily a

heads-up about what happened to Dr. Martin and that Chief Gerard was questioning Grace. If anyone knows how long-winded Chief Gerard can be, especially if he's barking up the wrong tree, it's Emily."

"That explains it. On my way back for this meeting, I called the restaurant. Marcus answered and when I said I needed to see Grace in my office this afternoon, he never asked why. He simply asked, 'What time?' When I said four, he indicated he'd make sure she was on time."

"Emily must have filled him in."

"Makes sense. You're here for the rest of the day, right?"

"Yes. I can stay a little late if necessary, but I have to make a mandatory appearance at six-thirty for dinner with Mr. Rogers and my mother."

Harlan grinned. "I gather it's steak night at the retirement center."

"You gather right."

"Okay, let's get this show on the road."

She followed Harlan into his office. Whether the others remembered from their previous meetings or because it was instinctive, the wingbacked leather chair, closest to the door in the conversation area of the office, was waiting for Harlan. Carole and Phyllis were on the couch, with Buddy wedged between their feet and the coffee table. Rather than sitting in the matching winged chair situated at the opposite end of the coffee table, Glenn had left that one for Sarah and was rolling Harlan's desk chair from its usual position behind Harlan's big oak desk to where everyone else sat.

As Glenn dropped his six-foot-plus frame into the chair, the image of a tiny car at the circus that kept emptying clowns popped into Sarah's mind. This wasn't quite as pronounced, but there definitely was a difference between the way the two men appeared when sitting in the desk chair.

Normally, because the chair was behind Harlan's desk, people didn't see how high up Harlan kept its hydraulic setting. He attributed it to working ergonomically, but Sarah thought it was so he wouldn't appear to be swallowed by the massive piece of furniture. She couldn't imagine if Glenn had tried sitting at the desk instead of rolling the chair closer to the conversation area. The one time Sarah, who was tall enough to look down on Harlan's bald spot, tried to slip behind the desk, there hadn't been room for her long legs without touching the wood above them.

"Glenn, would you prefer to sit here?" Sarah asked.

"No, I'm fine."

Sarah didn't look in Harlan's direction. He didn't have a Napoleon complex or anything like that, but she wasn't sure if he would be annoyed with her making an issue of him probably being half a foot shorter than Glenn. Instead, she focused her gaze on Buddy. "Carole, Buddy looks like his forever home suits him perfectly. He was always such a sweet dog, but I think he seems even more content now."

Carole gave the large dog a loving tap. "I don't know about that, but I can't even think about the time I didn't have him in my life."

"I feel the same way about RahRah and Fluffy. If you'd told me a few years ago two animals would be the most important things in my life, I would have laughed or told you, 'Don't be ridiculous, I already had a rat.'"

"A rat? You had a pet rat?" Phyllis said.

The others, who were more familiar with the story of Sarah's life, laughed.

"My ex-husband."

Harlan tapped his pen on his ever-present yellow legal pad, effectively stopping the continuation of this tangent of their conversation. "I think we better get on with the purpose of this meeting. As you know, at our last meeting, when we discussed the idea of making the Wheaton Animal Shelter a no-kill facility, we each took a few specific assignments. Phyllis, you were going to do a little more definitional research for us. What have you found?"

Phyllis smoothed out a piece of paper on her lap. "Our no-kill shelter would be a place that even when we're full doesn't kill healthy animals or those with treatable conditions. Euthanasia is reserved only for animals posing a danger to Wheaton's public safety or who are terminally ill."

"But," Carole said, "I remember reading somewhere that there can be a percentage of healthy animals put down and it still will be considered a no-kill shelter."

Phyllis nodded. "Ten percent is the number, but we want to make it our business not to make that our practice."

Sarah was glad their goal wasn't going to be 10 percent. She wished it could be no percent, but she wasn't sure if there were any methods the Wheaton shelter could employ to have a zero-threshold tolerance level. When she'd thrown out the question during their first meeting, Phyllis quickly replied that a lower tolerance level could be reached by raising money to expand services, building a bigger volunteer base, modifying the protocols involved with housing and medical service, and doing outreach to promote more fostering and other ways to minimize how many homeless animals actually came into the shelter. Everyone had taken her answer to heart and made a commitment to keep their shelter well under 10 percent.

Harlan cleared his throat and thanked Phyllis for her report. "It sounds to me that if we go forward with this, major fundraising is still going to be a necessity to fulfill our mission. Any new developments in that area?"

"The city is willing to go along with another YipYeow Day," Sarah said. "That and the Blessing of the Animals was a big success."

"In combination, those two things proved to be an excellent fundraiser and we got a lot of animals adopted too, but it isn't going to be enough." Harlan looked around. "Any other ideas?"

Carole reached down and patted Buddy again. Sarah knew Buddy wasn't a service dog, but there was no question touching the semi-blind, aging dog seemed to give Carole more confidence to speak. Considering the trauma Carole had gone through recently, Sarah was glad to see her so excited and engaged in helping the shelter.

"I was watching an old movie on TV the other night where the kids in the film raised money for a project by having a talent show. It would be easy to do and would be a good way to involve more of our community in our project."

Phyllis nodded in agreement. "If different Wheaton citizens were the talent and invited their friends to attend, we could get a big crowd—maybe most of Wheaton."

"We could charge an entrance fee, sell tickets, and ask for extra donations," Sarah said. "Plus, we can get a space big enough that we can show off some of our animals available for adoption."

Glenn groaned at his sister's idea. "Do we have to hold the show in a barn?"

"No," Sarah said. "I bet Pastor Dobbs would let us use the common room in the Little Brown Church like we did for the Blessing of the Animals."

Harlan disagreed. "We need to think bigger than that. Why not make this a Wheaton extravaganza and hold it at the civic center? We might be able to pull off using both exhibition rooms like we did for the Food Expo. Otherwise, I bet we could set up chairs and fill the room that has the stage area."

"Emily and Marcus oversaw the retail and worker food side of the expo. I'm sure they'll agree to have the Southwind Group sponsor or at least handle a refreshment area. For YipYeow Day, Cliff put together some staging to showcase our dogs for adoption. He might still have that or could make something we could use, but how are we going to decide who's in the talent show?"

"I can't sing two notes on key, but the Harlan Endicott law firm will put up five hundred, two hundred and fifty, and one hundred dollars for prizes. That should help us attract a crowd of entries. I'd say let anyone who wants to enter. We can always do different rounds to weed it down to a finalist round. But we'll need to have a fair way to judge the competition."

"Glenn?" Carole said. "Dr. Vera?"

All eyes turned to look at Glenn. "I play the guitar a bit, but only for myself. Dr. Vera, who practices with me, isn't only an excellent veterinarian, but a talented musician. She plays in a group with some of the junior college's faculty members. Maybe, through her contacts, she can find us the judges we need. I'll ask her."

"Great," Harlan said. "We've got two fundraisers. I'll still chair the fundraising committee and reach out to corporate donors. Sarah, will you please finalize the date for YipYeow Day with the city? Also, would you check with Pastor Dobbs to see if he's willing to do another Blessing of the Animals? I'll find out when we can get the civic center for the talent show while Glenn talks to Dr. Vera about having her and her friends judge the competition. If Emily and Marcus agree to take the food responsibilities off your shoulders for both events, that would leave you and the rest of your committee with the basic logistics and promotion."

Sarah didn't see herself as a fundraiser or committee chair, but she wasn't going to buck the only boss who gave her a job after her divorce. Besides, having done YipYeow Day once, she could pull that off again. "I'm a little worried about the publicity end of things."

"That won't be a problem," Phyllis said. "I can handle PR, tying it into our needs for adoptions and fostering homes, but I'd like to involve a friend. She's new to Wheaton, but she's been doing a lot of the marketing for the annual charity run and ride that one of the local running groups does with the Wheaton Wildcats. I know she has some free time on her hands."

Phyllis's friend sounded perfect to Sarah. Although Sarah was almost as afraid of trying to drive a motorcycle as she was of cooking, she was quite familiar with the Wheaton Wildcats, a local fun motorcycle group that many of her friends belonged to. "I noticed the advertising for the run is quite a bit better this year. If she'll do it, that would be great. What's her name?"

"Lynn Martin."

Sarah and Harland looked at each other. It didn't seem like the right time to announce that Lynn Martin had recently become a widow.

"That would be fine, Phyllis." Harlan glanced at his pad again and closed it. "Even though he's not here, I'm sure Cliff will be responsible, after I call him, for anything that might involve construction." He winked. "That will teach him not to come to a meeting."

Carole stopped petting Buddy. "But . . ."

"Don't worry, Carole. When Cliff and I talked yesterday, he offered to handle any aspects of this project that might need a builder or a building supervisor. I think that covers everything." He stood.

Everyone followed suit. He held his office door and said "goodbye" as they filed into the waiting room.

The last, other than Harlan, to leave the room, Sarah twisted her watch on her wrist to see its face. It was almost three-thirty. Harlan had done a masterful job of wrapping this meeting up before Grace arrived. Normally, he insisted on walking any client or guest to the front door, but today Sarah automatically assumed that role. She glanced over her shoulder. The movement of his office door slowly closing caught her eye. In the second before her view was eclipsed, she glimpsed him pushing his desk chair back into its place behind his desk.

Phyllis and Carole departed quickly, but Glenn lingered. He looked toward Harlan's closed door before meeting her gaze.

"I haven't seen you lately, Sarah. How are RahRah and Fluffy doing?"

"Knock on wood, they're both fine."

"Must be the excellent veterinarian care they get."

Sarah grinned. "Must be."

"Well, you'll have to bring them by the clinic so they don't forget who I am."

"I'll do that."

Glenn put his hand on the doorknob. "Or I could always stick my head in and say hello to them if you'd let me pick you up and take you to dinner tomorrow night. What do you say?"

"I'd like that." Once the words were out of her mouth, Sarah didn't believe she'd said them. She was still in mental shock at accepting a Saturday night date with Glenn while he told her he'd pick her up at seven.

The time set, Glenn rushed out of the office, his mission seemingly accomplished. Through the glass of the doorway, Sarah watched him go down the sidewalk with what she interpreted as a distinct swing to his step. She felt just the opposite to what she imagined his mood was.

Sarah sank into her chair in her cubicle. She stared at her computer screen, but her mind was racing too much to work. She needed to be available to help Grace. How could she have accepted a date with Glenn? One minute they were kidding around and the next they were going out? What had she been thinking? Why had her acceptance rolled off her tongue so easily? What about Cliff?

On one hand, Sarah could argue her relationship with Cliff was on and off again. They took a step forward and then circumstances slowed things down. A good part of the problem was her reluctance to get involved with anyone again. Her marriage might have seemed like a fairy tale when she said "I do," but by the time the rat told her "I don't," Sarah was hard-pressed to remember its magical moments.

Cliff had issues too, but Sarah had to admit they'd worked through a great many of their external roadblocks. Now, she didn't know if accepting the date with Glenn was putting a nail in the coffin of her relationship with Cliff or a way of testing the strength of what Cliff and she might have.

Maybe that was the problem. She'd learned from the best at doing the worst. Wasn't her accepting a date with Glenn exactly like when Bill Blair began going out with his bimbo? Thinking rationally, she assured herself it was different. She wasn't married, nor had Cliff and she ever agreed not to see other people. They just hadn't during the last few months.

In her mind, she wasn't sure how to resolve her feelings about Cliff or Glenn, but she knew she only had a little over twenty-four hours, if she went on the date, to figure out how she felt about Glenn. Sarah didn't have that kind of luxury of time before she saw Cliff again. She'd agreed to join her mother this evening as one of Mr. Rogers's guests for steak night. The odds were Cliff would be a guest too.

The office's front door buzzer brought her out of her thoughts. Seeing Grace and Mandy, Grace's partner, on the monitor brought Sarah back to the world of what really mattered. She buzzed them in. Their presence put her dilemma on a back burner in lieu of worrying about Grace's problems.

Chapter 9

"It wasn't as bad as I thought it would be," Grace told Sarah, leaning on the wall between Sarah's desk and the waiting room.

Sarah wasn't sure if Grace was referring to her time being questioned and giving her statement or the difficulty of wrapping up the last details of Southwind's prep. Sarah hoped Grace wouldn't minimize everything when she talked to Harlan simply because she wanted to get back to work. She wished she could convince Grace how important it was to get the facts straight earlier rather than later. That rehashing the details now would benefit the creation of her defense, if it became necessary.

It was clear to Sarah that if she hadn't called Emily and explained what was going on and if Harlan had talked to Grace instead of Marcus, Grace wouldn't have left the restaurant or mentioned Harlan's request to Emily or Marcus. As it was, Sarah bet Emily probably threw Grace out of the restaurant with enough time to be here at four only after repeating multiple times that Marcus and she could cover any fires that broke out.

Chivalrously extending his hand, Harlan gestured for Grace, Mandy, and Sarah to step in front of him into his private office. Sarah and Mandy did, but Grace stopped in front of him.

"I don't see what we have to discuss. Me coming here now seems like a waste of your time and mine. Chief Gerard seemed perfectly satisfied with my explanation of the blood on my apron and why Dr. Martin and I got into our shouting match."

Sarah couldn't believe Grace didn't seem to comprehend how much trouble she potentially was in. For someone who'd tussled with the law when she was younger over what was comparably malicious mischief, how could Grace have blinders on when there were so many witnesses to her shouting match with Dr. Martin moments before he was murdered?

She waited for Harlan to lay the facts out in black-and-white for Grace, but he didn't say anything. Instead, he again used his hand to guide her to the conversation corner of his office. Once Mandy and Grace settled themselves on the couch and Sarah and he again took the winged chairs, Harlan picked up a pen and fresh legal pad from the table.

"Before I go any further, we need to discuss Mandy's presence."

Mandy reached over and held Grace's hand. "There's nothing to discuss. Grace wants me here."

"I understand that, but Grace needs to know your presence technically negates any claim she might make about this conversation being privileged. The attorney-client privilege doesn't apply with extra people present, except in certain situations."

"But I think we fit one of those exceptions. We may not be tied together as family, but I have information pertinent to today's events."

"Mandy, you may be a paralegal, but whether you could be seriously qualified as an exception to today's events is debatable. Even if you have pertinent information, that doesn't mean you sitting in on this meeting doesn't invalidate the attorney-client privilege."

Grace raised her hands. She motioned Harlan and Mandy to both stop talking. "Harlan, it's settled. I want Mandy here. I have nothing to hide from her."

"That's irrelevant."

"I don't care. Plus, she has something to add. If someone challenges our attorney-client relationship, let's deal with that problem then. Personally, from the way it went with Chief Gerard when he questioned me and took my statement, I'm sure he understands the situation and will start looking for the real killer."

"Don't underestimate Chief Gerard, Grace. He's like a bull in a china shop. This is simply the lull before the storm. You're his prime and probably only suspect."

"I don't understand. He seemed so open this morning."

"It was part of his interrogation strategy. The more you're comfortable with your interrogator, the more likely you'll talk. The hope is that the more a person talks, the person will either admit things or say things that are contradictory."

"I'm not worried. What I said to Chief Gerard was the same thing over and over. You say he's only looking at me, but what about the other people who were on the floor? Chief Gerard also seemed interested in the fact Dr. Martin had multiple wives."

"Isn't it usually the wife or butler who did it?" Sarah interjected.

Harlan gave her a hooded-eye stare that made her think he'd just swallowed a sour pickle. "Sorry, none of them have blood on their apron."

"But I explained how it got there. Chief Gerard understood."

"You may have laid it out in simplistic terms," Harlan said, "but Chief Gerard is from the school that follows the blood or the money. As far as I can tell, he doesn't think there's any money for him to trace. That just leaves him with the conviction that the trail of blood always leads back to the killer. In this case, he's also looking at the skill involved in murdering Dr. Martin using the ice pick method."

"The what?" Sarah asked.

"It's a way of stabbing someone so they bleed out quickly from the puncture wound without a large spatter. Someone with knife skills and the background of running with a gang who understood the ice pick method makes a prime suspect for Chief Gerard."

Grace crossed her arms over her chest. She raised her head, her jaw jutting forward. "If Chief Gerard is so sure I did it, why didn't he arrest me? Why didn't the school terminate me?"

"The college isn't going to dismiss you outright until there's a formal arrest or reason to do so. The school may, under the guise of protecting themselves and you during an ongoing investigation, put you on temporary leave until things are resolved. As for Chief Gerard, he was burned in the past when he jumped the gun based upon a half-brained hypothesis rather than facts. Consequently, he took some classes and now takes his time, waiting for the forensic evidence to come back from the lab. If he thought you were a flight risk or going to disappear like a bleep from his radar, he'd have detained or arrested you. In the meantime, he'll check out every detail of your story."

"Well, that shouldn't be a problem. I told him everything." Grace pushed her lips forward in a way that reminded Sarah of how Emily pouted when the twins were five or six.

Keeping his head lowered, Harlan doodled something on the pad in his lap. "Everything except the truth."

Grace stood and in one step rounded the coffee table. Even though she was on the wing side of his chair, she towered over Harlan. Harlan didn't even bother raising his head to acknowledge her presence. Instead, he continued writing on his pad, something he often did while listening to a client.

Sarah wondered if Harlan thought his silence while he doodled encouraged clients to talk.

"I told Chief Gerard the truth."

"Only up to a point. You telegraphed loud and clear there was something you were avoiding every time you hesitated or shifted away from what he asked. It was apparent you either were hiding something or not telling the full truth."

Harlan put his pen down on his pad. "Grace, I've known you a long time and have seen you keep your cool with authority figures. Today, between blinking and your body language, it was obvious you were leaving things out. You're not a good enough liar to get away with it.

Believe me, if—or should I say *when*—you're arrested, letting others tell your full story from their perception won't serve you well."

Grace steadied herself for a moment by resting her hand on the high-tufted wingback of Harlan's chair. She returned to the couch depleted, as if Harlan had punctured her as easily as a pin thrust into a balloon. She reached for Mandy's hand.

Mandy placed her hand over Grace's. "Harlan's right. You know I sit in on lots of insurance fraud or accident case depositions and the physical and speech tells or cues he's talking about are exactly what we look for. You've got to be honest about everything."

"But—"

"There isn't any *but.* You're only going to get yourself in deeper if you try to keep me out of this."

Perhaps Harlan sensed the same aura of vulnerability in Grace that Sarah did, because he softened his tone. "What really happened when Dr. Martin came back to your classroom?"

"Like I told you. When he came in and shut the door, he was serious but calm. I don't know why, but I thought he was going to apologize, so I waited for him to speak."

"And did he apologize?"

"No. He let me have it about my teaching abilities and personal life. I was stunned."

"By his criticism of your teaching?"

"No, by his horrible homophobic comments about my personal life. At first, I was simply surprised and not sure I was hearing what he was saying. Then, the more he went off on me and my relationship with Mandy, I came down to his level and responded."

"With both barrels?"

Grace shook her head no. "Not at first. I was yelling, but I still had control of what I was doing and saying."

"But you lost it at some point?"

Grace nodded.

"What did Dr. Martin say that crossed the line? How did he provoke you to respond to his tirade?" Harlan asked. "Chief Gerard and I both know you've managed to stand up to a lot of bullying in the past."

Grace was still, as if gathering her thoughts. When she did speak, it was slowly, enunciating each word. "Harlan, I guess what set me off was the joy he took in lording himself over me. I didn't really think about it until now, but he played on everyone's weaknesses. Dr. Martin knew being part of the faculty meant a lot to me, so that's what he went after. He manipulated me."

"That's an interesting observation and matches what you told Chief Gerard when you gave your statement, but what else did he say? What button did he push that caused you to respond so loudly others heard you?"

"Our fight was overheard?"

Sarah frowned. She was unsure how Grace couldn't know she'd been overheard. "Grace, don't you remember hearing Dr. Williams tell the campus police chief that you were guilty and that everyone had heard you arguing with Dr. Martin not even thirty minutes earlier?"

"I wasn't paying full attention to what everyone was saying, especially Dr. Williams. He's always so pompous, I normally tune him out."

"Well, what about when Fern and Chief Gerard were talking? She not only told him the same thing Dr. Williams shared with the campus police chief, but she added more details about how you accused him of being out of line and made it clear you wouldn't take this kind of behavior from him."

"I guess I wasn't listening or processing everything that was going on around me." Grace glanced to the floor before finally looking back at Harlan. "I didn't realize people heard us. Things got out of hand. I'm a little ashamed because the words we were slinging were nasty. Much of what we both said was so hurtful that my mind keeps blurring in and out on our confrontation."

Harlan bent toward Grace. "That's why you need to tell the truth. No one, including Chief Gerard, believes you were so mad and upset simply because Dr. Martin challenged your teaching skills. Anyone knowing you is fully aware you don't blow up easily, so Dr. Martin had to have gone after you about something else. You've talked in generalities the last few minutes. I need to know what you can remember him saying."

It was obvious from Harlan's demeanor he already knew the answer, but for the love of her, Sarah couldn't imagine what could have gotten under Grace's skin so deeply. In the time since Sarah had known Grace, she'd always been cool and collected, able to take things in stride while keeping hidden any emotional reaction. Either Sarah didn't know the real Grace or absolutely nothing involving Grace and Dr. Martin was adding up.

"Grace, you've got to tell Harlan," Sarah said. "Believe me, sharing everything with Harlan made a big difference when he represented both Emily and my mother when they were each accused of murder. If you remember, Emily made it more difficult because she kept things close to her chest, almost too long. Please, help Harlan help you."

Grace clamped her lips together as if that would keep the words from spilling out.

Her reaction irked Sarah because Grace's behavior was wasting time. "Grace, whatever you think you're hiding is going to come back to bite you if you don't tell him everything."

"Sarah, it isn't important. I don't want to get anyone else more involved in this mess."

Harlan interrupted. "Let me be the judge."

CHAPTER 10

Sarah willed Grace to get a move on and tell Harlan what was really going on. As Grace began to speak, Sarah silently was thankful that this time her mental telepathy worked.

"I already told you that after berating me about my teaching skills, Dr. Martin changed the subject to my personal life." She stopped and looked at Sarah and Mandy before focusing on Harlan. "You know I keep my professional and personal lives separate. Dr. Martin blindsided me by launching into some very nasty remarks about the impression Mandy and I being a couple might have on my students. I hadn't ever gotten the impression he was a religious fanatic or had any strong beliefs against same-sex relationships, so I was completely shocked by how vicious he was."

Grace squeezed Mandy's hand tighter. "I couldn't figure out why he was so biased against us and why he was bringing it up now. In the short time he's been in Wheaton, Mandy and I haven't run into him where I would have introduced them to each other, but he knew all about her. He not only was aware where she worked as a paralegal, but that she taught self-defense classes, which he suggested both of us might need in the future. It was his continued slurs that got to me."

Harlan looked at Grace while he tapped his pen on the pad. "So how do you think he found out and what do you think riled him up today?"

"I have no idea how he made the connection, but Dr. Martin . . ."

Sarah interrupted. "By chance, was he at that cocktail party or whatever it was that you went to before the term began? You know, the one when I covered a shift at the restaurant for you?"

Grace grimaced and snapped her fingers. "That could have been it. I know I never introduced Mandy to him one-on-one, but he could have seen us there together. Maybe somebody else said something about us being a couple."

Harlan stopped tapping his pen against his pad. Waving it at her, he caught Grace's attention again. "Let's assume that was when he saw you together, but it really doesn't matter. Grace, I've known you since you were a teenager. Over the years, other people have said things about you. Even if you couldn't easily ignore them, you did. What happened today?"

"Once I got over being stunned by the hateful things he was saying, I held myself in check and calmly told him my personal life had no bearing on my teaching. His response was to use even more abusive language, including an inappropriate slur. That did it. Something snapped."

Sarah understood. There'd been many times Jane said or did something that made her snap. It might not seem like much, but it was the cumulative impact of her words or actions. Although Dr. Martin's comments had all been concentrated in a short period of time, he obviously hit a nerve by using some objectionable reference that opened the flood Grace had been holding back. Sarah kept her face neutral as Grace continued.

"I'm proud of who I am and that I'm with Mandy, and I told him that. Look, I may have been loud and far from deferential to my superior after what he said to me, but I will swear on a stack of Bibles in any courtroom that Dr. Martin was alive when I turned my back on him and walked out of my classroom. In fact, he was still ranting at me."

Now, Harlan looked up. "Are you saying you physically left Dr. Martin in your classroom by himself?"

"Yes, Harlan. That's exactly what I'm saying. He was in the front of the room, near the first prep table, yelling at my back when I walked away from him to meet Sarah."

Sarah remembered how flustered Grace seemed when she came running down the steps to where Sarah waited on the bench. "Grace, didn't your walking out on him make him even madder?"

"Probably, but at that moment, I didn't care. I'd stood up for myself and what I believe in, but I knew if I didn't leave, I'd truly cross the bounds of professional propriety. I guess I could have gone to the ladies' room or simply stepped into the hall, but it was getting late, so I went to meet you and hoped he'd be gone by the time I came back to clean up my classroom."

Harlan resumed tapping his pen. "How many times did you come back?"

While Harlan waited expectantly for Grace to respond, he tapped in a steady rhythm. Sarah wanted to shout at him to stop. The noise wasn't loud, but it was annoying. From the way Grace raised her voice, Sarah couldn't tell if the tapping was getting on her nerves too or if it was the way he'd posed his question. It felt as if he wasn't believing her or still thought she was hiding something.

"What do you mean, Harlan? How many times? I've told you everything now, so I don't know what you're trying to get at. When I left Dr. Martin, I took the stairs to the first floor, went outside, and found Sarah. We talked as she re-bandaged my hand, and we came back up together. That was the only time I went back to my classroom after I walked out on Dr. Martin." She stared at him for a moment, as if defying him to challenge what she was saying, but then looked to Sarah for confirmation.

Sarah nodded. "When Grace and I got back to the third floor, Dr. Martin was already dead. Franklin had called the campus police and paramedics and was blocking everyone, including Grace, from going into the classroom. He suggested we might be more comfortable closer to the elevators than in front of the classroom doorway." She paused to take a breath.

"Harlan, considering how many possible suspects there are, if you include everyone on the floor and throw in Dr. Martin's wives for good measure, surely Chief Gerard has more suspects than Grace."

He laid his pen and pad on the coffee table and frowned. "Remember, Chief Gerard follows the trail of blood or money. In this case, he hasn't found anything leading anywhere but to Grace."

Maybe Chief Gerard couldn't find anyone except for Grace and, come to think of it, Wanda, with Dr. Martin's blood on them, but perhaps he'd missed a trail that led to money.

Talking over whatever Harlan was starting to say, Sarah leaned forward and spoke directly to Grace. "What was it you wanted to talk to me about today? You said it had something to do with Jane."

Narrowing her eyes, Grace scrunched up her face. "I'm not sure what Jane wanted has anything to do with this."

"Grace," Mandy said, "if Dr. Martin or the college was involved, it may have some bearing on what's going on. Let Harlan decide the importance of whatever Jane wanted from you." Again, Mandy held Grace's hand.

Grace shifted her gaze to Sarah. "I promised Jane I wouldn't tell Emily and Marcus."

"I gather my name didn't come up when Jane made you promise not to share any of this with Emily or Marcus?" From Grace's silence, but blinking eyes, Sarah understood the fine line Grace was walking. "I'm right, aren't I?"

"Normally, I wouldn't have told you either, because technically my promise was meant to cover everyone involved with Southwind, but Emily and Marcus have been so good to me, I couldn't let them be blindsided by Jane's proposal."

"What proposal?" Harlan asked.

"Last week, Jane met with the college's president, Dr. Green, Dr. Martin, a few other staff members, and two city council members. She proposed what she thought was a win-win for the school and Wheaton."

"With that group at the meeting, it must have been an interesting proposal."

"It was. Jane wants the college to assume ownership or simply lease her building and restaurant to use as a hands-on hospitality experience location for its students. Unlike the school's dated kitchens and simulated hotel area, Jane's Place would provide students with practical hotel and culinary experience running its state-of-the-art kitchen, dining rooms, and upstairs bedrooms. She proposed trying to get the city to make a small monetary grant by suggesting that its sponsorship would reap Wheaton a large benefit."

Sarah understood how the proposed partnership would allow the college to advertise to prospective students the opportunity to be trained in a top-of-the-line facility, but she couldn't see how the program would benefit Wheaton. "What's the connection with Wheaton? It doesn't have anything to do with the college's hospitality programs."

"True, but the addition of the upstairs bedrooms for a lower-than-market rental because they're student-run would let the convention bureau add a group of more reasonably priced hotel rooms to its available accommodations list for things like weddings or conferences. It would be another selling tool for Wheaton's Convention Bureau."

From Pastor Dobbs insisting on having YipYeow Day and the Blessing of the Animals on back-to-back days so his wife, the convention bureau's assistant director, could take credit for booking an event resulting in the rental of several hotel rooms, Sarah understood the strength of

Jane's argument. The availability of lower-priced rooms was a definite attraction when organizations considered Wheaton for a meeting or to accommodate overflow from conferences or sporting events held in Birmingham.

"Is that the only benefit Wheaton would get for becoming a partner with Jane's Place and the college?"

"Not according to Jane. She maintained Wheaton could also boast the partnership as an example of Wheaton participating in another forward-thinking concept, because the city would be able to take partial credit for helping students gain exposure to all aspects of culinary and hotel management. Finally, according to Jane's scenario, the partnership would be an economic windfall for Wheaton."

"How?" With Wheaton's small population and its incorporated area only being around five square miles, it seemed to Sarah the word *windfall* might be a bit of an exaggeration on Jane's part.

"Jane told them that because Wheaton would have an exclusive elegant place for events or meals, where it received a deeply discounted rate instead of having to pay the going rates of other local restaurants, there would be immediate fiscal savings. She said—"

Sarah cut Grace off. "But Southwind always gives the city a discount or group rate."

"Maybe, but discounted versus at cost or free is a big difference."

Harlan let out a low whistle. "Jane's offer sounds enticing. How do you fit in?"

Grace looked from Sarah to Harlan and back to Sarah. "Jane was sure her proposal was a slam dunk, but instead of jumping at her offer of Jane's Place, the committee took it under advisement. When Jane came to me, she said that during the meeting, she got the feeling Dr. Martin was the kingpin in making any decision. She thought involving me, as a prized alumna and now adjunct instructor, might give her a leg up swaying a favorable vote. I'm sure after the meeting Jane heard the rumor that with whatever he touched, Dr. Martin wanted to know what was in it for him."

Sarah snickered. "Sounds like classic Jane." The soberness of Grace's face made Sarah stop mid-snicker. "Grace, did Jane offer you something more if you acted as her shill?"

"When I refused to accept her executive chef position, Jane asked me to be the program's on-site central operations manager and liaison with the college. She said she'd get it through as a salaried CJCC staff position—I'd do the work and Dr. Martin would get the credit for the program's success."

"That position seems administrative rather than letting you do what you love in the kitchen."

"That's true, but as Jane pointed out, the position would come with insurance and the ability to pay into the state's retirement system." Grace lowered her head. "I lost my student health insurance when I graduated, and I've only been able to afford a basic plan since then."

Aware of Grace's diabetes and finances and knowing Emily and Marcus weren't offering Southwind or Southwind Pub employees a group health plan, Sarah could see how Jane's offer would resolve a major worry Grace had been carrying around post graduation. Sarah clenched and released her hands as she debated how to respond.

This was exactly the kind of master maneuvering Jane did. Sarah could picture Jane presenting the position to Grace as a win-win situation and, in a sense, it was. Even though Sarah felt it would be a horrible situation for

Grace in the long run, she couldn't begrudge Grace good health insurance. Noticing Grace still averting her gaze from Sarah's, it dawned on Sarah that Grace was omitting something. "Is there something else you aren't telling me?"

"Only what I was going to tell you originally—that if Jane's proposal is accepted by the city and college, Southwind and the Southwind Pub would almost certainly take a big financial hit."

The idea of a financial hit when Southwind was just getting on its feet caught Sarah's attention and made her shiver. "How?"

"If the college accepts Jane's proposal, she thinks the Southwind Group will lose a lot of business, because Jane would not only get all of the events sponsored by the college, but the culinary students would bring in their friends for happy hour. In addition, Jane believes the school and city, paying her a guaranteed flat monthly facility rental fee or some type of subsidy per student, would promote Jane's Place over Southwind. Even while she's waiting for them to decide on her proposal, Jane's hosting events featuring faculty members to show the college and city officials how effective partnering with Jane's Place will be."

What Grace was saying made sense to Sarah. In the past, Jane consistently went for the most underhanded ways to obtain her goals, rather than simply relying on straightforward transactions. The difference here was Jane wasn't playing to Dr. Martin's male vanity. Instead, she was offering the college and city the ability to take credit for the project. Of course, knowing Jane, there probably was a way she planned to gain recognition later.

CHAPTER 11

Sarah gunned her car's engine. By the time Harlan and she finished talking with Grace and Mandy, it was after six. She was glad to know Grace was going directly home with Mandy—Emily and Marcus had insisted, considering the events of the day, that Grace take the night off. Sarah wished she didn't have to go to steak night at the retirement center. Because of her swirling fears about Grace being arrested, Chief Gerard's narrow search for suspects, and what she'd just learned about Jane's newest threat to the Southwind Group, Sarah really wanted to go straight home to RahRah and Fluffy or to Southwind to talk to Emily.

In the end, though, she knew taking an hour or two for dinner was easier than having a confrontation with her mother, who Sarah needed to remember to call, as her mother preferred, Maybelle. As it was, her mother wouldn't be pleased with her not being on time. Maybelle would have counted on Sarah leaving work at five. Based upon her car's clock, if she continued making all the lights between the office and the senior living center, she would only be ten minutes late for dinner.

She wished there had been a few extra minutes to stop home to freshen up and check on RahRah and Fluffy. RahRah would be okay no matter what time she got back, but it would have been nice giving Fluffy another walk or, better yet, bringing her to the retirement home to visit Mr. Rogers. She whipped into a parking space. At least, she could take comfort in that she'd left her pets plenty of water and food before returning to the office.

Sarah slipped into her seat at the table in time to hear her mother and Mr. Rogers assuring Cliff for probably the zillionth time how steak night was always good, so he should definitely order steak. Glancing around the filled dining room, she couldn't help but think the same exchange was probably happening between most of the other residents and their guests.

When the waitress came to the table, Cliff, Mr. Rogers, and Maybelle ordered the steak. Sarah asked for the broiled chicken breast without any sauce. Maybelle and Mr. Rogers tried to convince her to change her order. Sarah bit her tongue rather than get into a fight about why she thought eating chicken and fish was healthier for her than red meat. Besides, she'd seen enough things stabbed today.

Sarah politely declined their suggestions and repeated her order.

"At least," Maybelle said, once the waitress left the table, "you didn't get the sauce. George and I have noticed they not only use the sauce on the chicken, but on all the different types of prefrozen patties they serve."

Mr. Rogers hastened to add more information. "Because we can't tell what the patties are from tasting them, whenever we see one of those dishes on the menu, we call it mystery meat with sauce à la—"

"Mysteria." Maybelle finished for him.

Sarah rolled her eyes.

Veering from their lighthearted jesting about the food, Maybelle turned to her daughter and gave her the look only a mother can give an adult daughter. "You're late."

Under the table, Sarah felt Cliff's hand find hers and lightly squeeze it. As good as it felt, she couldn't help but think about the date she'd made with Glenn. Despite her twinge of guilt, Sarah left her hand where it was.

"Before you got here," Cliff said, "Uncle George asked about how Fluffy and RahRah are getting along. He hoped you might bring Fluffy with you tonight."

Sarah glanced from Cliff to Mr. Rogers. She knew how much Mr. Rogers cared about the little white dog he'd rescued after it was abandoned and left roaming in their neighborhood. The bond between Fluffy and him had been unbreakable until, after an injury, Mr. Rogers was hospitalized and went to rehab. During that time, Sarah, volunteered by Maybelle, took Fluffy in.

When Cliff and Mr. Rogers felt it best, during his long recovery, to sell his two-generation family home on Main Street and move into the Sunshine Retirement Home, Mr. Rogers was devastated to discover the retirement home didn't allow pets. He only sold his house to Jane after Sarah agreed to keep Fluffy. Considering what a pain Jane was, Sarah sometimes thought her life would have been easier if she'd refused to take Fluffy in. Of course, those feelings disappeared every time she hugged the little ball of white fur.

"I'm sorry. I planned to bring Fluffy, but we were off schedule at work all day. As late as I already was, I couldn't go home and pick Fluffy up. Mr. Rogers, I'll try to bring her by this weekend. Monday at the latest."

This seemed to satisfy Mr. Rogers, but her mother raised an eyebrow and cocked her head in Sarah's direction. "Don't tell me you're involved in the murder at the college."

Sarah answered her mother, but kept her gaze on Cliff's face. She didn't want to ruin tonight's dinner by upsetting either her mother or Cliff, both of whom felt she should leave sleuthing to the professionals. "Only tangentially. I was at the college with Grace when her program chair, Dr. Martin, was found dead. Because I was afraid Grace might be implicated, I called Harlan."

From the serious look on her mother's face, Sarah knew the inquisition was about to begin. "And?"

"Protecting Grace is as far as my involvement in this goes."

"Is everything okay with Grace?" Cliff asked.

Sarah shrugged. She couldn't talk about a case or potential case they had going on in the office. Better to shift the conversation. "Mother, I mean Maybelle, how did you know someone had been killed at the college?"

"We heard all about it on the news. As you can well imagine, it was the lead story on this afternoon's five o'clock report. They didn't even run a national story first."

Mr. Rogers leaned forward, his ever-present bow tie bobbing against his Adam's apple. "It was the noon teaser, so we all tuned in for the entire story at five. Our TV room was packed!"

Sarah could imagine there hadn't been an extra seat or space to squeeze another wheelchair into the TV room when the news came on. She understood the residents' curiosity and excitement. Wheaton was the kind of town that boasted having few, if any, crimes. Most of the ones reported, until the murders of the past year, were anything but newsworthy. One of her favorites was a series the local news ran when there was a rash of thefts. The most recent occurred during a rainy two weeks when people left umbrellas outside their front doors. They soon went missing. It took a week before the local police caught the yellow Lab wandering the neighborhood amusing himself by taking any umbrellas he found.

From the level of excitement in Mr. Rogers's voice, Sarah could tell a news story mentioning murder was something he and the other Sunshine Retirement Home residents followed with great interest. Thinking of them as armchair quarterbacks, she wondered if Mr. Rogers or any of his friends ever called the police station with crime-solving suggestions. She could easily imagine them searching the internet or comparing theories and fact patterns from their favorite mysteries.

Sarah wished she was as equally immersed from afar in the recent rash of TV stories about murders in Wheaton as the retirement home's residents. For there to be more murders in the last six months than the past sixteen years combined was a true aberration. Unfortunately, she'd been involved in all the recent ones. This was a record she didn't want to extend.

"Excuse me, Mr. Rogers, what did you just say?"

He stared over his pince-nez glasses at her. Sarah squirmed. She didn't know if she was reacting more to his stare or the reproving look she felt her mother was giving her for not only being late, but then not paying attention to the dinner table conversation.

"I said, of course you can well imagine how shocked everyone here was when we realized the person killed was one of our extended family members."

Sarah was confused. If she remembered correctly, Grace had mentioned Dr. Martin was only forty-two. That was way below the average Sunshine Retirement Home age. Although a few of the residents were in their sixties, most of the younger ones were in their seventies. She looked at her mother. "Did Dr. Martin live here?"

"No. His mother does. It's a pity. She has early-onset dementia." Maybelle pointed behind Sarah to a table across the room. "That's her sitting at the table by the bay window."

Turning in her chair, Sarah looked behind her at the table her mother indicated. Sarah did a double take. Discounting the gray-haired woman, who she presumed was Dr. Martin's mother, Sarah was shocked at the presence of the other three people.

CHAPTER 12

Sarah wouldn't have expected to see any of the three at the retirement home, let alone with Mrs. Martin. The one with the perfectly coiffured hairstyle and St. John knit suit was Eloise, a dear friend of both Maybelle and Sarah and the newest member of the city council. The other two were Franklin and Wanda, the students from Grace's class.

Sarah didn't know the connection between the four people at the table, but a glance at their plates told her they'd all gotten the message that tonight was steak night. "Mom, what is Eloise doing at that table?"

"Having dinner with Kait Martin."

"That much I figured out, but why? How do they know each other?" Despite living in Birmingham for several years, Sarah's parents had done business, banked, and hung with so many friends in Wheaton that her mother's grapevine let Maybelle usually know things well before Sarah heard a whisper about them.

"They were good friends through their high school graduation. You remember Eloise stayed in Wheaton and started working at the bank right out of high school. Kait went to Carleton Junior Community College and studied accounting for two years. After she received her degree, she took a bookkeeping job in Atlanta. That's where she met her late husband. I don't remember exactly what he did, but he was some sort of executive, so she stopped working after they had their only child."

"Dr. Martin?"

"That's right. Anyway, Kait and her family moved around the country a lot because of her husband's job, but Eloise and she annually exchanged Christmas cards. When Dr. Martin took the Carleton job, he contacted Eloise to suggest places where his mother might live because she was showing signs of early-onset dementia. He didn't think it was safe for her to live alone or with him and his wife. Since Kait moved in, Eloise visits once or twice a month."

A noise between a sniff and a snort made Sarah and Cliff look in Mr. Rogers's direction.

"Her son put Kait here to get her out of his way. It's a disgrace." He banged his fist on the table.

Cliff dabbed his mouth with his napkin. Sarah was sure it was a subterfuge to avoid his uncle seeing him grin at his uncle's intense reaction. "Uncle George, that's not a particularly nice thing to say."

"Nice, shmice."

Sarah coughed and hid her own mouth behind her hand as Mr. Rogers continued. She could tell from the way he waved his hands that this was going to be one of his long-winded tirades. Being his neighbor, she'd long ago learned how he loved to examine everything from a historic perspective. The thing was, while his ramblings might do with some editing, they were usually right on the money.

"The truth is the truth. That son of hers rarely comes to see Kait, and his new wife never visits."

"Maybe his wife and mother don't get along," Cliff said.

"How could anyone not get along with Kait? I've known her since we were kids. Sure, she's slipping a bit, but she's the sweetest thing. Of course, not as sweet as this sourpuss."

Although he smiled at her mother, Sarah was surprised Maybelle didn't take offense at Mr. Rogers's remark. She would have thought her mother would have replied with some choice comment or left the table in a huff. Instead, Maybelle glanced toward the table by the windows and then carried on as if Mr. Rogers hadn't said anything about her.

"I don't think that's the reason his wife doesn't visit." Now it was Maybelle's turn to act like a professor enlightening her class. She leaned forward and almost whispered, "This wife isn't his first one."

"More like the third," Mr. Rogers interjected.

Maybelle ignored him and kept talking. "She came once. She's quite a bit younger than him, which probably makes people in our age group seem ancient to her. Personally, I bet places like this and the people in them scare her. Besides, Kait and she really don't know each other. He only married her a year or so ago. Kait still recognizes people and things she's familiar with, but just like she can't get the hang of her phone or the television remote, I doubt getting to know a new daughter-in-law would be easy for her."

Mr. Rogers again slapped the table with his hand. "Kait may not recognize her son's new wife as a family member, but you don't have to be bosom buddies to visit someone. Besides, Kait's known her son the few times he came."

They all stopped talking as the steaks were served. Although Sarah wasn't all that fond of red meat, she had to admit her mother and Mr. Rogers were right about steak night. Their steaks looked beautiful.

Without waiting for Sarah's chicken to arrive, Mr. Rogers picked up his steak knife and cut himself a healthy portion. He raised his fork. As he twisted it around, Sarah could see the steak was perfectly seared on the outside and pink on the inside. Instead of putting the bite in his mouth, he resumed the conversation. "When Kait's son shows—I mean, *showed*—his face, he only stayed a few minutes. There was always a pressing meeting or dinner he had to attend. I don't think he ever cleared his schedule for steak night."

"That's one of the reasons Eloise started coming to steak night at least once a month," Mr. Rogers and Maybelle said simultaneously.

Unsure what the connection between Kait's son not coming to steak night with Eloise joining Kait once a month was, Sarah posed her question to her mother and Mr. Rogers.

While Mr. Rogers swallowed his piece of meat, Maybelle clarified things for her.

"Shortly after Kait moved in, Eloise began visiting her. On one of those visits, Kait confided that, although there were lots of people living here and many activities for her to participate in, there were times she felt lonely. You know how kindhearted Eloise is. Despite her many obligations, she decided joining Kait for steak night periodically would be fun for both of them."

"That's really nice of her."

Mr. Rogers swallowed another piece of steak. "That's Eloise. No matter how busy she is, she finds a way to make time for other people. I tell you, if it weren't for Kait's granddaughter and Eloise visiting, Kait would be like a lot of people here. Forgotten."

Sarah wasn't sure how things had jumped to Kait having a granddaughter, let alone one who visited. Glancing at the others sitting with Eloise, it slowly dawned on her that Wanda might be Kait's granddaughter. Sarah did the math.

Eloise was older than Maybelle. If Sarah was nearing thirty and her mother almost sixty, assuming Kait married early and had her son while she was in her early twenties, she could easily have a child Dr. Martin's age. Using that premise, at forty-two, Dr. Martin might have a daughter Wanda's age.

"Is Wanda Kait's granddaughter?"

"That's right. After Wanda enrolled at Carleton this year, Eloise and Kait decided she would be a perfect match for Eloise's nephew, Franklin. He's a year ahead of her at school."

Cliff groaned. "Matchmaking."

"Don't knock it, nephew. In the right hands, it can be quite effective." Mr. Rogers smiled at Maybelle.

Sarah wasn't sure if it was a change in the dining room's lighting or if her mother blushed.

"Now, George, I'm not a matchmaker." Directing her

comments to Sarah, Maybelle ignored whatever he said in response. "Kait and Eloise knew if they gave Franklin Wanda's phone number or orchestrated a date, it would go nowhere. That's why they decided to invite them each to a steak night, but make sure they all sat together. They figured the young people would be relieved to have each other to talk to instead of their old fogey relatives. As you can see, the plan worked. By the end of that first dinner, the kids clicked."

Devious. She almost hit her forehead with her hand. No wonder Mr. Rogers had teased her mother about matchmaking. In their own way, Mr. Rogers and Maybelle had done the same thing with Cliff and her on various steak nights.

"Better yet," Maybelle said, "not only have the two young lovebirds found each other, but being starving students, they gladly come and eat as Kait's guests every Friday night. Eloise joins them once a month or more often if she has the time."

Cliff reached across the table for the salt. "They're definitely regulars. I've seen them here almost every time I've joined Uncle George for steak night." Putting the salt back on the table, Cliff muttered to Sarah. "They're really cute together. Don't you think?"

Unsure if Cliff was referring to Wanda and Franklin or his uncle and her mother, Sarah ignored him and concentrated on her mother. Seeing her mother's reaction to the young couple, she wondered how much wider Maybelle's smile would be if she'd been the one to make the match.

Taking her mother's explanation of the relationship between Kait, Wanda, Eloise, and Franklin and comparing how Franklin and Wanda reacted to Dr. Martin's death, Sarah felt something was off. Although when she'd first seen them on the culinary floor, Wanda was somewhat teary-eyed and upset, she wasn't acting like a person who only moments earlier learned her father was murdered. It seemed to Sarah that rather than being stoic, Wanda should have exhibited a stronger emotional reaction.

Even Grace, who didn't particularly like Dr. Martin, adamantly fought with Franklin about getting into her classroom and trying to help Dr. Martin. Grace reacted with anger, sorrow, and shock. Maybe, by the time Grace and Sarah got there, Wanda was in a state of shock, but shouldn't Franklin have consoled his girlfriend rather than played Keystone Cop? In retrospect, it didn't seem to Sarah that either of them reacted how she would have expected. Surely, it should have been more intense. Sarah looked across the table at Maybelle. If she found her mother dead, propped across a prep table, Sarah would have gone to pieces.

Thinking back to the time she thought Fluffy ate something and seemed deathly ill, Sarah remembered being such a basket case she could barely get her act together to take Fluffy to the vet before the clinic closed. In fact, rather than take a moment to grab her car keys and drive, she picked Fluffy up and ran down the long driveway and across Main Street to the renovated house that contained the clinic. Sarah could still remember her heart pounding as she banged on the clinic's locked door, praying a veterinarian heard her.

No, the more Sarah thought about it, Franklin and Wanda's subdued reactions didn't make sense. Surely, Wanda should have had more trouble following the discussions going on with Chief Gerard, but she'd easily piped up how Dr. Martin picked up Grace's jacket.

It was possible Wanda and Franklin had gotten themselves under control before or after she saw them and were now keeping it together to break the news to Kait, but something felt off. Sarah cut and swallowed a piece of her chicken. She didn't really taste it. Her mind was racing a mile a minute trying to understand Wanda and Franklin's detached reactions or deduce what they might be hiding. The only way she was going to figure out exactly what was going on was to go a-sleuthing.

Chapter 13

Sarah's fork clinked as she rested it on her plate. She stood and draped her napkin haphazardly over the back of her chair. "Excuse me for a moment. I want to say hello to Eloise."

Maybelle gestured with her knife to the chicken on Sarah's plate. "Now? You're still eating."

Already behind her mother, Sarah gave Maybelle's shoulders a light squeeze. "You were right about the chicken. It's just this side of mystery meat. While the three of you finish your steaks, I'm going to pop over to their table. They look like they're finishing up, and I haven't seen Eloise in a while. I want to catch her before she leaves the dining room. I'll be back in a minute."

"We'll be on dessert by then." Cliff pointed to a dessert buffet table set up in the middle of the room. "Remember, unlike the meal, they don't take dessert orders. It's a buffet and you know how fast the good desserts go."

"Save me a bite of yours." Sarah was out of earshot before he could grumble to her, as he usually did, that, considering her definition of a bite, she needed to get her own dessert.

Eloise must have seen Sarah coming, because she stood before Sarah reached the table. Sarah was overwhelmed by the scent of Chanel No. 5 as the two women embraced. Peering over Eloise's shoulder, Sarah acknowledged the other people at the table. "Sorry for barging in on you, but when I saw Eloise, I had to come by to say hello."

Ignoring the "that's okay" reactions from those at the table, Sarah focused her attention back on Eloise. "It's been weeks since I've seen you. What have you been up to?"

"Juggling. The new job's keeping me hopping. There's a lot to learn. What about you?"

From a few stories on the news, it was obvious to Sarah the time and effort Eloise was putting into getting up to speed as Wheaton's newest councilwoman was paying off. Sarah bit her tongue, knowing she was telling a little white lie. "The usual. Happily, nothing too exciting."

"How are RahRah and Fluffy?"

"They couldn't be better. RahRah rules the roost, with Fluffy loyally following. Their interaction is more like siblings than a cat and a dog."

"Speaking of siblings, where are my manners? Sarah, I don't think you've met my friend Kait, her granddaughter Wanda, or my sister's son, Franklin."

Kait verbally acknowledged the introduction. Wanda

and Franklin responded with a slight nod, but neither said anything. She couldn't believe they didn't recognize her, so she assumed that, for some reason, they were uncomfortable seeing her. Perhaps they were afraid she'd say something about Dr. Martin's death that would upset Kait. Or, it dawned on her, maybe they hadn't told Kait about his death yet. Sarah decided to be careful how she worded what she said.

"Actually, I already met Wanda and Franklin earlier today, but, Kait, I'm delighted to meet you."

In response to Sarah's greeting, Kait slowly raised her face toward where Sarah stood. "Oh, do you go to school with Wanda?"

Sarah wasn't sure if Kait had bad eyesight or thought Sarah was younger than twenty-nine. "I wish I did, but I simply happened to be at the college when she was there today."

Eloise raised an eyebrow. "That's not your usual stomping grounds. What were you doing at Carleton?"

"Visiting Grace. She's an adjunct this term. In fact, she's teaching the knife skills course Wanda and Franklin are taking. Grace and I had planned to visit between the end of her class and when she had to be at Southwind."

"At Carleton?" Kait interrupted. "My son is on the faculty there. Do you know him?" Her lips formed a pout as she didn't wait for Sarah to answer. "My son used to be a good boy. He says he's busy between being a newlywed and having a big, important job, but you know how that is. Doug never comes to see me anymore. It's almost like I don't have a son."

Kait relaxed when she reached out and patted her granddaughter's arm. "Wanda, here. She's a good girl. She visits me at least once a week. Wanda is a very good girl."

Sarah wasn't sure how to respond. She didn't want to agree with Kait, nor did she want to say something praising Dr. Martin or excusing his behavior. Besides, technically, Kait no longer had a son who could come to visit her. She wasn't sure if Kait had been informed about Dr. Martin's death or if she simply was blocking out what had happened to him.

Rather than say something wrong, Sarah directed her comment to Eloise. "As you may have heard, there was some excitement after Grace's class today."

Eloise shifted her gaze from Sarah to Wanda and back again to Sarah. She shook her head in the negative. "Wanda and Franklin filled me in. That's one of the reasons I decided tonight was perfect for us to get together for steak night with Kait. We knew we had a lot to talk about and decided it would be easier to have a nice dinner together first."

As Eloise spoke, Sarah noticed Wanda rested her hand next to Franklin's until their pinkies touched. When he didn't pull away, Sarah decided to see how far she could explore their togetherness and today's events. "Wanda, Grace told me how wonderful you were when she cut her hand. She really appreciated your help."

"It was nothing."

Sarah glanced over. Eloise had moved to Kait's far side. In order for Kait to talk directly to Eloise, as she was doing, Kait's head faced away from Sarah, Wanda, and Franklin.

"I wouldn't say that. Most people wouldn't have reacted as fast as you did. I just want you to know I think it was pretty special." Sarah lowered her voice almost to a whisper. "And, I'm sorry about your loss."

When Wanda didn't respond, Sarah said, "I also could

swear Grace said something about Franklin and you leaving the classroom shortly after she dismissed class. Did you come back because you forgot something?"

Wanda took her pinky away from Franklin's and met Sarah's gaze. "No, I didn't forget anything. I knew Ms. Winston stayed to clean up her classroom. And . . . well . . . I was worried about her doing it alone. Considering how deep the cut in her hand was and that I'd only made a makeshift bandage for it, I was sure she shouldn't be handling the cleaning supplies we use in our prep kitchen. They're harsh and you have to be careful with them. To be honest, I didn't think Ms. Winston could focus enough. She was still pretty upset with the way Doug treated her in front of all of us."

Doug? Sarah was surprised Wanda called her father by his first name, especially because Grace and almost everyone else seemed to refer to him as Dr. Martin or Malevolent Monster. She crossed her fingers behind her back. "My understanding from Grace was she wasn't concerned for herself. Her fear was for the student who was helping with the demonstration in front of the class. The one Dr. Martin took to task."

Although Sarah glimpsed Franklin shift in his seat, he didn't volunteer he was the student.

Wanda appeared to be unaware of his movement. "Franklin was the one Doug went after. Maybe Ms. Winston was more concerned with what Doug said and did to Franklin, but, believe me, Doug got his licks in against Ms. Winston too. We all heard him. He basically accused her of being incompetent and unable to teach us."

"How did you and your classmates react to what Dr. Martin said about her?"

"Most everyone was surprised at how he blew up and

went after Ms. Winston and Franklin. Doug's actions were way out of bounds, but that's nothing new. Ask my mother."

Sarah was surprised to hear a tinge of bitterness in Wanda's voice. She looked to see if Kait reacted to the change in volume and the tone of Wanda's words, as well as the reference to Wanda's mother, but Kait was engaged in conversation with Eloise and apparently not listening to their exchange. Still, Sarah chose her words carefully. She didn't want to be the one who told Kait her son was dead.

"I don't think I understand how your mother plays into this morning's incident with your father."

Wanda's facial muscles tensed. Franklin patted her arm. "He's gone. You can let it go."

"No, I can't." She pulled her arm away from him. This time, as Wanda spoke to Sarah, she kept her voice low and her head turned away from Kait. "Excuse me if I sound a bit harsh, but Doug Martin wasn't my father. He was my stepfather and he wasn't a particularly good one."

Sarah was taken aback. She hadn't realized Wanda and Dr. Martin's connection wasn't biological.

"Besides being a lousy stepfather, he wasn't a nice man," Wanda continued. "If you were on his good side or had something he wanted, he could be charming. But if you fell out of grace with him, beware. Doug went after you no-holds-barred. He used people for his own benefit and then discarded them."

It was obvious Wanda felt Dr. Martin had dealt with her mother in the way she was describing, but Sarah wondered how much of his Malevolent Monster nickname was earned by being the same type of tyrant with the people he worked with at the college. The thought excited her. There might not be blood, but maybe there was a money tie-in she could follow that Harlan could use to send Chief Gerard down a different investigative trail.

"I heard some of the faculty had a nickname for him. Was it because of this kind of behavior?"

Wanda laughed. "Whoever on the staff dubbed him the Malevolent Monster was far kinder than I would have been. That's probably because the faculty was limited to using a nickname against him instead of standing up to Doug."

"That doesn't make sense to me. Dr. Martin was new at Carleton, so why would tenured faculty members be afraid to rile the feathers of an interim chair? I'd think if he behaved as badly as you're describing, some of them would have complained to the college's president or done something else to get rid of him."

Wanda shook her head. "The open secret at CJCC is that Dr. Green plans to consolidate the culinary and hospitality curriculum programs into a single department. He brought Doug in to head it. Doug's culinary-program interim chairman title is a placeholder until they announce the consolidation and give him a bigger title like department head, vice president, dean, or mini-god."

"But, if his behavior was so horrible, I would think the faculty would want to prevent him from becoming their permanent boss."

"It's not that simple for most of the staff. CJCC's culinary and restaurant-hotel management courses were only expanded to meet associate degree requirements two years ago. Until then, most of the courses were taught by part-timers or adjuncts like Ms. Winston. Some of the staff was converted to full-time and others were hired, but most are still working toward tenure. They're afraid if they rock the boat, they'll lose their jobs and maybe won't be able to get another one."

"And Dr. Williams?"

This time, Wanda snorted. "He's still clinging to the belief he'll be named to head the merged department on merit. Fat chance of that."

Sarah was taken aback by Wanda's venomous attitude. "Then, wouldn't that be motivation for Dr. Williams to want to get rid of Dr. Martin?"

"If Dr. Williams had a backbone, yes—especially the way Doug treated him. Instead, Dr. Williams had been playing up to Doug so he at least could stay in charge of the hospitality-hotel management courses."

It made sense Dr. Williams would want the job, but be hedging his bet so he'd still have a job if he wasn't made head of the department. She couldn't wait to talk to Harlan about how tenure and job security might have played into Dr. Martin's murder. Surely, from Dr. Williams to the department's secretaries, there might be a way to bring a money tie-in to the case, which would provide Chief Gerard with more suspects.

Assuring herself Kait and Eloise were still talking, Sarah decided to take advantage of Wanda's wound-up state of mind to explore if Wanda's loathing of Dr. Martin and money might produce another financial lead.

"Your mother?" Sarah prompted.

Wanda crinkled her brow in a quizzical manner. "My mother was a trust fund baby. Her first marriage, when she was nineteen, can only be described as a merger of two companies, with me as the company dividend. They stayed together while my grandparents were alive, but once they all died, my parents divorced. I was six."

"That's a tender age to experience that."

Wanda stared at the table. "Yes, it is. But let's cut to the chase. Your interest is in Doug. He came into my life the day before I left for sleepaway camp when I was ten. He was newly divorced too, and a mutual friend fixed my mother and him up. They got married two days after I got home from that one-month camp session."

"Wow! That was a whirlwind courtship."

"Doug always believed in the adage of striking while the iron was hot." Wanda crossed her arms across her chest.

Taking note of Wanda's protective stance, Sarah backed off a bit. "I bet it was difficult for you to adjust to a new father in your life when you'd barely had time to meet him, let alone get to know him."

Wanda spat out her answer. "From day one, he told me to call him Doug. He never was, nor did he want to be, a father figure to me. I came home from camp in mid-July and was packed off to boarding school by mid-August. Doug had a sabbatical year and Mom and he wanted to travel or have a yearlong honeymoon. I couldn't miss school, so boarding school was the answer they came up with."

"Not a good experience?"

"The school was fine. Without it, I wouldn't be who I am today, so I have no complaints about that. My issue was with Doug. I received postcards from all over the world, but, during the years I was at school, he usually found a reason it was impossible for them to get back for the few days I was on break or he made sure they were someplace it wasn't convenient for me to join them. That's why, when I had vacations or holidays, I spent them with Grandma Kait." Leaning sideways, toward Kait, she gave her a side-to-side hug.

Reacting to the squeeze, Kait turned her head away from Eloise. Sarah couldn't decide if the expression on Kait's face was one of confusion or expectation, but there was no question from the softening of the lines of her face when Wanda said "I love you" that she understood her granddaughter's interruption.

"I love you too. A bushel and a peck?"

"Oh, no. Even more than that." Wanda squeezed Kait to her one more time before releasing her from their hug. Kait immediately turned back toward Eloise while Wanda, keeping her voice barely above a whisper, resumed her discussion with Sarah.

"By the time Doug walked out on my mom for Lynn, his present wife, he'd spent most of Mom's trust."

"How horrible."

Wanda met Sarah's gaze. "Don't expect me to cry for him. I can't honestly say I'm particularly sorry he's gone. Grandma Kait is the one I'm worried about."

Sarah didn't know how to balance Wanda's dislike for Dr. Martin against her obvious caring for his mother. Instead of following up on that remark, she'd go back to basics. "Still, it must have been a shock when you saw him."

"It was. I may not have liked the man, but it was definitely upsetting."

Sarah faked a small shudder. "I couldn't have kept it together."

"I didn't at first. Thank goodness Franklin was with me."

Considering how Wanda had appeared exactly opposite to what she was saying, Sarah decided against challenging Wanda's statement directly. Instead, hoping to elicit more information from her, Sarah opted to tread lightly by keeping her tone as caring as she could muster.

"You certainly didn't show how upset you were. In fact, by the time Grace and I saw you, I didn't realize you had a personal connection to Dr. Martin. My impression was that Franklin and you were in total control of the situation."

Wanda shook her head. "That's only because of Franklin. His criminal justice and intern training kicked in once we realized there was nothing we could do for Doug."

"Anyone could have done everything I did." Franklin moved his hand closer to Wanda's again. "Other than calling campus security and securing the site, I didn't do anything out of the ordinary, except make sure Wanda took some deep breaths. I was afraid she might pass out before the paramedics and the campus police arrived."

Wanda hit his arm playfully. "Now, Franklin, don't exaggerate. I was upset, but I wasn't hyperventilating or anything like that."

Sarah cut in before their playfulness escalated, catching Kait's attention. "Well, the way the two of you handled everything was impressive, especially considering your closeness with Dr. Martin."

"As I told you, Doug and I barely saw each other, let alone had a relationship."

That limited relationship probably contributed to Wanda's ability to compartmentalize Dr. Martin's death from her personal feelings. It made logical sense, but Sarah still wasn't sure she could have done the same thing moments after finding someone she knew apparently murdered. Trying to size Wanda up, she watched her reach toward Kait and brush a strand of hair away from her grandmother's face. Wanda's hand lingered on her grandmother's hair.

"At least Grandma Kait and I stayed close, even when my mom and Doug broke up. It may sound strange, but I feel closer to her than I do to any of my blood relatives."

Sarah knew exactly what Wanda was saying. When the rat divorced Sarah, Bill's mother and Sarah continued to have a close relationship until Mother Blair's death. It was because of a bequest from Mother Blair that she now lived in the carriage house with RahRah. "I fully understand."

"That's why I didn't want to miss tonight's steak night. I figured Doug's new wife wouldn't even think about coming here today, but I thought someone owed it to Grandma Kait to try to tell her what happened in person. She has good days and bad, but I felt she needed to know. Thankfully, Eloise agreed to come too, in case Grandma became more upset than I could handle."

"That was kind of Eloise. Kait seems to be enjoying this dinner."

"She is. If you'll excuse me, she's ready for dessert. I'm going to take her over to the buffet before her favorites are gone."

Sarah hadn't realized Kait and Eloise had finished their conversation. She wasn't certain if Kait had overheard anything Wanda and she said, but, considering Kait's interest in going with Wanda to the dessert buffet, Sarah didn't think she had.

Perhaps sensing Sarah's uncertainty, Eloise chimed in

once Kait, Wanda, and Franklin left the table. "I was glad my schedule let me join them for dinner tonight. Doug Martin may not have always been the most considerate son, but he was Kait's. No matter how little he came around, I can't imagine losing a child—especially in a way that isn't a natural death."

Chapter 14

Returning to her own table, Sarah paused behind her mother long enough to squeeze her shoulders. Glancing around the table, she found her dinner companions finishing up their desserts. In front of her place, on a small white saucer, was a fork with a bite of chocolate cake.

"What's going on here?"

"You only asked for a bite." Cliff put his coffee cup on the table.

Everyone, except Sarah, laughed.

Because her mother and Mr. Rogers had saucers under their coffee cups, she knew who the prankster was.

"That's exactly right." Sarah slowly picked up the fork and brought it to her mouth. Rather than devouring it, she nibbled at the cake. Without hurrying, she chewed and swallowed before taking another taste. Considering the size of the piece of cake on her fork, Sarah thought she was a magician stretching her eating of the morsel to three bites.

Placing her fork carefully on the side of her plate, Sarah picked up her napkin and, with exaggerated motions, wiped her mouth. "That was delicious. And just the right-sized bite. Thank you."

"Our pleasure," George and Maybelle said simultaneously.

This time Sarah and Cliff laughed at how once again George and Maybelle had said the same thing. Maybelle cut them off by asking how Kait was taking the news about her son.

Before Sarah answered, she saw a waitress with a coffeepot near their table. She signaled for her by holding up her empty cup. The waitress filled Sarah's cup and topped off everyone else's.

Once the waitress finished and left their table, Sarah turned toward her mother. "You asked me how Kait took the news?"

Maybelle nodded.

"They haven't told her yet. Eloise said they thought having a nice dinner before sharing the news with her in her room would make it easier for Kait to accept."

"That makes sense, though I don't see why they didn't simply tell her before dinner. With Kait's short-term memory problems, she probably would have forgotten by dessert." Maybelle tried to sip her coffee, but it was too hot. She picked up the spoon she apparently had eaten her dessert with, scooped a small piece of ice out of her water glass, and dropped it into her coffee.

Mr. Rogers nodded in agreement with Maybelle. "Kait is always pleasant, but her ability to retain information is limited. She's at that stage where she doesn't talk much or if she does, she tends to repeat a question she asked twenty minutes earlier."

"I hope I'm never in that situation. You should kill me if I am." Maybelle sipped her now-cooled coffee.

"Don't worry, Maybelle," Mr. Rogers said. "You're too ornery to lose your marbles. Besides, if you do, you won't remember."

"At least by then, if it happens to me, you old coot, I won't have to worry about you having all of your marbles either."

"Now, now, I may have a decade on you, but that doesn't make me decrepit. I'm still sharp as a tack."

"And equally tacky."

Fearing their personal sparring might escalate into a nasty war of words, as it had once in the past, Sarah started to interrupt the flow of their conversation, but her mother did it for her. Maybelle declared that, while they both had their wits about them, they should make the most out of every moment.

Mr. Rogers agreed with her. "Since I've become more comfortable living here, I've discovered there's a full range of activities offered. Whether it's arts and crafts, culture, a shuffleboard game, or a movie, there's always something going on. What's nice is we aren't limited to just interacting with the people who live here. Like steak night, there are lots of things we can invite guests to attend."

"Sunshine has an excellent political discussion group every Tuesday. George has brought me as his guest several times."

"That's right," Mr. Rogers said. "The problem is many of the residents don't take advantage of what's offered, especially the ones with cognitive issues, like Kait. Whether they feel overtaxed by the activity or are afraid of repeating themselves, they stop participating."

"That's why, with Emily's help, we're going to have a special program open to everyone who lives here, but we're going to make sure people like Kait take part in it."

Maybelle said "Emily," but Sarah felt sure her mother was about to rope her into whatever her scheme was. As if Sarah needed another project or activity—no matter how worthwhile it might be.

"We've arranged an outing for lunch on Sunday. The retirement home will provide the transportation and Emily's handling the food."

"That sounds delightful. Where are you going?" asked Sarah.

Maybelle shot an exasperated look at Sarah. "Southwind. The restaurant is closed, but Emily is going to open it just for us."

Sarah slapped her head. "Of course. I should have known that." She wasn't sure if her mother caught her sarcasm or not, because Maybelle never stopped talking.

"But there's more than simply having lunch. Those who attend are going to be able to help make part of their lunch."

Sarah threw her hands up in frustration. "Mom, they can't. There are rules about making food for restaurants. You know, the state has hygiene and other health regulations Southwind needs to follow. People can't simply come into the Southwind kitchens and cook willy-nilly, even on a day Southwind is officially closed."

"That's not going to be a problem."

At this point, Sarah didn't know if she should pull her hair out or what. Her mother didn't seem to be listening to her. She wondered if Emily knew all the details of what her mother wanted to do. Surely, Maybelle wouldn't jeopardize Southwind's health ratings and Emily and Marcus's livelihood for a good-deed luncheon. "But it is."

"Sweetheart, relax. It won't be a problem because none of the residents will be cooking in the restaurant."

"Huh?"

"With the restaurant closed, we're not going to be in anyone's way if we prep outside. That's why Emily, Marcus, and I are going to set up long folding tables on Southwind's side lawn. Come to think of it, don't you have a few of those tables stored at the carriage house?"

"I have three." Sarah stopped herself. She couldn't let herself be sidetracked. "But you can't do this. Cooking outside the restaurant doesn't solve the problem of serving anything the Sunshine residents prepare. Their food still won't be made in compliance with the health codes."

"Don't worry. We're not going to serve the Stained-Glass Jell-O they make. We'll set up the tables and, depending upon how many people come, give them different colored packets of Jell-O to work with, alone or in pairs. We'll let them prepare their Jell-O and then—and this is where you come in—you'll help take the bowls of Jell-O into the restaurant to chill a bit."

"Whoa, I think from when I made Jell-O in a Can, I learned Jell-O needs at least two hours to chill. What are you going to do with these people for two hours? Plus, remember we can't take the bowls into Southwind."

"Sarah, it's not going to be a problem. We're going to tell them Southwind has state-of-the-art equipment and a new freezing process. While the bowls are chilling, you'll either give them a tour of the carriage house or one of us will tell everyone the history of the main house. When the historical tour is over, we'll bring what they think are their original bowls back to their tables."

"They won't be their original bowls?"

"Of course not. We'll have chilled bowls ready in every flavor and we'll bring out the ones we need. Once we do that, we'll let everyone chop up their respective Jell-O flavors and mix them together in a few bigger bowls with clear gelatin. Depending upon what Emily wants to do, they'll either add whipping cream or condensed milk to their bowls before we take the new bowls away to chill. While the bowls are being removed, we'll invite everyone to go inside the restaurant for a feast that will feature their creations."

Sarah wanted to dig her heels into the ground, but that didn't seem possible in the dining room. "I'll say it one more time. You can't serve what they make in Southwind."

Maybelle frowned at her daughter. "We're not. While Emily and Marcus take everyone in through the front door for lunch, you and Grace will collect the bowls from the tables, but instead of bringing them into Southwind, you'll dump anything the Sunshine residents made into a garbage can on Southwind's back porch."

This time, Sarah didn't slap her head, even if she felt a little silly having not figured out the plan her mother and sister devised to avoid anyone cooking or serving food in the restaurant. She should have realized neither would put the restaurant in jeopardy.

Sarah chuckled, though, at the thought her mother was once again assigning her the garbage detail. In retrospect, Sarah had to admit her own behavior was part of the reason she'd always been tasked with KP duties. When

Emily and Sarah were kids, Emily shadowed Maybelle as she prepared dinner, while Sarah lay on the couch in the den watching *Perry Mason* reruns. The show came on at five. At five-fifteen Sarah emptied the dishwasher, five-thirty was when she set the table, she greeted her dad at five-forty-five, and as the closing credits rolled, Sarah and her family sat down for dinner. After dinner, Sarah was responsible for cleaning up and scrubbing the pots and pans. Consequently, being assigned kitchen cleanup was old hat to her.

She also had to admit her mother's scheme sounded perfect, if not a bit devious. Maybelle and Mr. Rogers were doing a good deed. The residents, or inmates as Sarah sometimes referred to them, were being sprung for the day, and it looked like everyone was in store for a fun time.

Chapter 15

Sarah and Cliff walked out of the retirement home together, talking about the shelter meeting he'd missed that afternoon and the proposed talent show. "I hope your ears were ringing. Carole stood up for you because she was afraid Harlan volunteered you to build the sets and whatever we might need to showcase the animals without your permission."

He laughed. "I wouldn't put it past Harlan to volunteer me for anything, but I told him last night he could count on me building anything needed for fundraising. That was nice of Carole to speak up for me. She's been a real asset helping with the shelter expansion plans."

Cliff reached for her hand. This time, Sarah avoided letting him touch her.

"Want to come back to the cabin for a nightcap?"

When Sarah hesitated, he reminded her it wasn't late yet. "It just feels that way with the clocks set back for daylight saving time."

"That's true. With it getting darker earlier in the fall, everything feels later to me. I forgot dining at the retirement home is always on the early bird side. A nightcap sounds perfect, but I need to stop by my place for a minute to take Fluffy out."

"That's no problem. I'll go ahead and be waiting for you. Where are you parked?"

She pointed to the few spots near the front door. "Over there. Second spot in the visitors' parking area."

Cliff let out a whistle. They strolled in the direction of her car. "You got lucky."

"You don't know. With steak night, the parking lot was full. Apparently, the one person not staying for steak tonight was leaving when I pulled in."

"It was meant to be."

"No question. If I hadn't gotten that spot and been able to come right in, Mother would have been even more annoyed with my tardiness."

"Actually, I think she was in a pretty good mood. Somehow or other, my uncle and she seem to be reaching a different place in their relationship. What do you think?"

"I agree with you. In the beginning she visited him regularly because she felt guilty she wasn't with him in the hall when he was hurt. She felt an obligation to help him while he was recovering, but that's not the case now. By the way, did you notice how often they're finishing each other's sentences?"

"Or how your mother took my uncle's zingers without giving them back to him?"

"That almost knocked me out of my chair. Mother

doesn't take anything from anyone, but she let his jabs roll right off her back."

"When you were away from the table, she even played straight man for one of his corny jokes."

"I think I'm glad I missed that." Sarah unlocked her car.

Cliff held her car door open for her as she slid into the front seat. "The funny thing is, I think she enjoyed doing it."

"While I didn't see that, I started to interrupt them when they were jabbing at each other because I feared they'd get into a fight like they did that one time, but then I realized they weren't mad. They were actually having fun, good-naturedly making digs at each other." Sarah started her car.

"Well, here's hoping it goes somewhere. Just think, we might be able to go on a double date with them." Mercifully, he closed her door before she could reply.

She waved at him as she pulled out of the parking lot and he turned to walk toward his car.

On the drive to Cliff's cabin, after her quick stop at home, Sarah's mind wandered. She knew one reason she'd accepted his invitation was her love for the bluff where his cabin was. As a child, she regularly rode her bicycle to the secluded piece of land where the bluff jutted out over the water. Never developed, it had been her quiet retreat from her mother's demands or the pressures of being a cheerleader's twin. She couldn't count how many hours she simply stared at the water and let her mind wander.

After her marriage broke up, it was the only place Sarah knew she could go where she wouldn't run into Bill. He had his finger in all different types of land development deals, but they were all urban or downtown-oriented. Unlike Sarah, he didn't love nature. He could never appreciate the beauty and serenity of the bluff or understand how being there made her feel.

That was why it felt like a double whammy when, a few weeks later, she saw the posted *Keep Out* signs. Finding out someone bought the bluff and its surrounding land was like losing another part of herself.

It was well over a year later that Sarah learned Cliff was the property's owner, when he invited her for a boat ride. After she accepted and he gave her the directions to his property, Sarah realized it was her bluff. Going there the first time, she'd been afraid of how his cabin and other physical improvements might have ruined the bluff, but instead, Sarah was amazed at how well he'd incorporated his design and his talent for construction into fitting the cabin and new road to it into the natural way the land lay.

From his cabin's main room or on its porch, the view to the water and of the sun rising or setting was unobstructed. He'd curved the road so cars wouldn't obstruct the view and placed railroad-tie steps from the upper part of the bluff down to where his boathouse was hidden in a curve above the waterline. Down there, with plenty of space, he not only kept his Jet Skis, motorboat, and pontoon, but he'd also built a second outdoor living room as part of his dock system. Many a night, during the past few months, they drank a bottle of wine by the water at sunset or took a ride on his boat.

She loved watching him captain his boats. With the wind whipping through his tousled dirty blond hair, any tension from the day faded from his face. Perhaps her favorite memory with Cliff was from their first boat ride together. He'd taken her out in the pontoon boat and as they came back toward shore, he let the boat idle quietly while he drew her attention to a nest high in a tree. She'd barely been able to make out the outline of the nest at first, let alone two birds cooperatively going back and forth, feeding their young.

It was tender moments like that that offset the times Cliff was impulsive. She could still remember the moment they'd passed at the bank when his attire, size, and over-the-top behavior made her think of Paul Bunyan. She still sometimes thought of Cliff as a gentle giant. For the past few months, they'd been finding their way together in an off-and-on pattern that, for the most part, seemed satisfactory to both. So, why had she accepted the date with Glenn?

Was it something in her subconscious? Was she trying to sabotage a good thing? Was she looking for more than she'd told Cliff she was happy with? There was no question Cliff and she had an emotional connection. So, why was she going out on Saturday night with someone else?

The good doctor was equally as tall as Cliff and both were intelligent. Where Cliff was wider across the chest and more obviously muscled from his years in the construction business, Glenn's lifting and moving of animals had developed strength in his sinewy body. The bottom line was that both men were physically and mentally attractive to her. The problem was she didn't think she could balance a relationship with both at the same time.

Chapter 16

Despite knowing Cliff would be waiting, she stopped at the curve in the road and stared in the direction of the water. It was too dark to see clearly. Slightly saddened to miss seeing the water, she drove on to the cabin. Climbing the stairs, she ran her hand along the polished wood banister rail, admiring its thickness and smoothness. It had taken Cliff a few years to build this cabin in his spare time, but his workmanship showed in every detail of its features.

Sarah jumped at the feel of two arms encircling her waist. She relaxed at the sound of Cliff's voice and the gentle peck on her ear. "Hey, are you daydreaming? I thought you'd be inside opening the wine I left chilling."

She cocked her neck at an angle and looked into his brown eyes. Only because he was standing a step below her, leaning in for the hug, were they almost the same height. "You made good time. I was down at the boathouse because I thought you'd still be a few minutes."

"I didn't want to keep you waiting."

He let go of her and jumped from the step he was on to the landing. She followed him into the cabin, but not into the kitchen. It wasn't more than a minute before he returned with a bottle in his right hand and the stems of two wineglasses and a wine opener dangling between the fingers of his left hand.

"You took things for granted, didn't you? What if I hadn't agreed to come back?"

"It would have been a fate worse than death. I'd have had to drink this bottle alone."

Sarah couldn't help but laugh at the somewhat angelic face he made. "Oh, we couldn't let that happen. Do you want to sit inside or on the porch?"

"It's such a nice night. If you don't think this fall air will get too cool for you, why don't we go out there? If you'd like some munchies to go with the wine, there's a block of white cheddar in the refrigerator and a box of crackers on the counter. I didn't want to open them if you didn't end up coming back tonight."

"You were going to stick with only the wine if I didn't come over?"

"Yup. Why waste a good block of cheese? Grab the cheese, crackers, and a knife, and I'll meet you outside."

Sarah rummaged through the kitchen. She'd been here enough to know where almost everything was. Besides locating the crackers and cheese, she opened the cupboard next to the sink and pulled out a plate on which to more neatly display the cheese and crackers. When she reached for a knife from the block on Cliff's counter, she froze. After the events of the day, her mind raced to what each of the knives in the block were capable of doing.

In the past, with her lack of interest in the kitchen, she hadn't really contemplated that a big knife might not be as effective a cutting tool as a small one. After what she'd seen today, she had a new respect for knives of all sizes. She wondered how many people who weren't in the culinary business or who, like her, had little to no interest in the art of finer food, knew much about the different knives that came in a typical kitchen block, let alone the additional ones anyone who was a serious cook purchased separately.

Sarah knew, for a fact, Emily's knife roll was her most prized possession. It was worth a fortune and only contained knives Emily felt fit her hand well and were up to the tasks she bought them for.

"Are you coming?" Cliff's voice from outside sprung her from her trance.

"On the way." Sarah carried her assigned items to the porch.

Cliff already was perched in one of the two comfortable wood chairs that were his outside fixture pieces. When she first came to the cabin, she'd been surprised to learn he'd built the cabin, dining room table, and most of his other furniture, but the chairs were store-bought. His logic had been on the money, though. Why spend the time crafting something that someone already had built to perfection when there were so many other things to create?

The wine was already open, poured, and breathing. Sarah put the cheese and crackers on the table in the space between their two wineglasses and sat in the vacant chair.

She picked up her glass and brought it to her lips. The cool red wine tasted good as it slid down her throat. "This is delicious, but you shouldn't have taken it for granted I was coming tonight."

The words were out of her mouth before she thought about how they might sound.

"Did you have other plans?"

"Not tonight, but I might have. You shouldn't take me for granted." Not thrilled with the sharp sound of her reply, Sarah finished off her wine and held out her glass for a refill.

Cliff refilled her glass.

She knew she needed to slow down or at least eat some cheese before she continued drinking, but she didn't.

He put his glass on the table and cut several slices of cheese. Putting one on a cracker, he offered it to her. She didn't take it, so he popped it into his mouth. "Better slow down. You didn't eat much at dinner. This stuff is good, but it's pretty potent on an empty stomach."

Irritated he was telling her how to behave, Sarah gulped almost half of her glass down. She knew she was being reckless, but tonight any expression of caring from him made her want to lash out.

Sarah wished she could pinpoint what was sparking such negative feelings on her part. Maybe, she had to admit, her willingness to accept a date with Glenn had something to do with it. Perhaps she wanted to drive Cliff away so she wouldn't have to feel guilty about her behavior.

"Don't worry about me," Sarah said.

"Can't help it. I do. I hope you're not going to get involved with that stuff at the college."

"That's not open for discussion. I already told you, my only goal is protecting Grace."

"Which is why you called Harlan. He'll take care of things with Chief Gerard."

She stared at the wine still in her glass. In some ways, because of Harlan hiring her when no one else would give her a job and then putting himself out defending her mother and sister, she'd tended to think of Harlan as a white knight. It was hard for her to admit it to herself, but his continued bromance with Chief Gerard was making her rethink her trust in him. She doubted Cliff had even given Harlan's friendship with the chief a second thought. "I hope so, but who knows how far he'll push. Those two are good buddies now."

"Now, Sarah, don't sell Harlan short. When it comes to prioritizing Grace or his friendship with Chief Gerard, Grace is the clear winner."

"You're so good at predicting winners, maybe you should go to the track."

Cliff stared at her. He raised his hand and reached forward.

Sarah flinched at his outstretched hand.

Instead of touching her, he picked up his wineglass again and ran his finger around its rim. "Sarah, I don't know what's wrong tonight, but if I've done something that offended you, I'm sorry. Tell me what's wrong."

"It's not you." She drained most of the rest of her glass. Leaning over, she refilled her glass but stopped to eat a few crackers and some cheese. She knew Cliff was watching her, but he didn't say anything. "It has nothing to do with you. It's today."

"Whew, you had me worried." He grinned, but got more serious when she didn't react. "Sarah, I can be a good sounding board if you want to talk about what happened today with Dr. Martin."

A tear escaped from Sarah's eye.

Cliff put his wineglass down. This time, he leaned in front of the small table and wiped it away with his thumb. "Sarah, what is it? What's wrong?"

Sarah clutched her wineglass more tightly but didn't answer him. With her free hand, she wiped the same place on her cheek where he'd caught her tear.

"Sarah?"

She swallowed hard. Knowing she'd had enough wine for the moment, she put her glass on the table. "I'm sorry, Cliff. There's been a lot going on today and for some silly reason . . ."

Cliff stood and kneeled in front of her chair. He put his hands over hers where they lay in her lap. "You don't have to explain. Stuff happens and we all react to it in different ways at the oddest times. I'm here. I know I'm not always the most sensitive guy, but let me help you."

His kind words made Sarah feel worse. She couldn't hold back the tears. He pulled her closer to him and held her until the tears subsided. Only when there didn't seem to be any more coming did he rock back on his heels and, keeping his hands on her knees, wait for her to make the next move.

"Cliff, you're a great guy, but . . ."

"But? And what's with this you're a great guy?"

"I'm so confused. We've been having a good time, and I really care about you, but I did something today that makes me question everything."

"Sarah, I know I've come down hard about you not getting involved in investigations that should be in the hands of the professionals, but it's only because I care about you. I don't want you to get hurt, but today, you couldn't help yourself. Grace means a lot to you, and I understand you don't want her to be railroaded by Chief Gerard."

Sarah took a deep breath and let the words tumble out of her. "I accepted a date today."

She screwed up her face, waiting for Cliff's reaction. He didn't stand, rant, or rave. Rather, he quietly stayed as he was, kneeling in front of her with his hands on her knees. There was no smile in the eyes that met her gaze.

She looked away. "Cliff, did you hear what I said?"

He nodded. "Yes, you accepted a date today."

"Aren't you mad?"

"How can I be?"

Sarah started to cry again. "You're being so nice. I don't understand how you can be so understanding. We've been talking for months about having a relationship, and I was so mean when I thought you'd been going out with someone else. How can you be so calm when I, without even thinking for a moment, said 'yes' when someone asked me out for dinner?"

He put his hand under her chin, forcing her to meet his gaze. "Sarah, are we friends?"

She gulped. "Yes, of course."

"Friends first and foremost."

Sarah nodded.

"Sarah, you did what felt right to you in the moment. Accepting one dinner doesn't mean anything."

"But it does. Cliff, I know myself. If I were fully committed to our relationship, I wouldn't have considered, let alone accepted, the invitation to dinner."

"Probably not, but we've never been exclusive. In fact, being realistic, maybe I'm a little relieved you accepted an invitation. Look, I care for you deeply and I think you do the same for me." He held up his hand so she wouldn't speak. "But I bring a lot of baggage to our relationship. Considering the events since we met, I haven't always been the easiest guy to be with. I know there have been times where I've seemed to run hot and cold because I can't set aside the negative stuff that comes from my family ties."

"But we've worked past that. It isn't a barrier to me."

"Maybe not to you, but it still is for me. Believe me, I've given this a lot of thought. I care deeply for you, but every time we seem to be moving forward, something reminds me of the bad stuff and I pull back. You've been one of the best things in my life these last few months. But, Sarah, accepting a date without thinking twice doesn't mean you care for me less or that you're a bad person, but maybe it means we need to take a break and see where things go."

Surprised at herself, Sarah realized the tears had dried and the funny feeling in the pit of her stomach was gone. She felt a sense of relief. At the same time, it dawned on her that she wasn't quite sure if she was breaking up with Cliff or he was breaking up with her.

"You're being awfully generous. It's almost as if you've been looking for a reason to hit the *stop* button on our relationship and I've given it to you."

Cliff went back to his chair. He picked up his wine and took a long drink of it. "That isn't the case or at least it wasn't consciously. Whether you never accepted a date or I had gone out with that other person, I don't think it would change where we are today."

Sarah was about to make a sharp retort when she realized Cliff was right. Being with Cliff wasn't her end-all.

It had been a new beginning post–her ex, the rat. For the first time in a decade, Cliff had made her feel valued and safe, and for that she was thankful, but the comfort she'd gotten from him didn't make her heart sing.

She thought back to when she'd first met the rat. Nothing else had mattered. Bill was the only thing on her mind day and night in those first months of dating and, she liked to think, she'd been the same for him. It was only later, after he'd put her down so many times, that she lost her confidence. Cliff had roused a side of her she'd forgotten she had, but he hadn't stirred all the feelings of romantic love the rat had before his bimbo days.

Sarah put her wineglass on the table. "Cliff, I think you're right. I love you, but I don't love you."

"And I hate to say it, I'm the same way. I cherish you, but I can't take away the parts of our mutual past that are a barrier in my mind."

Sarah picked up the wine bottle and finished it off in Cliff's glass. "Here's to us."

They clinked their glasses together and drank to each other. She offered Cliff the cheese-and-cracker plate. He took one and she did the same. Sitting in silence in the dark, they finished off the cheese and crackers.

"Cliff."

"Yes?"

She held up her wineglass again. "Friends, I hope, forever. You've given me so much, but let's drink to what may be the perfect relationship: my mother and your uncle."

Cliff laughed and tapped his glass against hers. As the sound of the glasses hitting each other rang out, Cliff added to her toast. "And to always subconsciously knowing what's right or wrong and doing what's right."

CHAPTER 17

Walking into the carriage house, Sarah felt like the weight of the world was off her shoulders. The gut-wrenching feeling she'd had at Cliff's cabin was gone and, best of all, Cliff and she were in a good place. She knew in her heart that it was more than words to think if she needed him or he needed her, they'd be there for each other. Her mind kept straying down different paths, all of them tinged with an element of relief.

For a moment, Sarah thought it might be the wine thinking for her when it crossed her mind that she no longer had to feel guilty if Cliff criticized her for getting involved in police business. Now, if she could just figure out a way to get her mother off her back. Then again, if Cliff and she were right and Maybelle was busy with Mr. Rogers, maybe Sarah would be totally free of disapproving eyes looking over her shoulder while she tried to prove Grace's innocence. The reality was that, no matter what anyone said, she was going to help Grace. Patiently waiting for things to work out for her family and friends wasn't something she could do.

Sarah was glad when RahRah and Fluffy met her at the door. A few loving pats for each of them, a quick walk for Fluffy, and Sarah comfortably changed into her pajamas and kitten slippers. She positioned herself on the floor of her bedroom with her back against her bed. Fluffy lay quietly at her side while RahRah climbed into her lap. Stroking her Siamese cat, she relaxed even more as she called Emily. The good thing about her twin was she rarely judged.

Much as she wanted to brainstorm with Emily, Sarah hoped, because it was Friday night, Southwind would be too busy with customers for Em to answer. When her call went directly to voice mail, Sarah was disappointed but happy. She left a message for Emily to call her back as soon as possible to discuss what was going on with Grace.

Remembering that Emily and Marcus insisted Grace take the night off, Sarah dialed her number next, hoping to check up on her. Mandy answered.

Sarah asked to speak to Grace.

"I'm sorry, Sarah, she's not here. She went out for a drive to clear her head. Is there something I can do for you?"

"No, I simply wanted to check on her."

"She'll be fine. I'm taking care of her."

From her tone, Sarah envisioned Mandy sitting on the other end of the phone line with a chip on her shoulder that she dared Sarah to knock off. Remembering Maybelle's belief that a honey tongue got you further than

Sarah knocking the chip off would, Sarah added a bit to her natural drawl. "I'm sure you are. Grace is lucky to have you there tonight. This has been a horrible day for everyone. How are you doing?"

"I'm fine. Just fine."

"Well, if you need anything—anything at all, please know you can count on me, as well as Emily."

There was a pause before Mandy quietly said, "Thank you."

Their call ended, Sarah dropped her phone on her bed. Giving her full attention to RahRah and Fluffy, Sarah confided in the two furry members of her backup sounding board. "I wish we could figure out how to help Grace. Despite what I said to Cliff, I know Uncle Harlan is going to do the best he can. The problem is, I think we're missing something. Maybe like Cliff and me, it's something Grace or I know subconsciously."

RahRah raised his head and purred at her.

"RahRah, do you agree?"

Rather than making another sound, her Siamese cat simply cuddled his body closer to her. Sarah responded by holding him tighter and rubbing her cheek against his fur as she shared her thoughts with him.

"I tell you, RahRah, nothing in this world makes sense. Emily and Marcus are finally seeing a profit at the Southwind Pub and are turning the tables twice a night at Southwind, but Jane is about to throw a wrench in their plans by partnering with Carleton College and the city to keep Jane's Place afloat. The college hasn't opted in yet, but Dr. Martin was the major holdout. Without him blocking the vote, it's a no-brainer the college will take advantage of being able to offer its students state-of-the-art equipment and the opportunity to gain practical experience operating the culinary and hospitality sides of a restaurant-hotel establishment."

RahRah squirmed, but Sarah didn't release him. The warmth of his little body was comforting while she tried figuring out what she was missing that might exonerate Grace.

"Now, let me see. According to Grace, Jane already is planning special events tied into the college as a means of binding the two together. For example, Chef Bernardi, who also is an adjunct instructor at the college, is Jane's special open-house guest Sunday afternoon. If he likes the facilities, it's another endorsement for Jane's proposal and figurative nail in Southwind's coffin if it diverts too much business. Plus, if Jane gets a crowd out for Chef Bernardi, other faculty members could see a benefit of the partnership if it offers them an opportunity for more visibility in the community—especially if their tenure quests become competitive."

Sarah decided she would make a special visit to Fern's office when she finally went to pick up information about classes and enrollment. Fern was a pretty straight shooter, so maybe she could give Sarah a handle on how many culinary and hospitality faculty members were under consideration for tenure and if there was a limit on how many could be granted it. "Obviously, RahRah, if there is a limit, everyone would have wanted to be on Dr. Martin's good side. If any weren't, some might have had a motive to kill him. Don't you agree?"

RahRah, either agreeing or having had enough of Sarah's brainstorming, shook himself hard against her arms until she loosened her grip. Freed, ever so slightly, RahRah jumped to the floor. Landing on all fours, he steadied himself and made a beeline for the kitchen. Sarah didn't follow him. She knew exactly what spot she'd find him lying in. "Well, girl," she said to Fluffy. "Aren't you going to go with RahRah?"

Fluffy stirred but didn't leave. Instead, she stretched her head across Sarah's knee until it landed in Sarah's lap. Sarah gently rubbed the soft area behind Fluffy's ears. "Every now and then a little alone time is perfect, right?"

The puppy thumped her tail almost in rhythm to Sarah's strokes. "You may not respond as much as RahRah, but you'll put up with my brainstorming, huh?"

Fluffy raised her head, as if making it easier for Sarah to reach, then stretched upward, planting a wet kiss on Sarah's cheek before standing on all fours. Without looking back, Fluffy tottered off, taking the same path to the kitchen RahRah had.

"You're deserting me too? Be like that. Remember, though, I have a long memory."

Because Fluffy didn't hesitate in her quest to reach the kitchen, Sarah was sure her comment didn't have much of an impact. She was about to add another zinger when her cell phone rang. Caller ID showed Emily's name.

"Hey, Em. Thanks for calling me back."

"No problem. Up for company? I'm at the big house. Things at Southwind are quieting down to a point Marcus and the staff can handle closing without me, so I thought if you'd like a visitor, I'd come back to the carriage house."

Knowing how Emily rarely left before closing, Sarah was concerned. "Is something wrong?"

"Other than Grace, no. Well, maybe, but it's probably nothing a little hot chocolate and one of our brainstorming sessions can't solve. Do you have any hot chocolate or milk?"

"Better bring some milk from the restaurant. I haven't had a chance to do a grocery run lately."

"Will do. Leave the door open and the light on, and I'll be there in a few minutes."

Chapter 18

While Emily prepared their hot chocolate, Sarah took two mugs marked with the F.O.W.L. logo for Friends of the Wheaton Library out of her dishwasher and placed them on the counter. She figured it was more than a fair trade. While Sarah filled Emily in on what had happened today and how Grace was the chief suspect for Dr. Martin's murder, she unpacked the goodies Emily brought. The care package included egg salad, salmon, pasta, and vegetables. Sarah was certain she wouldn't have to make a meal for herself until midweek.

"I'm worried Chief Gerard isn't looking for another suspect any more than he did with Mom. That's why I need to help Harlan . . ."

"Grace is why I wanted to talk to you tonight."

"She is?" Sarah was glad to have Emily to brainstorm with. Unlike her mother and Cliff, it felt good to know

Emily not only wouldn't chastise her for wanting to help Grace, but she also wouldn't try to talk her out of doing a little investigating on Grace's behalf.

After a final stir, Em rested the wooden spoon on the brightly colored spoon caddy Sarah kept by the stove. It was one her mother had brought home as a gift from one of her recent trips.

While Emily watched the chocolate, Sarah reached into her pantry for a package of chocolate chip cookies. "They're store bought, so they aren't as good as yours."

"They're fine for tonight." Emily took the pot from the heat and poured the deep chocolate liquid into the F.O.W.L. mugs. "Do you have any additional theories for Harlan and Chief Gerard to pursue?"

"Yeah, I do. Harlan thinks Chief Gerard believes in following the blood or the money. He's stuck on the blood on Grace's apron as solving the case, but what if we can establish a money trail for him?"

Emily blew on her mug. "What do you have in mind?"

"Well, if there are faculty members who thought Dr. Martin was going to prevent them from receiving tenure, one might have killed him to avoid being unemployed or blackballed from getting another job. By extension, Jane could be a top suspect too."

"How?" Emily asked as they took their hot chocolate to the table.

The twins carefully stepped around RahRah, who lay stretched out in his spot on the linoleum. Fluffy, who was under the table, didn't budge when the twins' feet invaded her space.

Sarah cupped her hands around her mug, her elbows resting on the table. "Jane's Place is financially hurting.

Dr. Martin was Jane's stumbling block to her proposal being accepted. Getting rid of him might have opened the door for the committee to adopt her plan."

"I don't know. Much as I don't like Jane, I see her as a conniver, but not a murderer."

"Murderers don't necessarily come packaged the way you think they would. Hopefully, I can uncover something that will force the professionals to look at someone beyond Grace." Sarah flipped her long dark hair out of her face as she sat back and tasted her hot chocolate. "I appreciate the hot chocolate, Em, but tell me, what's on your mind?"

After taking a sip, Emily licked her lips. "I had a weird call this evening."

"From whom?"

"Dr. Williams, the head of the hospitality program at Carleton."

Sarah was surprised. She couldn't imagine why Dr. Williams would call Emily. "What did he want?"

"He wants me to teach the knife skills course for the remainder of the term."

"You? What about Grace?"

"Apparently, with Dr. Martin gone, Dr. Green appointed Dr. Williams as the acting chairman of the culinary program while he still performs his hospitality program duties. Under the circumstances, Dr. Williams indicated the powers that be felt it best that Grace stay out of the classroom until this matter is resolved, and he was carrying through their instructions. Of course, he assured me, it will only be a short-term gig until the cloud of suspicion around Grace is cleared."

"That's a laugh. He was the one who threw Grace under the bus to Chief Gerard."

Emily's eyes opened wide. "He didn't mention that. He was very complimentary about Grace and her teaching skills, but insisted the matter was out of his hands."

"But why you? Why not Jane? She's the one trying to do a deal with the college. Wouldn't it make more sense for them to bring her in as a substitute adjunct?"

"Maybe, but he said Grace recommended me to temporarily take her place."

"Grace *what?*"

"That was my reaction, so when I hung up from him, I checked with Grace. Apparently, Harlan warned her this might happen."

Thinking back to the conversation when Grace was in Harlan's office, Sarah remembered Harlan had explained to Grace and Mandy the school might want to quiet things down by getting her out of the classroom. Sarah had hoped it wouldn't come to that, but apparently Harlan had a better feel of things than Sarah did.

"Anyway," Emily said. "Thanks to Harlan, Grace wasn't blindsided when she got the call from Dr. Williams, trying to smooth things over just before our dinner service. Grace kept her wits about her and did some negotiating. I understand it took several phone calls between the college and Grace to work everything out."

"What did she ask for?"

"She asked for and received the rest of her salary for this term, whether or not she goes back into the classroom. Grace also requested that I be offered the opportunity to finish teaching the course."

Sarah watched the way her sister was holding her head

down while she ran her fingers around her mug. "Em, did you give Dr. Williams an answer yet?"

"Not yet. I told him I needed a night to think about it, but what I really wanted was the opportunity to talk to you first."

"Why?" Sarah put her mug on the table a little harder than she meant. Liquid sloshed over its rim. She jumped up and grabbed a paper towel to clean up the mess she'd made. "I don't know what I can add, but I'm glad to listen."

"My first inclination was to say no, but Grace begged me to take the offer and to talk to you about the reason why I should teach the knife skills class. She was adamant and said that if I didn't do it, it would be to the detriment of all of us. Her somberness frightened me, so I didn't want to give Dr. Williams an answer before I talked to you. With juggling tonight's dinner service at both restaurants, there wasn't time for me to catch you any earlier than now. I'm here for you to fill me in on why I should say yes."

Sarah thought about why Grace was so insistent Emily take the job and why she wanted Emily to talk to her to understand Grace's motivation. For a moment, Sarah wasn't sure what Grace wanted from her, but then it dawned on her what she could tell Emily that Emily didn't know. She wasn't sworn to secrecy, like Grace was about Jane's proposals and their possible impact on the Southwind Group.

Grace was being smart. If Grace couldn't be in the building as the Southwind Group's eyes and ears, involving Emily would mean a Southwind person was on the inside with immediate knowledge of Jane's different proposals. Sarah quickly filled Emily in on Jane's idea to have the community college and the city partner with her to make Jane's Place a practical culinary and hospitality experience for students.

In a few words, she explained Grace's concern about how the proposal might hurt Southwind. She also told Emily why Grace might need to consider jumping ship for the retirement program and health benefits, but how her loyalty to Emily and Marcus had made her figure out a way to get around her promise of secrecy.

"That's so Grace. I wish we could come up with something to address health benefits for her and all our employees. We've got a good staff and don't want to lose any of them, particularly Grace. Marcus and I got quotes for offering our employees a health benefit plan, but, until recently, we simply couldn't afford it. In a way, I'm glad we haven't gone through with it yet, because if Jane's proposal is accepted, we might not be able to handle the cost of implementing a plan."

"With you taking Grace's place, maybe you can prevent Jane's proposal from being accepted. Or you can be the one the school partners with."

"Perhaps. I'll keep my eyes and ears open, but I have no intention of trying to sway things the way Jane will. If we create a partnership, it will be done aboveboard."

Considering her sister's nature, Sarah was sure that anything Emily and Marcus achieved would be because of hard work and merit.

Emily finished the last dregs of her hot chocolate. She rested her chin on her hand. "I still don't understand one thing."

"What's that?"

"If the only holdout was Dr. Martin and he's gone

now, why would Dr. Williams not put Jane into Grace's slot and go forward with voting and accepting Jane's plan?"

"I've thought about that for the past few minutes and think I have a plausible explanation. The word on the street is Carleton's president is going to combine the culinary and hospitality programs into one department. Dr. Martin was presumably brought in recently to run it. Without Dr. Martin in the picture, maybe Dr. Williams assumes once he's doing the job, Dr. Green will give him the position permanently. Consequently, Dr. Williams doesn't want to rock the boat. If he was ordered by Dr. Green to reach out to you, that's what he did."

"I guess that makes sense." Emily twirled a piece of her hair. "Or, maybe the college is going to seek additional proposals."

Logically, it worked for Sarah, but the question nagged at her whether Dr. Williams had made any effort to convince the college's president Jane should teach the class. Based on watching Dr. Williams by the elevator, she thought he could easily play both sides, depending upon how he thought he might benefit. Perhaps there was more tension behind the scenes than Grace was aware of, or there was more than one holdout to Jane's plan.

Emily nibbled on a cookie. "Anything else come to mind as to why I should or shouldn't take the job?"

"The only other thing I can think of is the tenure issue I mentioned, but I don't think anyone will care if you teach the class for the remainder of the term. They won't see your temporary presence as a threat to them. Grace said a lot of people are eligible for tenure or working their way to receiving it. I've made a mental note to go see Fern Runskill to see if she can enlighten me on the subject. If I find out anything that seems significant, I'll let you know."

"Thanks. I'll do the same if I learn anything while I'm teaching."

"Are you going to call Dr. Williams tomorrow and take the job?"

"It's what Grace wants, and you certainly made a good case for me to accept the offer to protect our business interests."

Sarah smiled. It always amused her when Emily or Marcus included her when talking about something to do with Southwind. In her mind, she viewed herself as a glorified landlord rather than a partial owner.

"Now that you'll be on campus and keeping an eye on Jane, do you know she's having some public food demonstrations at Jane's Place that apparently tie in with faculty members? I think it may be another way to ingratiate herself with the culinary and hospitality staff members. The first one is tomorrow afternoon at two with Chef Bernardi."

"I'd heard she was doing something like that with Chef Bernardi tomorrow afternoon, but I didn't understand the significance of how it tied in with a plan to partner with the college. Now that I do, I guess I'll need to be there. Want to go together?"

"Not really, but I will. I'm dog-walking in the morning, but I'll make sure to be back to go to the demonstration."

"You'll have plenty of time to get home after walking the dogs." Emily pulled the cookie package to her and grabbed a second cookie. She swallowed a bite. "Has anything else jumped out at you that might help Grace?"

"The first two things, which I've already brainstormed with RahRah and Fluffy, were possible motivations tied to Jane's plan or tenure. Besides Jane, there are a lot of other people who might have kowtowed to Dr. Martin but still hated him. Based upon how he ridiculed faculty and students alike in public, someone might have been angrier than they let on. If one of the people he shamed was a tenure candidate, I doubt a vote of no-confidence would be considered a ringing endorsement for getting another job. Both seemed like possible motives, but I didn't get far with either one, so I was in the process of switching gears when my sounding board deserted me and you called."

Emily finished her cookie. She pushed the bag toward Sarah.

Sarah took a cookie. "I have one more idea."

Chapter 19

"What if the involvement between the college and Jane's Place isn't the reason Dr. Martin was killed? What if it has something to do with his personal life? We know he wasn't on particularly good terms with his stepdaughter or ex-wife."

"We do?"

Sarah gave her sister a quizzical look before remembering she hadn't been at dinner with her tonight. She quickly brought Emily up to date on her discussion with Wanda, Franklin, Eloise, and Kait. "Although Kait made a home or safe place for Wanda during her school breaks, there's no question Wanda blames Dr. Martin for her mother ostensibly abandoning her."

Using the back of her hand, Emily wiped a cookie crumb from her mouth. "There may also be some unresolved anger if Wanda feels Dr. Martin looted her legacy by taking financial advantage of her mother and she thought he was going to do the same thing to Kait."

"I hadn't thought about that angle. My mind was wandering more to his new wife. If there's a glimmer of truth to what I heard some of the faculty tell Chief Gerard, Dr. Martin may not have been on the best of terms with his current wife."

"Eloise should be able to fill you in more about Wanda and Kait. Personally, I don't think Eloise would let Franklin be involved with someone she thought might be a murderer."

"You make a good point, but as we know, people do things for emotional reasons. Wanda obviously had a lot of pent-up anger against Dr. Martin. What if his going off on someone else she loved was simply too much and she snapped? You know, an uncontrolled passionate reaction?"

Emily shook her head as she took Sarah's and her empty cups to the sink. Coming back to the table, she closed the bag of cookies. "I well know protecting someone you love may cause a person to make a bad decision, but murdering someone goes over the line in my mind. Wanda goes on our suspect list, but you mentioned his ex-wife."

"I'll check with Eloise, but I didn't get the impression she's in Wheaton. That brings me back to Dr. Martin's present wife, Lynn. You remember that rhyme we used to jump to when we were kids? The one that went *Went upstairs to get my knife. Made a mistake and stabbed my wife*. Perhaps it's the reverse here? Maybe she got him first."

"That's pushing it, but if anyone knows about the behavior of a rat, it's you. Still, I don't think we have enough to go on here. Have you ever met his new wife?"

"No. His personal life is an area we need to find out more about." Sarah made a mental note to add a discussion about Dr. Martin and Lynn to her planned conversation with Fern. She also decided she'd better try talking to some of the other faculty members whose offices were near his. The suggestion that his wife dropped in at odd times or tended to wait for him in the Coffee Bar wasn't necessarily grounds for murder, but what if, in a moment of anger, she stabbed him?

To this day, Sarah could remember the gut-wrenching sensation she felt when she learned the rat was two-timing her with Jane. It wasn't too far-fetched to think Dr. Martin's murder was a violent emotional reaction when she found out her husband was cheating on her. After all, anyone nicknamed Malevolent Monster probably wasn't going to win a Mr. Congeniality contest, even with his own wife.

"There's something obviously still bothering you. You've laid out lots of theories, but you don't sound convinced about any of them. From what you've said, besides Grace, you've got lots of possible suspects for Harlan and Chief Gerard to look at. Right?"

"In a sense." Sarah held up her fingers as she ticked them off. "They should consider anyone who was on the floor when Grace and I got there. That would be Wanda, Franklin, Chef Bernardi, Fern, Nancy, Dr. Williams, and the people who waited to be interviewed in their offices who I don't even know. The same holds true on the tenure issue, because most of the faculty is working its way toward tenure."

Sarah put her hands back on the table. “I don’t think I have enough fingers to count everyone. When I add in family, there’s Wanda, but also Wanda’s biological mom, Dr. Martin’s new wife, Lynn, and Kait. There might also be someone at the retirement home who has a connection to Dr. Martin that I haven’t discovered yet. Someone mentioned that because of Kait, they considered Dr. Martin to be part of the Sunshine Retirement Home family.”

“That’s a long list of potential suspects. Surely Harlan can find enough motivation for most of them to raise doubt if Grace is arrested or tried. What’s really bothering you? What’s going on in your head?”

“Frustration.” Sarah frowned. “You’re right. No matter how I put the pieces together, I’m not getting anywhere with my theories that I think will make sense to Chief Gerard. The only thing I feel certain of is that even though Dr. Martin didn’t visit his mother often and she’s convinced he wasn’t a particularly good son, Kait isn’t a suspect because of her dementia and her inability to leave the Sunshine Retirement Home without assistance. I also doubt anyone at the home had it in for Dr. Martin simply because he didn’t spend enough time there. He paid his mother’s bill when it was due, and that’s what they care about. Consequently, that means we can probably rule out anyone at the retirement home.”

“But that isn’t what’s bothering you, is it?”

“No, Em, it isn’t. Sadly, I have to admit that if I were Chief Gerard and I was committed to following the money and the blood, Grace would be my primary suspect too.”

Chapter 20

Harlan had just leashed Sallie, a retired greyhound racer, when Sarah arrived at the animal shelter for their Saturday dog-walking session. She was a few minutes late because she'd opted to call Emily when she remembered that, in the fervor of last night's brainstorming session, she'd forgotten to ask her sister if Southwind would handle the food for the two shelter fundraisers. Sarah figured it was better to be late and, in this case, report a positive answer if Harlan brought up the subject.

He patted the stately greyhound, who stood by his side. "I'll wait for you at the beginning of the path. Sallie here is ready to stretch her legs."

Sarah quickly checked her assignment list. Now that Buddy had been adopted and there had been a high rate of adoptions after YipYeow Day, she happily had all different dogs to walk this week. Much as she enjoyed walking and playing with the same dog on back-to-back Saturdays, she knew it was better when her list didn't have a repeat name, because it meant a dog had found a forever home.

Reading her list, she heard a bell peal. She smiled at the sound. When Phyllis became the shelter's director, she'd hung a brass bell that the staff rang when an adopted dog or cat was leaving. The adopting person or family thought the certificate, snapshot, and animal were the adoption takeaways, with the bell simply being the icing on the cake, but Sarah had discovered that to Phyllis the ringing of the bell had a deeper significance. Apparently, one of Phyllis's favorite holiday movies had a line about angels getting their wings when bells rang. Phyllis felt the ringing of the shelter bell meant the adopted animal had found an angel. The concept both amused and pleased Sarah.

Based upon her list, she retrieved Dr. Jamie from her kennel. She thought it was an odd name for someone or the staff to have given the little fawn-colored pug. Nothing about the puppy suggested anything medical to Sarah. Once she leashed Dr. Jamie, Sarah went outside to join Harlan.

Instead of being near the beginning of the trail waiting for Sarah, as he had promised, he was about a quarter of the way down the path running at top speed, with Sallie loping ahead of him.

Sarah couldn't help but chuckle at the contrast between Harlan pumping his short legs for all they were worth and Sallie's elegant stride. There was no question Sallie was a beautiful dog, but her long legs were her best feature and now Harlan's nemesis. No matter how hard he ran, Sallie, without really picking up her pace, could easily outdistance him. Seeing Harlan pulling on the leash to slow Sallie down, she wondered if Harlan finally understood he couldn't outrun Sallie.

Looking at the shorter, stubbier dog heeling perfectly next to her, Sarah was surprised at how well-behaved Dr. Jamie was. She marveled that Dr. Jamie hadn't pulled and tried to join Harlan and Sallie. For the fun of it, she ordered the dog to sit, lie, shake, stay, and come. Each time, even though there were distractions, including Harlan and Sallie coming back to join them, the muscular dog stayed focused on obeying the commands. Only when Sarah bent and rewarded Dr. Jamie with a hug did the dog break from being in a command-response mode to cuddle against Sarah.

"Someone took the time to teach you lots of tricks before you moved in here. I wonder why anyone gave you up for adoption?"

"Why do most of these dogs come to the shelter? Some are unwanted, but others, like the one you have there, were obviously well-loved. Maybe their owners moved, died, or simply couldn't afford to keep their pets and, unlike RahRah and Fluffy, there wasn't a new, ready-made home for them."

Sarah hadn't realized she'd spoken aloud. She was glad she'd been able to provide a home for RahRah and Fluffy. Knowing they were secure made her wish she could take more of the sheltered animals home with her, but she couldn't. She could only work to help them get adopted and, in the meantime, give a few a break by walking them on Saturday mornings.

"Their backstories are what I'd like to know about each of the dogs we're walking today. I don't have one on my list that I've ever walked before," Harlan said.

Sarah peeked at his face, still flushed from running with Sallie. It was interesting he wished he knew the backstories of the dogs he walked. In a way, that was what he did with his clients. By getting the bigger picture of what was going on in their lives and what motivated them, he helped them in more than a superficial way.

There was no question from what Grace and Harlan had said to Chief Gerard, Harlan's involvement in more than Grace's legal problems had turned Grace's life around. Sarah also could attest that her own hiring, when no one else would give Sarah a job, gave her the opportunity to earn a decent wage while gaining confidence in herself after her divorce. More recently, his quiet encouragement and questions about her future were what had prompted her to consider taking some classes. "My list is all new too, but I always think that's good, don't you?"

"Usually, especially since Phyllis's been here, but remember this isn't a no-kill shelter yet. Every now and then . . ."

Sarah knew what he was going to say. It only increased her desire to work to raise the funds necessary for the Wheaton Animal Shelter to not only become no-kill, but to be able to function below the 10-percent figure. "Harlan, I thought our meeting yesterday was a good one. Just so you know, I checked with Emily and the Southwind Group is on board to handle the food for both fundraisers."

"That's great." He made a check mark in the air with his finger.

Sarah laughed. "Do you think we'll be able to accomplish our goal soon?"

"Not soon enough, but we have a lot of good people working on this. Many times people think about the no-kill part, but don't address the other outreach and adoption programs necessary for successful and sustained implementation. Thanks to Phyllis's vision, we've really looked at the broader scope of being a no-kill shelter rather than jumping in and being surprised."

Harlan's reference to looking more broadly made Sarah wonder if Chief Gerard had widened his search for Dr. Martin's murderer. Sarah posed the question to Harlan.

He shook his head. "Grace is still front and center for Dwayne, but at least this time he has expressed a willingness to look into the people in the hallway a bit more than he would have done in the past."

"How deep do you think his investigation will go? From what I've learned, a lot of people had motives and, with Grace not being in her classroom, opportunity."

Harlan pulled Sallie up short so quickly Sarah and Dr. Jamie almost collided with them. The pug calmly stared at the staid greyhound. The relaxed stance of both were in direct contrast to how Harlan's facial muscles were tightened into a scowl. "From what you've learned? Please don't tell me you're out there investigating again. Haven't you learned your lesson yet?"

Sarah resumed walking Dr. Jamie. Over her shoulder, she called, "Fine, I won't tell you. But I do think some of the relationships and behind-the-scenes things I've discovered might help you defend Grace. They go to the money instead of the blood."

Harlan caught up to Sarah. "Don't you understand that, unlike the professionals, when you stir things up, you're liable to get hurt?"

"That's not going to happen."

"You can't know that."

Sarah's gaze met his. If eyes could brim concern, Sarah was convinced his did. It unnerved her. They'd already had this discussion, and she wasn't any more interested in pursuing anything beyond their friendship and employment relationship than before.

She stumbled.

Harlan reached his hand out to grab Sarah, but before he could reach her, Dr. Jamie, digging into the path with his muscular legs, successfully provided the solid base she needed to regain her balance.

Harlan pulled back his hand in midair. "Looks like the little guy was all you needed."

"This time." She kneeled and gave the pug a hug.

He nudged his large, wrinkled forehead into her. It was moments like this she wished she could provide a home for each animal she walked.

Sarah looked to where Harlan and Sallie stood in front of Dr. Jamie and her. "Harlan, I appreciate your concern, but I promise I'm being careful."

"You've said that before and look what happened in the past."

Sarah stood and faced him. "Those times were different. Besides, someone has to stand up for Grace."

"I'm doing that."

"I know you are, but . . ."

"But what?"

Sarah started walking Dr. Jamie. She motioned for Harlan to follow her with. "Come on, let's walk these dogs and I'll explain my *but*. It isn't a big deal. After all, weren't you the person I called immediately to help Grace?"

The four fell into a step rhythm. "Harlan, you're able to handle the legal maneuvers and strategies, as well as any dealings with Chief Gerard and the other law enforcement people, but even as kind as you are, people view you as an authority figure. I'm different. People identify with my lack of kitchen skills and not-so-perfect life."

"Now, Sarah, we've talked about this. You're not incompetent. Whether in the office or the kitchen, you can follow a recipe."

"Maybe, but not with the flair and expertise of Marcus or Emily. If I had to label me, I'd call me meat loaf to their steak."

Harlan started to interrupt her, but she didn't let him.

"Meat loaf is comfort food. It doesn't look like much, but it goes down smoothly. In a similar way, although I have an anxiety attack thinking about being in the kitchen, if someone else cooks, I'm able to blend into the background serving it. The same thing often happens when I talk with people or raise a question that makes them think I'm not sure what they're saying. People get comfortable and then, without realizing it, they share things they didn't mean to tell me. You know, things about themselves, other people, or something they saw."

Sarah paused to take a breath.

"Sarah, meat loaf can be cut with a knife or even a fork very easily. I don't want to see that happen to you."

"Now you're the one being dramatic. Besides, I promise I'll be careful and only talk to people in public places."

Having reached the end of the path, they paused to give Sallie and Dr. Jamie a treat. As they began their trek back to the shelter, Harlan picked up exactly where he'd left off.

"This isn't funny. I'm dead serious. Whoever killed Dr. Martin used a knife. Knives not only are sharp, but they require close personal contact to be deadly. Chief Gerard believes this murder was a crime of passion or impulsivity."

"You know Grace. Even though she has those traits, you can't believe either of them apply to her to the extent she'd commit a crime."

"I don't. That's why I'm representing her, but that's also why I'm worried about you. I agree with Chief Gerard about the murderer acting in the moment, but think about the way Dr. Martin was killed. The knife thrust into his neck was deadly, but small. Whoever killed Dr. Martin was standing close to him. From what we know about Dr. Martin, he surely wouldn't have stood near someone if he thought there was a chance the person would turn on him. I don't know who murdered Dr. Martin, but even being in a public place might not save you. For your own safety, you've got to stay out of this."

"I wish I could."

Chapter 21

Having finished her dog-walking shift, Sarah hurried home to check on her pets and grab an egg salad sandwich, using part of the bounty Emily had brought over the night before. Emily's egg salad was to die for. It was quite popular on the lunch menu. Emily swore it was simple enough that Sarah could make it, but Sarah knew that probably wasn't true. Rather than try and fail, Sarah made sure her sister knew how much she appreciated care packages, especially ones with Emily's egg salad.

Finished with lunch and knowing RahRah and Fluffy were settled, Sarah walked up the driveway from the carriage house to the property's big house. She knocked on the back door that led into Southwind's kitchen, but didn't wait for anyone to answer before she let herself in. The kitchen was empty.

"Hey, Em," Sarah called. "I'm here. Ready to go?"

For a moment, there was no response, but then Emily and Marcus entered the kitchen. Based upon Emily's jeans and simple blue oxford cloth shirt that matched her chameleon blue-green toned eyes, she not only was ready to go, but ready to blend into the crowd observing Chef Bernardi.

Sarah looked Chef Marcus up and down, taking in his blue-and-white–striped balloon pants, Southwind white jacket, and orange clogs. She smirked. "Not joining us, I gather?"

"Why, am I overdressed?" Leaning against the island in the middle of the kitchen, the big man giggled in the way that always made Sarah laugh because it so didn't match his mountainous size. Instead of the deep-throated chuckle she expected, his reaction to something funny was more like the sound someone who swallowed helium from a balloon made when they tried to talk right afterward.

"No way. There's lots I can do around here that will be far more beneficial than watching Robert do one of his pastry demonstrations. I understand his advertised topic is 'The Versatility of Pastry Knives.' "

"Marcus, you're kidding, aren't you? Surely, considering everything that happened yesterday, he's going to modify the topic."

"I doubt it. Flexibility isn't one of his strong suits. If it was, he might still be in business. He'll gamble, which is another one of his passions, that he can get by with this. I'm not sure either of you are going to get much out of his demonstration."

Emily kissed Marcus. "Maybe not, but I still want to

go. It's a way to see what's going on in Jane's Place. Maybe I'll pick up some information or ammunition about Jane's plan and the college's reaction to it."

"I doubt if anyone on Jane's staff or from the college is going to talk to you about the proposal, even if you ask about it outright. We're considered the enemy."

"If her plan goes into effect," Emily said, "we may be the wounded enemy. I may not learn any dirt, but it's a good way for me to remind people about the Southwind Group's existence. I'm not going to stand by and let them ruin our business. We've worked too hard to let Jane take it away from us."

Marcus got quiet.

"Marcus?" Emily went to hug him, but he shrugged her off.

"Are you accusing me of doing that? Of standing by and letting that woman destroy our business?"

Emily wrapped her arm around his well-developed bicep. "Not at all. I know how hard you've worked to make Southwind what it is and how much of a partner you've been with the city and the college. I want them to see my face and tell me why, without talking to us or giving us the chance to offer them a similar program using the big house's upstairs bedrooms, they're adopting Jane's proposal. It seems to me that the college should have posted a formal request for proposals rather than going with Jane's Place."

Sarah could see Marcus's bicep muscle relax. Emily had gotten through to him. This was one of those times where the contrast between their personalities, not to mention the size of her former cheerleader sister and Marcus's linebacker physique, made her question their pairing. But, as she periodically acknowledged to herself, only they could decide what made them happy.

Watching the two of them, even now, get to the brink of an argument but work it out made Sarah feel good about their relationship, as did the kiss he bent and bestowed on Emily's head. "Be good. See you when you get back."

Emily squeezed his arm before totally releasing it. "Don't forget, we'll need twenty portions to serve tomorrow."

"No problem. I've got it under control, though why you want me to waste my time making Stained-Glass Jell-O for twenty people, when I could simply make one flavor and be done with it, is beyond me."

"Think of it as doing a good deed. The retirement folks will be so excited when they see their Jell-O served to them." Emily signaled Sarah to follow her out the back door.

Now it was Sarah's turn to giggle at the image of Marcus, while they were gone, making two sets of the different flavors of Jell-O and then having to come back and cut each color from one of the sets up and mix them to make each person's individual stained-glass creation. Maybe this was another way Marcus demonstrated his love for Emily. She was sure there were plenty of other things he could have been doing while Em and she went to Jane's Place.

As they walked down the driveway toward Main Street, Sarah saw a few people already making their way up the walkway to Jane's Place. The irony that the front doors of Jane's Place and Southwind almost faced each other wasn't lost on her. It fed the competition between the two restaurants, as well as between Sarah, Emily, and Jane.

"Em, I met Chef Bernardi when his booth was near Southwind's at the Food Expo. Both he and his delicious pastries were to die for."

"Considering the events that occurred at the Food Expo, I wish you wouldn't phrase it that way."

"No problem. But what happened during the past few months? Grace told me Chef Bernardi doesn't have his shop anymore and that he's been teaching courses at the college and moonlighting a bit with his desserts."

"That's right," said Emily.

"Although I hadn't gone by lately, I was under the impression his business was successful. The pastry shop always seemed busy when I was in it."

"It was. The problem wasn't a lack of customers, it was that Robert lost his shirt—and in turn, his business—gambling."

"That's a shame. I had no idea."

"Most people don't. It took everything he had to square himself. We talked to him about doing some pastry work for Southwind and the Southwind Pub, but the price he quoted was more than we could afford. I have a feeling that's what a lot of his potential customers discovered."

"But Dr. Martin hired him?"

"To teach a few classes. From what you've told me, my only question is: What strings are attached?"

"Well," Sarah said, "I guess, under the circumstances, I shouldn't have been as surprised to see him waiting with the others when I went to Grace's classroom with her. He was talking with Fern when we got there, but, from the way he was dressed, I don't think he'd been working in the other prep classroom."

"He has an office up there. I'm just wondering if things are tighter for Robert than he's been letting on. I know how nervous Marcus and I were until things fell into place for us. I was a basket case."

"And desperate."

"Don't remind me. I admit I made a lot of bad decisions out of fear. Come on, let's hurry. I'd like to get a seat for the demonstration."

"To blend in better?"

"No, because I expect to be on my feet working my tail off during dinner tonight. It's the beauty of Saturdays. From the reservations, we're expecting to turn each table at Southwind at least twice."

"That's great to hear. Do you expect that much business at the pub too?"

"We don't take reservations at the Southwind Pub, but it's been hopping the past few months on Saturday night. I anticipate we'll have a good night tonight. There are a few ball games and fans love our big-screen TVs."

"If you expect to be that busy at both places, will you be running between the two tonight?"

"Not tonight. Because of her hand, Grace isn't functioning at full speed. I'm going to work the kitchen at Southwind with Marcus, while Grace is going to handle front of the house and expediting at the Southwind Pub. Our staffs are small but good, as you know, so Marcus, Grace, and I can pretty easily lead in either restaurant for any shift."

Reflecting on how integral Grace was to Southwind's operation, Sarah thought it was a shame her lack of health insurance might force her to take another position. She'd be a real loss to the Southwind Group.

"Em, after our talk last night, I started thinking. Is there any chance you can get an individual health insurance policy for Grace or subsidize a portion of it?"

"I'd certainly like to because I don't want to lose her. We already looked at that option, but the numbers don't work. Much as we don't want to ignore this, Marcus and I have to put it on a back burner until we know what the college is going to do with Jane's proposal."

Sarah scuffed her shoe against the curb as she finished crossing Main Street. "I know Grace has been loyal, but if she's cleared and Jane's proposal goes through, I don't put it past Jane to pressure Grace about accepting the job again."

"I agree, but there's nothing we can do about it today, so let's go listen to Chef Bernardi."

Chapter 22

Sarah had to give it to Jane. She'd gone all out showcasing her restaurant. Decorations hung in the entry and waiting area emphasized various types of cookies, cakes, and other sweets. Sarah presumed each of the pictured desserts were part of Chef Bernardi's repertoire. Sarah wondered if this was subliminal advertising, because even catching the decorations out of the corner of her eye made her hungry for one of his delectable decadent desserts.

Jane had apparently anticipated this type of reaction because she'd removed the tables from the dining room and pushed the chairs back along the walls. Except for a few strategically placed high-top bar tables people could cluster around or put a drink down on, most of the floor space was open. The exception and focal point of the room was a centrally placed round table.

Although people were milling around the table, Sarah was able to worm her way to a spot from which she could see everything Jane had put on it. Both outer sides of the table were set the same way: clear plates, cocktail napkins, two platters of sweets that looked very similar to the ones pictured in the entry, and a tray piled high with bite-sized sandwiches. Rising from the center of the table was a cornucopia decorated with flowers, fruit, and cheese that seemed to hang in midair.

Fascinated, Sarah moved closer to the table to get a better look. The cornucopia, she realized, was made from a tan-colored burlap material stretched over what appeared to be a metal skeleton or formed shell. Each of the things that seemed to be floating were pinned to the centerpiece's frame with a miniature dagger-shaped toothpick. Sarah leaned forward and yanked out a stiletto-shaped toothpick. As she popped the cheese cube, which had been speared on the toothpick, into her mouth, her sister whispered in her ear.

"Jane apparently wanted to keep the theme of this week going."

Sarah turned her head to look at Emily. "Huh?"

"Besides that dagger you're holding in your hand, look what Jane put at the centerpiece's base."

Flipping her head forward so her gaze followed Emily's directions, Sarah realized the bottom of the cornucopia was surrounded by partially-cut mini-wheels and wedges of cheese. Each one had a small knife or cheese cutter stuck at different angles so guests could serve themselves. Sarah felt the arrangement cleverly showed how knives could have different purposes. She doubted other people's thoughts would jump to murder, but it was a natural landing point for hers. In retrospect, Sarah guessed she should have cut her cheese from the wheels and wedges rather than yanking one of the decorative daggers from the centerpiece.

"Come on, Sarah. Jane's got the back room set up for Chef Bernardi's lecture. Let's see if we can still find a chair. I don't know what she did to advertise this event, but I think she's going to have a full house."

Emily went into the next room, but Sarah paused long enough to pick up a plastic plate and cut herself a few chunks of Jarlsberg and Brie. Adding two little desserts to her plate, Sarah contently took a napkin and went in the direction Emily had gone. Hopefully, Emily had found them seats.

The back room felt full not only because it was a smaller room than the first dining room, but because Jane had set up four rows of chairs, auditorium-style, facing a podium. She had squeezed the tables and chairs normally spread through the room closer together toward the back of the room.

Sarah didn't see Emily when she glanced at the people sitting in the rows of chairs. Uncertain, she stood rooted in place until she noticed Emily waving to her from the table farthest to the right. Sarah wasn't sure if the table afforded a view of the podium, but at least they'd be able to sit while they listened.

Just as she put her plate of goodies on the table, the microphone barked and cracked with Jane's voice before she was entirely drowned out by a high-pitched sound. Jane tapped at the microphone and started to speak, but again the painful whistle came from the microphone. Someone jumped up and adjusted the microphone's sound and Jane began again.

"I'm Jane Clark and I want to welcome each of you to

Jane's Place. As you know, not only do we serve lunch and dinner Tuesday through Saturday, but next month we plan to add a champagne and jazz brunch on Sundays. Our food, which is farm to table, is prepared in-house and, I'm pleased to announce, beginning with what you have been tasting from the table in the other room, Wheaton's own Chef Robert Bernardi has agreed to supervise all dessert-making for Jane's Place. Today, he is going to tell us a little about the versatility of pastry knives. Please join me in welcoming Chef Robert Bernardi to the podium."

A round of applause went through the room. Sarah and Emily each clapped briefly. Sarah used the moment to pop one of the sweets into her mouth. It was as heavenly as she remembered. At the thought of periodically stopping in at Jane's Place for coffee and dessert, a pang of disloyalty went through her. Afraid her twin might read her mind or notice how much she was enjoying the last morsel of chocolate icing clinging to her fingers, Sarah looked toward the podium. Like she had thought at the Food Expo, Chef Bernardi was as easy on the eyes as his dessert was going down.

"Thank you all for coming, today. I'm delighted my dessert-making will be associated with Jane's Place, but, for those of you interested in learning to bake my chocolate divinities or many of my other sweets, I'll be teaching a six-week Saturday course open to anyone in the community through Carleton Junior Community College beginning next month."

Chef Bernardi pointed into the audience. Sarah looked in the direction he was pointing. Although she had glanced at those seats when she was looking for Emily, she hadn't really focused on who was sitting in the auditorium-styled rows. Now, Sarah saw Wanda and Franklin were sitting with a group of young people. Because most were wearing jeans and T-shirts with the Carleton logo, Sarah assumed they were students. Chef Bernardi confirmed her assumption when he gave a special thanks to the many Carleton students who had come out to support his first Jane's Place demonstration.

"I especially want to thank pastry student Wanda for helping platter today's desserts and, I want to tell each of you, if you sign the pad by the hostess desk on your way out, you will receive ten bonus points." Chef Bernardi glanced around the rest of the room. "There aren't any bonus points for the rest of you, but, at the conclusion of this demonstration, there will be more desserts for you on the table in the other room."

His remarks served as an icebreaker before he went into his more serious presentation. "For a pastry chef, or even a home chef, a pastry knife is the most versatile knife you can own."

Sarah leaned over to Emily and whispered, "Is he right? Is it?"

Emily shrugged and wrinkled her face. "It's one of those. To each his own. For him, it is. I wouldn't be without one in my knife roll, but it isn't my favorite knife."

A "shhh" from the woman sitting next to Emily stopped Sarah from saying anything else. Instead, she turned her attention to the podium, where Chef Bernardi held a very long and menacing knife in the air.

"With its blade being between ten and twelve inches long, a handle that adds a few more inches to its overall length, a serrated edge, and a rounded flat end, the pastry knife can be used for almost anything you might possibly want to cut. Because of its serrated edge, you can slice bread with it or if needed, use it as a carving knife." He turned the knife so people, especially those sitting close to him, could see its sharp cutting edge. "Not a knife you want to get your finger in the way of."

Chef Bernardi held the knife facing the ceiling again so everyone could see its rounded flat end. "As you can see, this end is quite a contrast to the knife's serrated side. The beauty of it is it can be used as a spatula or a palette for spreading, which differs from so many other knives that have the same serrated sharp edge, but end in a point. Whether you're a pastry chef or not, I submit this is a knife everyone should own. Now, let me show you some practical applications of how I use my pastry knife."

During the next thirty minutes, Chef Bernardi described the finer points of using and choosing a pastry knife. In each instance, whether cutting or spreading, he demonstrated his point by using the knife. He concluded the last fifteen minutes of his lesson by using the knife to help make his special flourless chocolate cake.

The room was quiet as he talked and prepared the cake for the class. Because she didn't see an oven or even a microwave, both of which Emily and the other competitors had at the Wheaton Civic Center Food Expo six months ago, Sarah wondered how Chef Bernardi planned to bake his chocolate confection, especially with the limited amount of time he probably had left.

The mystery was solved when he reached to what Sarah presumed was a shelf below the top of the podium and brought out a finished cake he had already prepared. The audience properly oohed and aahed at the finished dessert. When she thought about it, she realized that was exactly what Marcus was doing back at Southwind with the Stained-Glass Jell-O recipe.

Once the presentation ended, the crowd, despite Jane's invitation to sample the appetizers and desserts in the other room, began to thin out. With fewer people in the room, Sarah was able to see that besides the pocket of students sitting with Wanda and Franklin, there were other people associated with the college and Jane's proposal in the audience.

Fern Runskill, Dr. Williams, and a few members of the Wheaton city council were at a table exactly opposite to where Emily and Sarah sat. Sarah easily recognized Eloise and Anne Hightower, but she wasn't sure if a man whose back was to her was a councilman, someone from the college, or a random person using an extra seat at the table. To Sarah's surprise, Kait Martin was also seated at the table.

Sarah waved at Eloise, hoping to catch her eye, but it was the council president, Anne Hightower, who waved back. Sarah cringed. Sarah hoped Anne, who was a master at evaluating and working a crowd, hadn't caught the face Sarah had made. Things between them were calm now and Sarah didn't want to upset that.

Despite being cognizant that Anne always had Wheaton's best interests at heart, Sarah tended to be wary of dealing with her. Somehow, no matter how much Sarah planned, Anne had a way of twisting things to come out the way she wanted.

Now that she'd been spotted by Anne, Sarah thought it best, or at least politically correct, to take a moment and say hello. She invited Emily to join her.

"I'm going to pass. This went a little longer than I anticipated, so I really need to get back and help Marcus with Southwind's dinner prep. You politick for us. Give them my best."

Sarah stuck her tongue out at her sister. Emily chided her for her high level of maturity. Both laughed as Emily left while Sarah worked her way across the room. Her success at reaching the other table before Eloise and Anne left was hampered by dodging several other people who were leaving.

Finally, getting across the room, Sarah slowed her step when she realized no one in the college and politico group had budged from their table. In fact, Jane and Dr. Bernardi had joined them and all had their heads together in what appeared to be a serious discussion.

CHAPTER 23

Eager to know what they were talking about, Sarah wasn't sure if it was better to walk up and join their group or sidle up and eavesdrop. The latter method of sleuthing won out.

Instead of going straight to the table, Sarah ambled in a wide circle until she ended up near the group but out of Jane, Eloise, and Anne's sight. Even though everyone in the group probably recognized her, she felt the others were less likely to interrupt their conversation to acknowledge her.

Within earshot, she pretended to fiddle with a napkin and plate that had been left on the next table. She recognized Jane's voice as being the speaker. "As you can see from how smoothly things went today, Jane's Place can offer you a facility that is a perfect match for your program. With our finished rooms upstairs and state-of-the-art kitchen, both culinary and hospitality students will be able to gain practical experience."

To Sarah's surprise, it was Anne who raised an objection to Jane's sales pitch. "Jane, that's well and good, but I'd like to see the numbers laid out. I get the feeling there may be some double billing or management issues that need to be addressed before we move forward."

"Everything is out in the open."

"That may well be, but I have a duty to make sure everything is accounted for in black and white before I commit to any project. Besides, if you want city money and support, the college will have to open this up for competitive bidding."

From their previous encounters, Sarah could tell from the saccharine tone of Jane's voice as she answered Anne that not only was Jane irked, but she was trying to hold her anger in.

"Anne, I'll get you those numbers, but I already presented them to the committee. For your information, there isn't a competitive bidder. I'm the only game in town."

"Not that I see. In fact, if I look out your front door and across the street, I see a competitor we need to consider."

"Southwind isn't in the business of letting students come in and run their operations."

"Maybe not run their operations, but, since you brought up this plan, I discussed it briefly with Emily a few minutes ago. She informed me that, if given the opportunity, Marcus and she would like to submit a counterbid."

"Southwind can't offer what I can," Jane said.

"You're right," Anne agreed. "They wouldn't let the students have free rein like you, but they'd create a curriculum, working with the college, which would be a similar practical teaching model for the students. Before Wheaton enters any partnership, I, for one, would like to have an opportunity to analyze both proposals and to see if there are any other alternatives that would make more sense for the city and the college."

No longer restraining from showing her irritation, Jane punctuated her retort by jabbing her finger at Anne as she leaned in her direction. "But, Anne, there isn't and hasn't been a counterproposal. You only sought one from Emily because of your brother's friendship with Marcus and your dislike of me. You and your brother, Jacob, have been biased against me for as long as I can remember."

Sarah didn't have to see Anne's face to know how tightly her lips were pressed together. Anne's measured response was as predictable as her expression. "I'm sorry you feel that way. It isn't true, of course. I'm simply doing the due diligence every member of the council must do before the city enters into any type of agreement."

Forgetting she was playing with the napkin as a means of eavesdropping, Sarah took a step closer to the group, trying not to miss Jane's next response. Whether it was Sarah's actual movement or hearing a noise behind her, Eloise turned her head and caught sight of Sarah. She called out for her to join them, effectively terminating the discussion.

Deciding a cheerful approach would work best, Sarah almost danced to the table. "Hi, everyone. I hope I'm not interrupting. I wanted to come over and say hello and tell Chef Bernardi how much I enjoyed his demonstration and today's desserts."

Chef Bernardi beamed. "Thank you. Do you enjoy making desserts?"

"I enjoy eating them more."

Everyone, except Jane, chuckled.

"There are many like you out there," Chef Bernardi said. "Sadly, not enough to have kept my shop open."

So that was what he was telling the public. Sarah played along, deciding it was better to help him save face. "I just heard that. I'm so sorry."

He waved his hand in a gesture that made it seem like it was meaningless or at least a fait accompli.

"Chef Bernardi, I did want to ask you about the difficulty level of that community class you mentioned. Is that something a beginner could handle?"

Next to her, Sarah knew the sound she was hearing was Eloise unsuccessfully suppressing a snicker. Ignoring Eloise, Sarah focused her attention on continuing to play up to Chef Bernardi.

"If you can measure ingredients and read a recipe, you should have no problem with my course."

"Of course, you might need some remedial training in how to turn on the oven," Eloise said.

Sarah averted her face to avoid looking at Eloise, who seemed to have something in her throat, for fear they both would break out laughing.

Fern stepped in smoothly. "Sarah, there are some flyers about Chef Bernardi's course in the administration office. I'd be glad to pick one up and mail it to you."

"That would be wonderful, Fern, but actually unnecessary this time. I've been thinking about taking some classes, so I plan to come by the college in the next few days."

"Make sure you stop by my office or, better yet, call or text me in advance and we can meet for lunch or a quick cup of coffee."

Sarah nodded. "I definitely will."

"That's so nice," Jane said. "Besides Chef Bernardi's course, Sarah, perhaps you could take a few of the other basic beginner classes. Maybe you'll eventually get good enough that your sister and that boyfriend of hers can hire you as their new pastry chef. I hear they're in the market for one."

"I don't know anything about that, but I guess you feel a need to keep your eyes on the competition." Even as she made her comment, Sarah knew it not only sounded snarky, but she'd lowered herself to Jane's level.

Embarrassed, Sarah hastened to repeat that she'd merely come over to say hello but needed to run, but Jane beat her to the punch. Jane guided Chef Bernardi away to another group who needed to meet Jane's Place's divine pastry chef.

As Sarah started to turn in the opposite direction from where Jane and Chef Bernardi were headed, a hand tugged at her arm. She glanced back to the table and then down, realizing Kait, who had simply sat at the table in silence during the entire discussion, was the person restricting her getaway.

"Don't let her get to you."

"Excuse me?" Sarah partially squatted to be on the same level as Kait.

"She's not worth letting her get under your skin. From what Eloise tells me, you're a fine and loyal person and you're going to find out who really killed my son."

"What?" Sarah jerked her head up and looked around for Eloise.

Eloise, who stood behind the chair she'd previously sat in, shrugged.

"I'm sorry about your son," Sarah stammered.

The way the happy look on Kait's face faded scared Sarah.

"I'm sorry." Sarah was glad to see Kait's features take on a more placid appearance.

"Don't be sorry, dear. One thing I've learned in life is it can end without any warning. I may not always remember everything, but I'm going to enjoy mine while I can. It's what Doug would want. Just as he would want you to find out who murdered him."

Still bent even with Kait, Sarah placed her hand over the older woman's. "I think you're a bit confused. I'm not a detective."

Kait tilted her head back and laughed. "Oh, I definitely am confused, but don't worry, I have enough of my marbles to know you're not an official detective. I don't always know where I left my keys or what day it is, but there are some things I can still grasp most of the time. One of them is you're a good person and Jane isn't. Of course, that may be because Eloise told me she likes you and neither Eloise nor Doug ever indicated a particular fondness for Jane."

Unsure how to respond, Sarah simply stared at Kait, hoping words would come to her.

"I see the cat's got your tongue. Eloise, explain to her I'm not completely off my rocker. Getting closer every day, but not there yet."

Sarah glanced from Eloise to Kait and back to Eloise.

Eloise threw her hands up in the air in an *I give up* type position. "Kait's right. Dementia is a wicked disease, but it's different every day. Kait has an early-onset diagnosis, but she's still very much able to come to a lecture like this and enjoy it. With support, she's also able to interact with people."

"Exactly. Let me put it this way: You wouldn't want me to be responsible for turning off the stove in your house and I'm afraid I'm starting to repeat myself or forget what I did a little while ago, but that doesn't take away from being able to feel who's a good person and who isn't. Jane took pleasure in riling you up, but you let her get away with it."

"I did and I shouldn't have."

"Psst, you're only human. But seriously, I was watching you listening just now. You may not be an official detective, but you're a pretty good snoop."

"Kait!" Eloise tried to look stern, but the break in her usual stiff-lipped façade gave her away.

"Eloise, the truth is the truth." Kait removed her hand from Sarah's grasp. "If anyone is going to figure out who really killed my son, it's you."

Even as she kept her gaze fixed on Kait's hand, Sarah's mind whirled. Maybe she was the one with the slightly addled mind. It seemed to her that Kait not only believed Grace was innocent, but she wanted Sarah to find Dr. Martin's killer because she didn't believe the professionals were going down the right path.

"Eloise?" Sarah asked.

Eloise nodded.

CHAPTER 24

Leaving Jane's Place after talking more with Eloise and Kait, Sarah reflected on how surprising Kait was. She'd made it clear it was time Sarah stood up to Jane. Kait also hadn't minced words talking about her son's death and what she wanted from Sarah.

It was somewhat amazing to Sarah that Kait, who was grieving the loss of her son, wasn't embracing the cry against Grace. Her reasoning and the things she said about Grace were exactly what Sarah believed. But, the more Kait talked about Grace's innocence, it became clear Kait's opinion was a gut feeling based upon nice things people, including Wanda and Eloise, had told her about Grace.

It also interested Sarah that, while Kait was sad about her son's murder and wanted his killer caught and punished, she didn't seem particularly enamored of Dr. Martin. The level of love and caring Kait demonstrated for Wanda didn't come through when she talked about her own flesh and blood. Sarah wondered if it had always been like this or if mother and son had grown more distant after Dr. Martin married Lynn. Maybe she called the shots?

There were so many things to consider, but the most immediate one, Sarah realized after glancing at her watch, was rushing home to take care of RahRah and Fluffy. Next, was getting ready for her date tonight with Glenn.

For a moment, the idea of whether to cancel the date went through her mind, but there really wasn't anything else she could do to help Grace this evening. Sarah decided to keep the date. It was frustrating not to know who killed Dr. Martin, but what was worse was going to be picking out what to wear tonight.

At home, having addressed her pets' needs, she opened her closet and stared at the clothing. Glenn hadn't told her where he was taking her for dinner. She knew it wouldn't be as casual as a morning trip to Buffalo Betty's for one of Betty's special chicken biscuits, but at the same time, she doubted he'd want their first date to be somewhere they'd be on display for everyone to watch during those awkward moments of getting to know each other. That pretty much ruled out the slightly dressier outfits she might have chosen for Southwind or, if he dared, even Jane's Place.

After holding a few outfits in front of the mirror hooked to her closet, she finally decided to play it safe with a pair of black knit pants and a gray turtleneck sweater. Black boots and a chunky silver necklace, with slimmer silver and turquoise earrings, finished off her outfit.

Five minutes before Glenn was due, Sarah was back in

her bedroom second-guessing her clothing choice. Fluffy offered no help. Instead, she seemed intent on taking an after dinner nap.

RahRah seemed more attuned to Sarah's predicament. He stood at attention with his eyes facing the mirror.

"Are you looking at me or at you?"

RahRah took a step closer to the mirror but maintained his erect posture. He didn't swat at the mirror or try to nose it like he sometimes did when playing with his reflection. Instead, he turned so it felt like he was staring at her. For a moment, remembering that staring cats were often fighting for territorial control, Sarah was alarmed. Only when she could have sworn RahRah's gaze softened and he blinked at her several times before letting out a purr did she relax.

"Why, you little monkey! You like me. That's what all the books say about blinking into your owner's eyes. You like me and I'm gathering you like what I have on." After one more purr, RahRah left the room. Sarah mockingly hit her hand to her head. "Okay, I'm losing it. Not only am I talking to my cat, I'm reading answers into his expressions."

The ringing of the doorbell woke Fluffy and ended Sarah's discussion with herself. Together, they answered the door. As Glenn, clad in dark slacks and a pink button-down shirt, stood in the doorway, an excited Fluffy jumped toward him. Sarah barely restrained her by grabbing her collar while saying "No."

Gently guiding Fluffy, Sarah moved aside to give Glenn enough room to cross the threshold. "As you can see, we're still working on not jumping on people."

Glenn kneeled and rubbed Fluffy behind the ears. "Hi, gal. How have you been?" His magic touch and soothing voice settled Fluffy down and had a similar effect on Sarah. Glenn's calm demeanor, very much like she'd seen from him in his office and at the shelter, projected a feeling of comfort. Her worries about being over- or underdressed went by the wayside.

With a final pat to Fluffy's head, Glenn stood and looked around. "Where's RahRah? I can't see one of my pals without saying hello to the other one."

Before Sarah could suggest RahRah was sunning in the kitchen, RahRah sashayed himself down the hall. Whether it was instinctive or not, Fluffy took a step back and RahRah filled her vacated spot. Rather than reaching up to Glenn, RahRah lay down and preened himself.

Glenn stayed still, not touching RahRah until the Siamese cat finished and poked his head toward him. Apparently convinced RahRah was ready to be engaged, Glenn smoothed his fingers across RahRah's head. Sarah watched as Glenn's tapered fingers eased back and forth until RahRah cuddled against his leg. Sarah couldn't believe her finicky cat was encouraging human contact.

She took it to be a mark of respect. "I think he likes you."

Still petting RahRah, Glenn cocked his head in Sarah's direction. "Maybe, but it probably is that he associates me with always being a ray of sweetness and light in his life when he comes to the clinic."

Sarah wrinkled her brow. "Sweetness and light? Aren't you ahead of the holiday season?"

"Not even thinking about things in those terms. If you haven't ever noticed, at the clinic, I pet, examine, and try not to do too many things that scare or hurt RahRah, or, for that matter, any animal. Carole or one of the other techs usually takes temperatures, gives shots, or does anything routine that might upset an animal. That's what I mean about associating me with sweetness and light or simply good stuff."

"But I've seen you give animals shots, and I know you do other procedures that can't be fun."

"True, but circumstances dictate what I do. The main thing is I don't want a pet to always associate a bad feeling with coming to the vet. It's enough that an animal doesn't feel well. We don't have to make it worse, if we can help it."

Sarah didn't know if she fully agreed with the good doctor. "Whether it's a shot or some other treatment, it seems to me most animals, at some point, experience pain during a clinic visit."

"Only within reason. We're a place to heal and help. Sure, there's pain, but we also try to make it so there are pleasant things that happen in the clinic. Hopefully, that keeps an animal from being as skittish at a later visit."

"I understand what you're saying, but I think it's easier said than done. At the shelter, I've seen a lot of animals who are absolutely petrified of being handled."

"That's usually because of the treatment they've received elsewhere. Their fears go way beyond being seen by a veterinarian." Rising from his crouched position, Glenn faced Sarah. "Hopefully, our shelter gives those animals a second chance."

"No question about that." Sarah knew there were many timid dogs that, after several weeks of being walked and loved on by different volunteers and the shelter staff, underwent a personality transformation. That wasn't to say many lost the baggage they carried, but they became secure enough, despite their prior treatment, to adjust well in their new homes. She had a feeling Dr. Jamie, the pug she'd walked this week, would be one of the dogs whose adoption resulted in a happy ending.

Glenn rested his hand on his stomach. "Enough about all that. I'm starving."

"Missed lunch again?"

"How did you know?"

Sarah leaned her head back slightly to get a better look at his well-toned physique. She didn't think he looked any worse for having skipped a meal, any more than when he'd arrived at the Southwind Pub earlier in the week equally starved. "I'm beginning to sense a pattern with you."

He held his hands up as if he were giving himself up to a lawman from the Wild West. "Guilty."

Despite his words and body language, his expression reminded Sarah of the look of a little boy who'd been caught with his hand in the cookie jar. "How often do you skip lunch?"

"Almost every day."

"No wonder you're ravenous by dinner. Why don't you adjust your schedule to give yourself a lunch hour?"

"I tried that, but I feel guilty taking a meal break if anyone who came in before lunch hasn't been seen yet. We're also usually busy during lunch hour with walk-ins."

Sarah thought of when she tried to take her pets to the veterinarian. It certainly wasn't lunch hour. "Why then?"

"Usually one of two reasons. A lot of people want to avoid a visit to the veterinarian, if possible. That's why, if their pet seemed a touch under the weather, they went to work and came home at lunch to check whether their animal was sick or merely lethargic. Seeing their pet, they realize the animal needs to be seen right away."

That made sense to Sarah. "What's the other reason?"

"They bring their pet in during their lunch break, hoping we'll give them a quick magic fix so they can get back to work without needing to take leave."

"I hadn't thought about that, but, in retrospect, the minute I think one of mine is ill, I'm ready to be on your front porch."

Glenn glanced at RahRah and Fluffy. "Well, let's hope these two stay healthy tonight. In fact, I'm hoping all the animals in Wheaton stay well so our evening won't have to be cut short."

CHAPTER 25

Sarah raised an eyebrow. Was Glenn already planning his getaway from their date? She knew Glenn wanted his veterinarian practice to offer some evening hours, but the other clinic staff members didn't.

"I don't understand. You make it sound like you're on call, but your practice doesn't have night hours. Instead, your group insists that after-hours and weekend patients go to the Animal Emergency Clinic on Spring Street."

"That's right, but like us, they're a small practice. Their three veterinarians alternate the nights they're on call. One of them is out on maternity leave, so I agreed to cross cover as the second backup for the practice until she comes back."

"Does that mean your clinic now has extended hours or are considering them?"

"I only wish. I'd like to, but the other members of the clinic would kill me. They like the flexibility of our present schedule. It gives them time to hang out with their families or take part in things they find fun. For example, Dr. Vera, who has, by the way, agreed to help us find judges for the shelter talent show, plays in a string group with faculty members from the college."

"One of those fancy classical groups?"

"Exactly. Black-tie attire and everything you can imagine that goes with it."

Sarah thought about the petite Dr. Vera holding a violin tucked under her chin. "From your description, I can just imagine Dr. Vera playing an A-note to tune her group."

"Not even close. Dr. Vera is the group's bass player. Her instrument and she are almost the same size."

Sarah tried to picture Dr. Vera and her bass but gave up. She'd have to go hear her play sometime. "Should I assume Dr. Vera is one of those opposed to the practice adding night hours."

"Vehemently. But I still think it would be nice not to have to rely on another practice for after-hours and weekends. Anyway, let's go have a pleasant evening. There's never been a problem since I've been covering for my friend, because they always have a vet and a vet tech on duty."

"I didn't realize a night practice could be so busy."

"Any time of the day can be busy when it comes to animals. Speaking of being swamped brings me back to the fact I'm hungry. Do you like Italian? If you do, we could try this little hole-in-the-wall I love. It's in the same strip center as the Southwind Pub. It's small and they don't take reservations, so we may have to wait or go somewhere else. If we can get in, though, I always think it's worth it."

"Little Italy?"

"That's the one. The restaurant matches its name in terms of size and seating, but the food is excellent."

"It's one of my favorites." Sarah reached for the keys she'd left in the bowl in the front hall and picked up her jacket from where she'd hung it near the door. "They make the best eggplant parmigiana in town and their tiramisu is to die for."

Taking Sarah's jacket from her, Glenn held it so she could easily slip it on. He leaned over her shoulder, as she straightened her collar. "Aren't you being a trifle disloyal to Marcus and Emily? I won't tell, but I bet they prefer hearing praise only for their restaurants, especially from a family member."

Her eyes crinkled as she put her hand to her chest. "This is one time they won't fault me. They love Little Italy too. As you can imagine, for Emily to sing the praises of another restaurant is a big thing."

"I bet."

"I'm very loyal to Marcus and Emily's food, but when it comes to Little Italy, they—or at least Emily—are in complete agreement with me about its eggplant parmigiana and tiramisu. She's so wild about both dishes that she's tried to make them for herself."

"For herself? If they're so good, why not nail them and put them on the Southwind and Southwind Pub menus?"

"Out of respect for Little Italy's owner, Sal Dominco. They're good friends and those are two of his specialties. As long as he's in business, she'll only make those recipes for her own pleasure. She's got the tiramisu down pat. It turned out to be such a simple recipe that she swears even I can make it."

She paused, annoyed with herself that not ten minutes into this first date she'd already made a self-deprecating remark about herself. Considering it was about her cooking, it wasn't something she would deny, but that wasn't the best way to start off the evening. She was relieved Glenn didn't have a comeback, but then she remembered he'd once mentioned having been in the audience when she demonstrated Jell-O in a Can.

"Emily's been trying to figure out the eggplant recipe ever since she first ate it. Her version tastes great, but, no matter what she does, she can't quite get Sal's recipe right."

"Couldn't Emily just ask him to share the recipe? I mean, there's only one owner and chief chef there, so Sal should know his own recipe."

"That's touchy. Normally cooks keep their secret recipes to themselves, but Sal and Emily are friends and have shared some recipes, including the eggplant parmigiana. Try as she might, though, there's something about Emily's that doesn't quite taste the same."

"Do you think Sal deliberately forgot to tell her one of the recipe's ingredients?"

"That was my first thought, so I suggested it to her, but Emily doesn't think so. She believes the difference is either how he measures something—you know, a pinch of this or that—or simply that little extra a good cook puts into every dish."

As Glenn started to say something, Sarah, keeping a hand on Fluffy so she wouldn't run out after them, motioned for him to go outside ahead of her. Releasing

Fluffy as she pulled the door partially closed, she looked at RahRah and Fluffy, both sitting quietly in the front hall. Although they appeared innocent, almost angelic, she reminded them to behave.

While she locked the carriage house door, Glenn went ahead and opened his car door for her. "Tell me, because you know the inside secret, what really is the little extra that good cooks put in every dish?"

"Love." Sarah slipped into the front seat. "Emily says a chef can't quantify it, but it's what distinguishes the food of top chefs from run-of-the-mill ones."

"And I always thought it was butter."

Sarah laughed. "Shh. That's the other secret ingredient."

Shutting her car door, Glenn went around to the driver's side, got in, and started the motor. Pulling out of the driveway, Glenn brought the conversation back to what they had been talking about. "I guess the love ingredient is probably true in most fields. If someone loves what they're doing, it comes through in the final product. In a slightly different way, that little something extra makes the difference in my field too."

"Because of how a veterinarian treats the animals?"

"It doesn't have to be a veterinarian. It can be a doctor, vet tech, receptionist, you name it—even a pet owner. The key is whether the person treats the animal in a routine manner or with an extra snuggle that demonstrates they care."

"I would think most people who want to work at an animal clinic are motivated by a love of animals."

"You'd be surprised. Some need a job and they like animals well enough to answer an ad to be a receptionist or whatever else we need that comes with a paycheck and defined hours. Others just have that special something that makes them want to go the extra mile. Don't you see that in the volunteers at the shelter?"

Thinking about people like Phyllis and Carole, she had to admit they more than filled his description. She couldn't say the same for everyone who participated in the shelter's recent YipYeow Day. Most of the volunteers worked on the fundraiser out of a genuine desire to raise funds to support the shelter's mission, to better the conditions of the shelter animals, or to promote animal adoptions, but there were a few who only got involved to grab media attention for their personal interests.

Three who quickly came to mind as volunteering only for their own personal gain were the present mayor, Anne, and Jane. There was nothing hidden about the current mayor or Anne's agendas. They both wanted to enhance their political chances for the next election by currying favor with animal lovers. Similarly, Jane's volunteering to sponsor a refreshment table was to advance her own brand as a chef and caterer by showcasing her food.

In the end, Sarah had to admit the mayor, Jane, and Anne were very much like the not-as-motivated job applicants and employees Glenn described. They served a necessary purpose for YipYeow Day, but their efforts could have easily been put forth for any cause. At least when Glenn and she got to Little Italy, Sarah wouldn't have to worry about whether love was apparent, because she knew it would be in every bite.

CHAPTER 26

"Sarah, I knew Little Italy would be crowded, but I didn't expect a thirty-minute wait. Would you prefer to go somewhere else?"

"And give up on the eggplant parmigiana? No way! I've been salivating for it since you mentioned Little Italy. Besides, by the time we go anywhere else, we should be seated here."

The soft sound of Glenn exhaling as they moved out of the way of the people behind them in line caught Sarah unawares. She hadn't realized he might be as nervous about this date and how it was going as she was. The thought that they might harbor similar feelings helped calm the fluttering sensation in her stomach she'd had since he rang the carriage house's doorbell.

Sarah glanced around the small dining room. One thing she'd learned from being around the Southwind

Pub and Southwind was to judge how long it might be before a table turned over. Assuming orders were being expedited in a timely manner, but people weren't being rushed, an hour and a half to two hours between sitting down and getting up would be about average. Because most of the patrons only appeared to be at the drinks and/or appetizer stage of their meals, the hostess had probably underestimated the time she quoted.

In the past, Sarah knew she usually had to wait for a table at Little Italy, but she didn't remember being misled about the wait time. If this was one of the Southwind restaurants, Emily wouldn't be pleased if one of her hostesses underestimated the time she told everyone. Emily understood patrons who weren't drinking at the bar, or noshing on something the restaurant offered as a means of placating them for waiting, tended to get annoyed if too much time elapsed. If they started their dinner on the wrong foot, it might, no matter how good the later service and food was, color their entire experience and opinion of the restaurant. Bad word of mouth was worse than no word of mouth.

When a cold draft from the door opening behind them blew on Sarah and Glenn, he took her hand and guided her to a spot near an alcove and planter that divided the dining room from the entryway. "This should be a little warmer while we wait."

From her new vantage point, Sarah had a better view of the guests in the dining room. She waved at a table where two of her neighbors sat. As they waved back, she looked beyond them and was surprised to see Chef Bernardi, Fern Runskill, Nancy Reynolds, and Dr. Williams sitting at a table in the far corner together. They were the last group she expected to see socializing. She debated whether to walk over and say hello, but decided against it because, while Fern and Nancy were intently sipping wine, the other two appeared to be engaged in a rather heated conversation.

Dr. Williams was sitting back, arms crossed, as Chef Bernardi leaned forward, saying something. Although Sarah couldn't hear his words, the quick movement of his lips and wide motion of his arms, followed by a sudden slamming of his palm on the table, made Sarah wish she could be a fly on the wall listening to their conversation.

Glenn's voice brought her attention back to him. "Little Italy is really hopping tonight. I can't believe how many people I recognize. Apparently, they're all out and their pets are home."

"Is that how you view people, through their pets?"

"Sometimes, but some I look at through a different lens." He stared at her.

Sarah squirmed. She directed his attention to the dining room. "I can't tell if they're happy or arguing. What do you think?" Sarah pointed in the direction of the foursome.

"Well, if I had to spin a tale from what I see, I'd say something has two of them worked up, but the women are either comfortable with the conversation, taking it in stride, know something the men don't, or are simply glad to have the bottle of wine to themselves."

"I almost believe you."

"You should. Believing me is a lot safer than you going over there."

Sarah shifted so Glenn and she were face-to-face. She forced a smile. "What's that supposed to mean?"

Glenn stared at his cell phone, but there was no announcement of their table to save him. "Remember, I've watched that curious mind of yours get you into trouble where you might have been seriously injured. I know you're itching to get into the middle of whatever is going on at that table, but I don't want to see you get hurt."

"I don't think talking to people at a dinner table can be classified as a dangerous activity."

"The problem isn't the conversation, but what the wrong person might think you, wearing your sleuth hat, could put together later." Glenn looked across the room, where the college folks sat. "They're probably talking about something to do with their department or debating politics, but it isn't something you need to thrust yourself into."

Sarah's face warmed. She opened her mouth, but Glenn cut her off.

"Please, don't get mad. I shouldn't have said anything. I'm sorry. Believe me, I'm not presuming to tell you what to do. If you want to go talk to the Carleton people at that table, do. I only spoke up because I'm worried someone might hurt you because you're so good at putting things together. I'm sorry. I was being presumptuous."

Her face cooled as she relaxed, realizing Glenn would prefer she left everything to the professionals, but that he understood she needed her freedom and that he'd overstepped the line. Sarah glanced at her hands. They were stinging slightly. She'd clenched her fists so tightly she'd been pressing her nails into her palms. "Don't worry. While I'm leaving this one to the professionals, Grace is my friend. There's no way I can shut my eyes if there's some way I can help her. That's part of the reason I'm curious as to what they're so worked up about."

"I already told you." He laughed. Although it sounded

forced, at least he wasn't being didactic like Harlan. "That's my special gift."

"Come again?"

"I not only can explain conversations from fifty feet, but I also have the talent to tell you what a book is about by merely looking at its cover."

She giggled. "No, you didn't mention these talents."

Glenn's phone beeped. He checked the text message.

"Is our table ready?"

"No, it's the emergency clinic. It's too noisy in here. Let me go outside and call them. I'll be back in a minute. Maybe our table will be ready by then." Without waiting for a reply, Glenn quickly went outside.

Alone, Sarah turned her attention back to the four faculty members. They didn't seem like they'd be social friends. She could see them throwing back a beer after work and complaining about whatever struck their fancy at the college, but she never would have pictured them having dinner together on a Saturday night.

Suddenly, she realized Fern was coming toward her. Lost in her thoughts, Sarah hadn't seen her leave the table. Had the group caught sight of Sarah and assumed she was spying on them?

"Hey." Fern breezed by Sarah into the alcove near where Sarah stood without stopping. Compared to Fern's usual friendliness, her brusque manner took Sarah by surprise until she looked up and read the sign above her head. Sarah laughed. The alcove led to the hall where the restrooms were. At least she didn't have to worry Fern was on a mission to censure Sarah for being the next Mata Hari.

There was still no sign of Glenn when Fern returned to

where Sarah was. "Are you alone? A few of us are having dinner if you'd like to join us."

"Thank you, but I'm here with a friend. He's outside taking a phone call away from all this noise."

Judging by Fern's flushed face, Sarah guessed the group, or at least, Fern, had had more than dinner. She decided, while Glenn wasn't here to reprove her, to see if Fern's tongue was loose enough to spill the beans on what was being discussed at her table. Maybe there was something the faculty members hadn't shared with the police.

Asking Fern a question or two wasn't like she was going to accuse any of them of killing Dr. Martin. No matter what Glenn thought, she couldn't let this chance go by. She might learn the tidbit that would be exactly what Harlan needed to force Chief Gerard to suspect someone other than Grace. "I saw all of you over there, but the group seemed to be having such an intense discussion, I didn't want to interrupt."

Fern gave a dismissive wave in the direction of her tablemates. "That wouldn't have been a problem. Dr. Williams wanted to get together to discuss how Doug's death is going to affect the future of a combined culinary and hospitality department. Doug had a plan for underwriting a new facility for the program but, now that he's gone, that probably went with him."

"I know you're in fund development, and I remember you saying you were upstairs because you delivered a report Dr. Martin wanted. For the fundraiser we're planning for the animal shelter, different people are assigned to solicit specific companies or donors. Does it work similarly at the college?"

"That's right. Because Dr. Green hired Dr. Martin, with

the idea that the two programs would be combined into a department housed in a new state-of-the art building, I was the one working with Dr. Martin on fundraising for the building. That's why I brought the report to him."

"I haven't seen anything in the paper about the two departments being combined or there being a campaign for a new building."

Fern shot Sarah a wide grin. "Neither has been, but ask anyone and they'll tell you both are the worst-kept secrets on campus."

When Sarah started to ask a follow-up question, Fern, swaying a little, put her hand up, signaling Sarah to wait. "Seriously, the most important part of a fundraising campaign is the silent phase. The idea of what is planned trickles out, but major soliciting is done before any of the information is made public. When the campaign is announced, there already is a matching challenge gift or a goodly sum of money raised to encourage smaller contributors to make a pledge."

"Then, if you were working with Dr. Martin, can't you still solicit whomever his major donor or donors were going to be?"

"Normally, yes, but it's not that simple here. Dr. Martin kept his cards close to his chest, so even I don't know who he hoped to make his big donor. That's why Dr. Williams wanted us to have dinner tonight. He hoped we could brainstorm who to reach out to. Unfortunately, none of us could come up with a plan to successfully entrap Dr. Martin's grieving mother or widow for a donation to build a Douglas G. Martin building on campus."

"Entrap? Surely you want them to donate out of the goodness of their hearts."

"Out motley crew isn't proud. We'll take money any

way we can get it. But, as I explained to Dr. Williams and Chef Bernardi, if either was his source, I'm not sure how he planned to pry their fingers open, let alone how we can."

Sarah raised her eyebrows. "Why don't you think he could have gotten them to make a donation?"

"He might have, but not us. His mother has been a supporter of the college since she graduated, but, from the development office's viewpoint, her bequest is set, but we'd need to know her present financial and mental capabilities before we could accept a donation from her to underwrite a building. We doubt she has the capacity to manage her own funds. If Dr. Martin was handling her financial affairs, we don't know who will replace him."

"What about his widow?"

Fern snorted. She steadied herself by resting her hand on the rim of the large planter separating where they stood from the dining room. "Lynn? That's a no-go. Apparently, she's been distancing herself from him as much as possible. Something went wrong there."

"Do you know what?"

"I don't, but Dr. Williams and Robert got literary explaining their relationship to me. They alluded to the bloom being off the rose or her finding greener pastures somewhere else. Consequently, they doubt she'll give the college two nickels in his memory."

"Whew!"

"Exactly. By that point in our conversation, with fundraising exhausted, the two of them and Nancy moved on to sparring over the role of adjuncts, faculty, and tenure."

"Is there a big difference between adjuncts and hired faculty?"

"Sure. Adjuncts only get paid for the class they teach

and have no benefits. They're easily dispensable. Occasionally, one gets moved into a regular faculty slot, but I wouldn't ever count on that if I were an adjunct. Anyway, I'm letting them argue their points while I explore the finer points of the bottle of wine we ordered."

"That sounds like a perfect plan."

Fern nodded in the direction of the others. "It is, except for one minor detail."

"Oh?"

Fern leaned forward and put her hand on Sarah's arm. She pulled Sarah closer, as if to confide a secret. "It's working too well." She laughed. "Sure you don't want to join me?"

"Thank you. Although your offer is tempting, I can't. As I said, I'm here with someone who's outside taking a call."

"Tsk-tsk. The cell phone is the scourge of today's world. How did we ever survive without them?"

"I don't know, but I think it's safe to say there are times we can't live with them, but I, for one, can't imagine how people once lived without them."

Fern laughed. "To tell the truth, I feel the same way. But the company line at the college is to turn them off. They interfere with learning. Speaking of interfering, I think I better move along. There's a tall, good-looking guy coming our way in a hurry who I have a feeling is looking for you, not me."

"Sarah," Glenn said.

"Glenn, this is Fern Runskill. Fern, this is Dr. Glenn Amos."

"Pleased to meet you, Fern. I'm sorry to interrupt you two, but—"

Fern stopped him with a raise of her hand that turned

into a farewell wave. "No problem. I need to get back to the other members of my party. Everyone's trying to hash out what's going to happen with the culinary and hospitality program after tomorrow's campus memorial for Dr. Martin."

"I didn't realize anything was planned," Sarah said.

"His wife thought because his mother only has a few friends left in Wheaton and Dr. Martin didn't have any friends or family, other than his mother, outside the college, a memorial on campus would be nice. Considering Dr. Martin's mother's ongoing allegiance and support of the college, Dr. Green immediately agreed to a Sunday afternoon memorial service."

"But Dr. Martin was killed on Friday. Because this was a murder, I'm not sure his body has been released yet. There hasn't even been a full business day for the autopsy to have been performed."

"Doesn't matter. Dr. Green doesn't care if Dr. Martin is there or not. Nothing was going on in the chapel tomorrow afternoon, so that's when the tribute service will be."

Sarah raised her eyebrows. She'd heard of services after cremations or before someone was buried, but not one planned because the chapel was available.

"You know," Fern said, "anything for a donation."

"I hate to say it, but when you put it in those terms, everything makes sense."

"Of course it does." Fern winked at Sarah. "If you want to come, it's tomorrow at five, but get your wine in tonight. They don't serve in the college chapel. Nice to meet you, Glenn."

She walked away, head erect, heels clicking against the tile floor. Sarah watched Fern for a few seconds until she realized Glenn was explaining something to her.

"Sarah, I'm sorry, but we have to go." He ran his hand through his hair. "That was the emergency clinic."

"I know." Didn't he remember she'd been standing there when he got the text and went out to make the call? Was he simply trying to clarify the reason they had to leave without dinner or was this one of those fake rescue calls to give him a reason to end the date early?

"This is the first time it's happened since I've been covering for my friend, but the doctor on duty is in surgery and there's an emergency coming in the tech thinks is going to need immediate treatment by a veterinarian. I'm sorry. I can drop you off at your house, but I don't think I even have enough time for you to get a take-out order."

"That's okay."

Without another word, they made their way through the people waiting for a table. When they got outside to the car, Sarah asked, "Would it be easier for you if I walked home?"

"No." He opened the door for her. "I have to go down Main Street anyway."

"Then drop me off in front of Southwind. It will be quicker for you."

"Thank you." As he started the car, his phone beeped. Glenn glanced at the text and mockingly hit his head with his hand. "Our table is ready."

"Figures."

They drove in silence on Main Street until they reached the Southwind driveway. Without offering again to take her to the carriage house, he pulled the car to the curb. As Sarah got out, Glenn leaned across the seat. "Rain check?"

"Of course."

"Good." He didn't specify when.

She had barely closed the door and stepped away from the car when he sped away. As his taillights faded in the distance, she reflected on the evening. She wasn't sure she fully believed him about having to go in for an emergency. Being honest, on a scale of one to ten, she bet they both would rate this date a big zero.

What had she done wrong? It wasn't that Glenn was mean to her, but, in retrospect, everything about the night, except when they'd been in her hallway with Rah-Rah and Fluffy, seemed stilted. Had her rebuke of his telling her what to do ruined the evening?

Whoa! That kind of self-blaming was what she'd fallen into with her ex-husband. Sarah was better than that now. One thing she reminded herself was that it took two to interact. There might not have been a spark during tonight's date, but not every date was perfect—and it didn't necessarily mean either of the two people were at fault. They just didn't click.

As she reached the carriage house, the final kick of the evening hit her. With her bare fridge, her dinner was more likely to be a can of tuna mixed with mayonnaise than eggplant parmigiana.

Chapter 27

Sarah stood on the sidewalk in front of Southwind with Emily. Two vans of retirees were scheduled to arrive at eleven-thirty. She had to agree with Emily that the weather was perfect for the group's outing. There wasn't a cloud in the sky and just a mere hint of a breeze.

Emily, Marcus, Grace, and Sarah had met at the restaurant at nine. While Marcus prepped the main meal, Emily set the tables inside Southwind for lunch, and Sarah and Grace prepared the side lawn for the Jell-O making.

They covered each table with brightly colored plastic tablecloths Emily had purchased. There was a different cloth for each table to match the color of Jell-O the table's four to six participants were responsible for making. After arranging them, Grace and Sarah agreed the mixture of green, red, yellow, orange, blue, and purple gave the lawn a very festive feel.

As her last task before joining Emily in front of Southwind, Sarah had double-checked that the two giant garbage bags she needed to trash the Jell-O the participants made were on the back porch. She didn't care about anything else to do with what she thought of as being a glorified art project for the seniors, except for making sure no health rules were broken in the process.

While Sarah confirmed the garbage bags were in place, Grace went back into Southwind to help Marcus. Before Sarah walked to the sidewalk on Main Street, she peeked through the back-porch window. Grace and Marcus were putting something on luncheon-sized plates that were spread out across one of the counters. Although she couldn't see what they were doing, Sarah knew exactly how each finished plate would look because Emily had shared the menu with her.

For simplicity, lunch was going to be the well-liked Southwind special consisting of a bed of lettuce topped with a tomato sliced to look like a flower whose petals were opening. She imagined Grace and Marcus placing a scoop of chicken salad in each tomato and garnishing the plate with crackers and fruit. In addition to the chicken salad special, the menu called for a chocolate dessert and the pièce de résistance—a slice of the molded stained-glass Jell-O.

Sarah wondered if any would question how they'd manage to get the Jell-O to chill so quickly that it could be sliced and served without being the least bit runny. She was sure if the question came up, Marcus was ready to spin a tail about refrigeration, freezers, and the beauty of modern-day appliances. Her random thoughts were interrupted by the arrival of the vans.

As residents emptied out of the vans, helped by the retirement home aides and staff members, Emily and Sarah greeted them. Somehow, despite the noise level of the group, Sarah heard Jane's voice rise above the din. She looked around to find her.

She was standing in the middle of Main Street. Behind her, on the sidewalk in front of Jane's Place, Chef Bernardi waved a giant poster board picturing an array of desserts. Already surprised by Jane and Chef Bernardi's interruption of the Southwind outing, Sarah was more shocked to see Wanda walking up the path to Jane's Place. Sarah couldn't imagine why, until she remembered Wanda was studying dessert-making under Chef Bernardi. Probably, she was assisting him with whatever was going on at Jane's Place today.

"Remember, after your lunch at Southwind, you're all invited to Jane's Place for a special dessert buffet prepared by Chef Bernardi," Jane shouted.

Sarah looked at Emily. "What?"

"I have no idea what kind of stunt she's pulling now." Emily crossed her arms and muttered something that Sarah couldn't make out.

Mr. Rogers and their mother approached the twins. They didn't seem surprised to hear Jane yelling from the middle of the street.

"Close your mouths, girls," their mother advised. "I gather no one informed you of this little addition to our outing?"

Emily shook her head. "Moth—Maybelle, when did this happen?"

"We found out in the van on our way over here. Apparently yesterday, the retirement home's social director brought a group to Chef Bernardi's presentation. She was so taken with him that she went up to Jane to discuss a possible outing, like the retirees were going to have to Southwind, but featuring Chef Bernardi. Jane immediately offered to have the group come across the street to Jane's Place after their Southwind lunch to meet Chef Bernardi and sample his desserts. Of course, the social director accepted the invitation."

"This is ridiculous," Emily said.

"I can't fully blame the social director. She's always looking for new activities for the residents and thought it would be a nice addition to the group's outing. Apparently, the ones who attended yesterday's lecture were quite taken with Chef Bernardi."

"Yeah, they thought he was cute. His buns, as well as his desserts, were quite the discussion at dinner last night," Mr. Rogers said.

Both Sarah and Emily laughed at his observation. Despite being amused, Sarah didn't think much of the social director's thought process. "Didn't she realize Southwind would be serving dessert as part of lunch?"

Once again, Mr. Rogers had a quick retort. "She thought by the time we got to Jane's Place, most of the group would forget they already had dessert. But don't worry," he assured Emily and Sarah, "they'll remember the Jell-O part of the outing."

Maybelle snorted. "Personally, I figure Jane just wants to use up the extra desserts Chef Bernardi prepared yesterday."

"There were a lot on the buffet table when Sarah and I left," Emily said. "I could really go snarky here, it's *so-o-*

oh easy, but today, I'm going to take the higher road. The one Jane's never tread on. Come on, let's go present Southwind in its finest light."

While Emily went off to help some of the guests get to the tables, Sarah simply stared at her. She felt certain that, although Emily was using her best cheerleader voice and demeanor for the sake of today's outing, Emily was as angry as Sarah.

Emily might assess things in terms of food usage and spoilage, but Sarah was more interested in ulterior motives. Yesterday's program let everyone know Chef Bernardi was associated with Jane's Place and how attractive events between the restaurant and the college could be, but a modified version for seniors who rarely left their retirement home didn't make sense—except as an opportunity for Jane to steal some of Emily and Marcus's thunder. Even without using up the leftover desserts, that alone probably was enough motivation for that witch.

Maybelle put her hand on Sarah's arm. "Take a deep breath and channel that energy into something positive. Follow Emily's lead and help us give these people a fun day. With Jane's luck, something will blow up in her face." She chuckled.

There were moments like this that Sarah felt a special kinship with her mother. As quirky and all-knowing as Maybelle often acted, it always amazed Sarah when her mother cut right to the core, especially when it was to a thought that was rattling silently in Sarah's brain. She instinctively knew her mother was right, but accepting her mother's advice and following her directive were two very different things. Sarah vowed to try.

She went to help the last people getting out of the van and was pleased to see one of them was Kait. Considering what Mr. Rogers had said about Kait not participating in many of the activities, Sarah was particularly glad she had agreed to come. She offered the older woman her hand.

Once Kait was on solid ground, Kait looked across the street at Jane's Place. She pointed at the house. "It seems so strange to see that as a restaurant. When I was a girl, I spent many hours over there playing with Joyce."

"I didn't realize you and Mr. Rogers's late wife were childhood friends."

Kait nodded. "Joyce was older than I was, but we spent a lot of time together because our parents were such close friends. She was like a big sister to me. I still remember being a bridesmaid when she married George and when they moved into that house after her parents gifted it to them as a wedding present. I guess I never thought George would sell the house, let alone permit it to be used as a restaurant."

Kait's face lost its smile. "It's sad to look at that house now. I wonder if they've changed the polished wood banister we used to slide down when Joyce's parents weren't home. It was one of the few things they forbade us to do, so we did it the minute they left us alone."

Not wanting to give Kait more time to reminisce about the house and her late friend, Sarah took Kait's arm and guided her to the side lawn, where the Jell-O tables were set up. Kait stopped again and glanced behind her toward Main Street. "I know things don't stay the same, but I'm not sure I like all these new developments and new ideas."

"It's a balance," Sarah said. "What color table would you like to be at? It's the Jell-O color you're going to make."

"Red, of course. I'm—or at least I was—a fiery one." When Kait laughed, Sarah joined in.

"Your wish is my command." Sarah seated Kait at the red table. Realizing there wasn't a staff member specifically assigned to Kait, Sarah positioned herself a few feet behind the red table. Except when she had to handle her other duties as assigned, it would be good to be an extra pair of hands if Kait needed them. She wanted to make sure she had a good time so perhaps Kait would join in more activities the retirement home arranged in the future.

Sarah looked around to see if her mother and Mr. Rogers wanted to join the red table, but when she saw them seated at the yellow table, she left them alone.

"Hello, everyone," Emily shouted.

Marcus and Grace stood next to her.

The group, in unison, yelled a *hello* back at her. There was no hiding the fact the retirees were looking forward to this outing.

"Welcome to Southwind. Many of you know my partner, Chef Marcus—take a bow, Marcus."

He obliged.

"Chef Marcus and I own the Southwind Pub. Recently, we opened this restaurant, Southwind. While our other location is more casual, we hope you'll enjoy this more upscale addition to the Southwind Group of restaurants. We have a special lunch planned for you made by Chef Marcus and our sous-chef, Grace Winston, but first, we're going to make a special portion of our meal together."

Marcus waved and went back to the restaurant, but Grace stayed outside.

Once Emily had everyone's attention again, she addressed the group. "We're going to be making Stained-Glass Jell-O. Each of your tables has a recipe card for the entire recipe, but as you'll see, there is a trick to this dish. We don't make it in one step. Instead, each table will prepare one color or flavor of Jell-O in the bowl on your table. Your color or flavor is the same as the tablecloth at the table where you are."

Emily interrupted her description of what they were going to do to point to one of the men moving toward another table. "No changing, now, please."

"But I like blue. Besides, my friend Billy is sitting there."

"I'm sorry," Emily said. "The blue table is already full. You're going to have to stay with the green, but, don't worry, before we finish, all your colors will be blended to make a stained-glass masterpiece. That's the trick: We'll take your bowls and let them get a little firm through a new refrigeration process we have. When we bring them back to you, you'll turn each bowl over, cut the different flavors up, and mix them together in a mold to make a beautiful rainbow of color."

Emily pointed in the direction of where Grace and Sarah stood by different tables. "Grace—who you already met—my sister, Sarah, over there by the red table, and I will be helping you. My mother, Maybelle Johnson, and her friend, George Rogers, have a special treat planned for you while we wait for the single-colored bowls of Jell-O to set up. They'll tell you more about that later."

After being given their assignments, the retirees worked diligently. At one point, Sarah looked up and saw the man who had tried to move from the green table earlier was now standing with his friend near the blue table. Both men were peering into the blue table's Jell-O bowl and laughing. Sarah wasn't sure what they found so funny, but she didn't have time to find out as the red table participants needed her help to finish their first Jell-O preparation.

In short order, Grace, Sarah, and Emily were able to take the big bowls of Jell-O to be cooled. As Sarah picked up the blue bowl, one of the blue-green boys as she now called the two octogenarians, slapped the other on the back and howled. She was puzzled but didn't stop to find out what was so funny.

From behind the house as she dumped the blue bowl of Jell-O, Sarah heard her mother's unmistakable voice announcing that, for the next fifteen minutes, she would be leading the group in singing some of their favorite songs, accompanied by George on his ukulele. Sarah paused for a moment to listen to the first notes of Mr. Rogers's music and her mother's clear, soprano voice. Within seconds, other voices were singing too.

Emily, who was returning from a trip to the garbage can–cooling area, stopped near Sarah to listen too. "I wasn't sure how Mom's idea for singing was going to go over, but she obviously knows her crowd. They really sound like they're having a good time." Emily nodded toward the bowl in Sarah's hands. "Better finish with that. We need to bring back the cold bowls in a few minutes."

"Will do. By the way, keep your eye on those two guys at the blue table—the one you told to stay at the green table and his buddy. They've been laughing and nudging each other like two high school boys. I'm not sure what that's all about."

"I'll try to find out." Emily walked toward the blue table while Sarah collected the empty bowls Grace and

Emily had stacked near the trash and carried them inside to put in the dishwasher. In the kitchen, Sarah found Grace near the counter on which sat identical bowls with solid Jell-O in each of the colors Sarah, Emily, and Grace had just dumped. As Grace checked her watch, Emily came through the doorway.

"How soon can we take these outside?" Emily asked.

Grace held up the arm with her watch on it. "Five more minutes."

"Okay. By the way, you were right about those two guys, Sarah. One of them has a flask and the two have been nipping at it."

"Em, they were laughing over the blue Jell-O bowl. You don't think they spiked the blue Jell-O, do you?"

"Probably, considering how funny they think they are, but it doesn't matter. Their bowl is in the garbage. When I take Mom her new bowl, I'll ask her what she thinks."

Once the five minutes passed, each of them grabbed two bowls, with different colors of Jell-O, and took them back to the appropriate tables. Emily explained the next steps to the group. She had half the people at each table cut and chop their color of Jell-O while the other people prepared basic gelatin in a mold. Those who had the soft gelatin molds went from table to table, where those with the chopped colored Jell-O added some of their pieces to each mold until every color was mixed in. When they finished, Emily announced that Sarah and Grace would collect the molds to get them cold enough to slice and serve for lunch.

While Grace took two molds to the back of the house, Sarah started to pick up the mold on the orange table. A woman sitting there stopped her. "Do you know if the lunch is gluten-free? I have a gluten intolerance."

Unsure, Sarah caught Emily's eye and signaled her sister over to answer the woman's question.

Relieved, Sarah made two trips back to the trash can with the molds from the green and yellow tables. When Sarah returned to the side lawn, she noticed Jane mingling with Southwind's guests. Sarah walked up to Jane. "What do you think you're doing?"

Jane was smooth as ice. "Just reminding everyone about the wonderful desserts Chef Bernardi has made. We want to make sure they leave room to sample his divine delights, but, then again, they shouldn't have a problem if Jell-O is the high point of their lunch. After all, I bet they get that at every meal at the retirement home."

"I think you better leave."

"Why, this is an open restaurant area."

"Not today," Sarah said quietly but firmly. "Southwind is closed except for this private party, and you're not part of it." Sarah felt Emily's presence before her twin touched her. She glanced at Emily and realized the retirees were now paying attention to the discussion going on. Sarah deferred to her more diplomatic twin before the retirees could begin chanting "food fight."

"Jane," Emily said, with a big smile on her face, "I think you've issued your invitation. Right everyone?"

Some of the eavesdropping retirees replied in the affirmative.

"I'm sure our guests will join you later, but right now it's time for our special Southwind lunch, so if you'll excuse us." Emily turned to the tables of people. "Let's go on in. It's open seating."

The retirees, hearing lunch was about to be served, immediately lost interest in the would-be confrontation. Emily tugged at Sarah's arm for Sarah to follow her inside, but Sarah shrugged free and stayed outside. Her gaze met Jane's.

"Cat got your tongue?" Jane said.

"No, I've got the cat, the carriage house, and all this." Sarah waved her arm toward Southwind. "And just think, without having to stoop to your level even once."

Smiling, Sarah turned her back to Jane and went inside to join the others. Her comeback might not have been snappy, but, for the first time, she'd made one. She felt pretty good.

Chapter 28

Inside Southwind, Sarah shot her sister a thumbs-up. She hoped Emily would accept that as an okay sign, despite the fact both were still seething at Jane. Glancing around the room, Sarah was delighted to see how happy everyone seemed. Jane might have an ulterior motive, but she was glad Maybelle and Emily did things for the right reasons.

Being honest, while the event showcased Southwind and might bring some traffic in their direction, the reality was most of the residents didn't get out much, nor did they have relatives who would take them to a restaurant like Southwind for anything except a once-a-year event like a big birthday celebration. Most, like Kait, were living a more isolated existence that depended on the retirement home's event planner and mealtimes for socialization.

That's why Sarah hated to see today's nice outing marred in any way.

Judging by the buzz in the dining room, dessert at Jane's Place was far from anyone's mind. Both the retirees and the staff accompanying them seemed happily occupied with the Southwind food in front of them. Although she didn't see Kait anywhere, Sarah spotted her mother and Mr. Rogers sitting at a table on the right side of the dining room. Her mother, catching her eye, waved her over.

"Yes, M—Maybelle. Did you need something?"

"Emily asked me to check on those two at the next table."

Sarah peeked at the next table, trying not to be caught staring. Both men were wearing collared golf shirts and pants she assumed they either now or once wore on the golf course. The slacks of the heavier man, who the other one had referred to as Billy, she remembered, had a repeating mini–golf-flag-stuck-in-a-hole pattern. The other one's pants were yellow with a faint pink-square plaid pattern. She didn't know which pair of pants she found more distasteful. Once again, the two were yipping it up in a way that reminded her of some of the high school football players who used to come around trying to catch Emily's fancy.

"Did you find out anything about them?"

"George did. He went and made small talk and they admitted spiking the blue Jell-O from a flask they brought. They thought it would liven up today's outing."

"That's horrible. Don't they realize a lot of the people here take medications that don't mix with alcohol?"

"Sarah, relax. No one is going to get the spiked Jell-O. The fun thing will be seeing whether, thinking the blue bits have alcohol, these two will get sillier from the placebo effect. Knowing them, I'm betting on it." Maybelle settled back, ready to see if they put on a show.

"Call me over if it gets amusing."

"Will do."

At that moment, with a bit of self-made fanfare, Chef Marcus appeared, carrying a platter of individually plated Stained-Glass Jell-O servings. From the oohs and aahs, it was clear Emily and Maybelle's subterfuge had worked. Satisfied things were under control, Sarah slipped outside to help Grace discard anything remaining on the tables and break them down.

Compared to the noise level inside the dining room, the area outside Southwind was like a tomb. Sarah was surprised. She expected to hear at least some sound of Grace cleaning up, but she was met with silence. She presumed Grace, with her usual efficiency, had finished without her help, or maybe that was hindrance, and gone back inside to work the kitchen with Emily and Marcus.

When she caught sight of the tablecloths still on tables, Sarah realized her assumption was wrong. More bothersome to Sarah was not seeing Grace anywhere cleaning up. She wondered if Grace had forgotten this was one of their tasks.

It was only when Sarah saw the yellow and blue tablecloths, neatly folded, but on the ground next to the red table, she became alarmed. She was uncertain why they had been dropped there, but she was sure none of the retirees had moved them from their original tables. It had to have been Grace.

Sarah walked up to the red table and glanced around to see if anything else was out of place. Her gaze was drawn across the street to Jane's Place and she somehow knew where she'd find Grace and Kait. Much as Sarah wanted to keep her feet from leading her across the street to Jane's Place, she couldn't.

Reaching the front door of Jane's Place, Sarah hesitated. If her hunch was wrong, this was going to be more than awkward. Taking a deep breath, she pushed the door open and stepped inside the main entryway. There was no one there. Jane, Wanda, and Chef Bernardi were in the dining room setting up a rising display of cupcakes in the middle of the same round table where the desserts served after his lecture sat again today.

Wanda stood on a ladder, carefully placing each cupcake Chef Bernardi handed her on whatever shelf of the display fixture he directed. Jane stood next to Chef Bernardi, alternately admiring the display or suggesting Wanda move a cupcake slightly to the right or left or to a different riser. Without complaint, Wanda, with a cupcake in one hand, used her free hand to manipulate the cupcake into the position Jane desired. There was no sign of Kait or Grace.

Sarah debated whether to back out of the restaurant, hoping the three didn't see her, but she still had a feeling something was amiss. Forcing herself to move farther into the room, she loudly said, "Jane, have you seen Grace or Kait?"

Apparently startled by Sarah's voice, Jane whipped around, bumping the ladder Wanda stood on. With both hands extended, Wanda fought to keep her balance. She dropped the chocolate-frosted cupcake she clutched as she scrambled to keep herself upright. It smashed upside down onto the center of Chef Bernardi's head before slipping down the shoulder of his white chef's coat. The next moments unfolded like a scene out of a Keystone Cops movie. Chef Bernardi tried to grab the ladder and Wanda. He caught the ladder but couldn't stop Wanda's forward face-plant into the top layer of the display. Displaced cupcakes flew in all directions.

As Wanda grabbed at air, trying to find a way to push herself away from falling into the desserts lying on the table, Chef Bernardi managed to get an arm around her waist and swing her away from the table. He slowly lowered Wanda to the floor. Once Wanda appeared stable on her feet, he released her from his grasp.

Sarah let out the breath she didn't even realize she'd been holding. As she exhaled, a twinge of guilt swept through her for starting this mess, but it was quickly followed by a wild moment of exhilaration that Jane had gotten her just desserts—or at least a taste of them. To Sarah's eye, it appeared that, except for the top layer of cupcakes, the remaining desserts would be salvageable.

A noise made Sarah and the others look back at the dessert table. At first, nothing seemed amiss, but then she realized the tower display had shifted. A creak grew to a whine as it slowly swayed. Chef Bernardi reached for the central post to steady the fixture, but he was too late. It fell against one side of the dessert table with a resounding bang. The cupcakes still on the display splattered onto the table, floor, Wanda, Chef Bernardi, and Jane. Sarah took a step forward, bent, and picked up an undamaged cupcake. She turned it in her hand, examining the delicate detail of its icing, before placing it on the table amid the crushed remains of Chef Bernardi's handiwork.

Cupcake remnants dotting her hair and sweater, Jane accosted Sarah. "What's wrong with you? What were you thinking sneaking in here like that?"

Sarah took a step back from Jane. "I'm sorry, Jane. I

really am. I didn't mean to startle you. I was looking for Grace and Kait and thought they were here."

"Here? At Jane's Place? Are you crazy?"

As Jane moved back into Sarah's personal space, Sarah stammered how she found the folded tablecloths abandoned on the ground near the red table. "Because of things Kait mentioned about playing in this house when she was growing up, it seemed logical Kait and Grace were here."

Jane cut off her explanation. "Is that the best story you can come up with?" She threw her hands up in the air. Grabbing Sarah's arm, Jane pulled her until they both could clearly survey the sorry state of the room, Chef Bernardi, and Wanda.

Sarah wasn't sure which was a worse disaster—the table and floor littered with fallen cupcakes and splattered desserts, or Chef Bernardi and Wanda. They wouldn't even need any makeup to be part of the mayhem and havoc insurance-company commercial she often saw on TV.

"Once again, you played detective and bumbled it. When you snuck in, couldn't you see that, except for the three of us working, there's no one here."

"Let's get something clear, Jane. I didn't sneak in. Your front door was open."

"And you took advantage of that to do your idiotic busybodying again? You're going to pay for this!"

"That's not fair. You're the one who bumped into the ladder and caused this mess."

"Fair? First, you destroy my restaurant and now, when I have a chance to regroup and start over, you come into my restaurant—uninvited—looking for two people who should be at your restaurant. You ruin everything for me!

You're a big one to talk about fairness." Jane glared at Sarah. Jane's hair and face were the same shade of red.

"That's enough," Sarah said. "Look at yourself. With your schemes and plans, what gives you the right to talk or pass judgment on anyone? Did you ever stop and think you get what you sow?"

"What?"

"Just what I said." Sarah wasn't sure if Jane was taken aback by Sarah's outburst, but she was. Holding herself together so the tears wouldn't flow, Sarah modulated her voice. "I don't think you even know how to act with a shred of moral decency. You—"

A whimpering sound came from the direction of the kitchen.

Cutting herself off midsentence, Sarah ran across the dining room.

"Stop!" Jane yelled. "Get out of my restaurant."

Sarah ignored her. She pushed the swinging kitchen door open and froze. Grace sat on the floor, her arms wrapped around Kait. A cast-iron skillet lay on the floor next to them.

Chapter 29

While Wanda cried, "Grandma Kait," Chef Bernardi pushed past Sarah and Jane. As he bent near Grace and Kait, Jane shouted at Grace. "Let go of her, you murderer!"

Grace raised her head, while tightening her grasp on Kait. "What are you talking about?"

It was Chef Bernardi who responded. "Wasn't killing Dr. Martin before he could get his mother to sponsor our culinary project enough? Now you've gone and killed her. Why?"

Sarah was absolutely confused. She couldn't comprehend the idea of Grace killing one person, let alone two, because of something to do with the college's culinary program. Speechless, Sarah stared at Grace, at the woman she thought she knew.

Grace met her gaze. "Sarah, what is he talking about?"

"Kait." Sarah, her tongue feeling like parchment, barely croaked the word out.

"What?" Kait ever so slightly lifted her head from Grace's shoulder.

As a flood of words flew from Jane's mouth asking why Kait and Grace were in the kitchen and what was going on, Sarah simply let out a sigh of relief. She knew whatever the explanation was, it could never be as bad as what she had thought happened. It bothered her that she had wavered in her faith in Grace, but Sarah was thankful her lapse of judgment was obviously proven wrong.

Either from hearing Kait's voice or Chef Bernardi's observation that Kait was alive, Wanda rushed to her side. The toe of Wanda's sneaker hit the skillet. The collision barely moved the pan. Considering the sound of the thud and Wanda's cry of pain, Sarah assumed, as she watched Wanda slide to the floor next to Kait and Grace, the pan got the better end of the crash.

Kait pulled away from Grace and sat on her own, reaching her arms out to Wanda. The young woman, tears streaming down her face, collapsed against the older woman. "I thought you were—"

"Hush." Kait patted Wanda's hair.

Jane pulled her cell phone from her pocket. "I don't know what you're trying to pull, Sarah, but neither you nor Grace were invited to be on these premises."

She punched three numbers into the cell phone and held the phone to her ear, waiting for a response. Apparently, someone answered. "This is Jane Clark from Jane's Place. I need you to connect me with the police. There's been a break-in at my restaurant."

"What! The door was open."

Jane ignored Sarah. "I'm perfectly safe. I have the two

confined to my kitchen, but please tell the police to hurry." She clicked her phone off.

"Are you losing your mind, Jane? There has to be a rational explanation for Grace and Kait being here," Sarah said.

"I'm sure there is for Kait, but as for Grace and you, you can tell it to a judge. I'm going to swear out a warrant for your arrest for breaking and entering."

Sarah met Jane's gaze. Without looking away, Sarah tried to reduce the tension in the kitchen by making a quick exit. "You're being ridiculous, Jane. This is all a big misunderstanding."

Still keeping her gaze locked on Jane's, she flicked her hand to catch Grace's attention. "Come on, Grace. Let's get out of here."

"Neither of you are leaving before the police come." Jane grabbed a long knife that was sitting in a butcher block on the counter near the kitchen prep area.

From its shape, Sarah recognized it as a cleaver.

"Sit on the floor next to Grace."

Was Jane going crazy? The way Jane brandished the knife, combined with the wild look in her eyes, gave Sarah second thoughts about leaving. Without any further argument, Sarah did as Jane ordered. As she sat, she wondered if Jane had lost it in a similar manner with Dr. Martin.

Once Sarah was settled near Grace, Jane seemed calmer. "Wanda, take your grandmother into the other room, please."

"What about the seniors?" Sarah pointed to the clock on the wall. "They're finishing up lunch at Southwind and are going to be here any minute."

Jane whipped her head around toward the clock.

"Thanks to you, there's nothing for them to come here for today. Chef Bernardi!"

"Yes?" He stood and moved closer to Jane. Besides the chocolate from the cupcake that had hit his shoulder, his white jacket now was smeared with even more chocolate, some red-orange that could have been from red-velvet or carrot-cake icing, and a streak of blue where he must have hit something blueberry.

"You need to go across the street and cancel our pop-up dessert event."

"But, look at me—this is how you want me to go over to Southwind?"

"We don't have a choice. I can't leave these two before the police get here, and Wanda is busy with Kait. Just tell their event person to explain to the group Sarah ruined today's treat at Jane's Place, but we'll make it up with a special outing soon. In fact, tell her I'll call her tomorrow and schedule something."

Still muttering, Chef Bernardi left the kitchen. From where she sat, Sarah saw him take off his white jacket. He had a T-shirt under it, but at least it was clean. She was sure some of the seniors would appreciate the form of the delivery so much they'd ask him to repeat the message.

Her fears of being alone with Jane and her cleaver for much longer were allayed when Officer Alvin Robinson came through the swinging kitchen door. He pushed it so hard it stuck in the open position.

"The police—or should I say, I'm—here, Jane. What seems to be going on today?"

Sarah was glad the responder was Officer Robinson. The recent addition to the Wheaton police force had consistently been a voice of reason in her past dealings with him. She felt certain he wouldn't accept Jane's rendition of the facts at face value.

Using the cleaver for emphasis, Jane pointed toward where Grace and Sarah sat on the kitchen floor. "Officer Robinson, it's very simple. Grace broke into my restaurant, apparently through the back door, while Sarah came through the front. Sarah destroyed the dessert display Chef Bernardi and I planned to serve our retirement home guests today. You can see the remnants in the dining room. The mess is everywhere. I want you to arrest them for breaking and entering, trespassing, and anything else you can think of."

Officer Robinson held his hand out. "Okay, Jane. We'll get this sorted out, but first, I want you to give me that knife."

"Oh, this little thing." She handed it to Officer Robinson. "I needed it to protect myself from Sarah and Grace. I'm so glad you're here now to take care of me." She batted her eyes at him.

"Jane's exaggerating. We didn't do anything she needed to be protected from, and we didn't break in." Sarah glared at Jane.

Jane thrust her face toward Sarah's. "You liar! The proof is in the pudding."

She turned toward Officer Robinson. "Even you can see Jane's Place is closed, Grace and Sarah are inside my building, and because none of the three of us in the building let them in, they broke in. This is an open-and-shut case. I insist on pressing charges."

Officer Robinson pointed to the dining room. "What about those two?"

"That's Wanda and her grandmother," Jane said.

Sarah seized the moment to explain her side of the story to Officer Robinson. "Wanda was working here with Chef Bernardi and Jane, but I think something triggered Kait, who has dementia, to leave the group having lunch at Southwind and wander over here. She used to play in this house with its former owner when they were children. I'm not sure of every detail, but I know neither Grace nor I did anything wrong today—especially not enough to be held here in the kitchen at knifepoint."

"It looks to me like we have a lot of things to sort out here. I think we better do it down at the station."

CHAPTER 30

Harlan held the door for Grace and Sarah as they left the police station. When Sarah started to thank him for coming to help them, he cut her off. "Not another word until we get back to my office."

The three continued the two-block walk in silence. Only when they were in the office did anyone speak, and it was Harlan, as he escorted Grace into his office. "Sarah, I think we need some coffee. Please put on a pot."

Without responding, Sarah dropped her coat on her chair and went into the office's little break room. She knew Harlan either was beyond mad at her or simply wanted a moment to talk to Grace in private, because coffee wasn't one of Sarah's other duties as assigned. Harlan and she took turns making coffee, depending on who was in the office first.

Once the coffee ran through their coffee maker, Sarah

stuck her head into Harlan's office. "Coffee's ready. Do either of you want anything in yours?" When both Harlan and Grace answered black was fine, Sarah returned to the break room and filled two mugs for them. She made one for herself with two packets of natural sugar and then carried the three mugs into Harlan's office. Grace was sitting on the couch, Harlan in his oversized leather wingback chair. Sarah took the matching chair across the coffee table from him.

"Grace was just telling me she saw Kait cross Main Street and walk toward the rear of Jane's Place. Why don't you fill Sarah in?"

"What happened, Sarah, was almost exactly like you told Officer Robinson when we were in the kitchen. I was collecting the tablecloths and had several in my hands when I reached the red table. As I started to pull that tablecloth off, I glanced across the street and saw Kait going up the driveway that Jane's Place and the veterinarian clinic share. I looked around to see if someone was watching her, but everyone, including you, was inside Southwind. She'd apparently crossed Main Street by herself. Because I didn't think she should be wandering alone, I dropped the tablecloths I'd folded onto the red table and ran after her."

"The breeze must have blown them off the table," Sarah said. "The folded cloths on the ground is what made me feel something was amiss."

"What happened next, Grace?" Harlan asked.

"I crossed Main Street, but, by that time, Kait was already out of sight."

Harlan made a note on the legal pad he was holding. "How did you know she was going into Jane's Place rather than the animal clinic?"

"I didn't. It was a hunch. Anyway, I ran up the driveway and caught a glimpse of her going into Jane's Place through its back door. I followed her."

"Was the door unlocked?"

"Definitely. Otherwise, I wouldn't have been able to get in. The door already had closed behind Kait."

"That means Grace didn't break in any more than I did, because when I went into Jane's Place, the front door was unlocked too."

"Sarah, let's not get into semantics right now. You're only lucky that, considering Jane and your past experiences with Chief Gerard and Officer Robinson, they're in the process of explaining to her that it would be better not to press any charges because her actions with that giant knife could have consequences for her. I'm pretty sure if you pay for the damaged desserts, this will all be resolved."

"But why should I have to pay anything when she's the one who bumped the ladder?"

"And you're the one who startled her by 'entering' Jane's Place when it wasn't open."

Sarah pouted. "It doesn't seem fair. She's the one who encroached on the nice outing my mother and Emily planned for the home's residents."

"I understand how you feel, but, trust me, in the end, this will be for the best. By the way, Maybelle told me to tell you not to worry about RahRah and Fluffy. Mr. Rogers and she went to the carriage house after lunch to play with them. They'll probably spend the afternoon, so you don't need to worry about rushing home to walk Fluffy or feed Fluffy and RahRah. They'll take care of them."

"That makes me feel better. I was about to ask you if I could dash home for a minute."

Harlan turned his attention back to Grace. "Did you figure out why Kait went over to Jane's Place?"

Sarah volunteered that Kait knew the house from her childhood and maybe it was a matter of old memories surfacing.

Grace shook her head. "I don't think that was it. When I came in, she was already sitting on the floor fingering the small cast-iron pan. She said something about the kitchen being a place that held memories for her, but it obviously was different now. That's when she teared up and started talking about how all things change and how memories fade."

"Her mind?" Sarah asked.

"Again, while that may be part of what she was referencing, I think she was seeing in broader terms. Kait mentioned a woman, who I now realize was Mrs. Rogers, and Dr. Martin. Then, out of the clear blue, she pointed across the kitchen at a wall and said something about it being a foundation wall that couldn't be moved when her friend's mother remodeled the kitchen. When I seemed perplexed, she said something about how the future always needs a solid foundation. She laughed and said it was probably the only idea her son and she ever agreed on. After that, Kait teared up again."

"What happened next?" Harlan asked.

"Kait made another comment about the house. I didn't quite catch it, but then she started crying in earnest. I didn't know what to do, so I held her until the sobs subsided and she grew quiet. That's when everyone burst into the room. Personally, I don't think in that moment she had the ability to respond to the racket Jane and Sarah created."

Harlan put his pad on the coffee table and picked up his coffee mug. He took a few sips, looking at Sarah and

Grace over the top of the cup's rim. "Some of what Kait said makes sense, but I'm not sure how much is a fact she was trying to convey versus delusional thoughts."

Sarah shook her head in disagreement. "I don't understand what she was saying to Grace, but while Kait is having short- and long-term memory loss, she's never seemed delusional when we've spoken. Eloise can give you a better idea on that. Eloise eats with her at least once a month."

Putting down his mug, Harlan picked up his pad and made a note. "I'll follow up on that. Okay, Sarah, pick up the narrative of what happened next."

"I heard a noise—probably one of the sobs Grace just described—and ran into the kitchen through the swinging door from the dining room. Jane followed, or should I say shoved me out of the way, so we both came into the kitchen at almost the same time. When I saw Kait and Grace, I thought Kait was dead. I stood there, stunned, but Chef Bernardi pushed past Jane and me and went to look for a pulse. Time slowed and sped. I can't speak for Jane, but my mind flew in different directions, trying to figure out what happened and how Grace was involved. It wasn't until Kait raised her head and spoke that I realized she was alive. I was relieved and I think Jane was too. She had Wanda take Kait into the other room, and that's when Jane went off the deep end."

"In what way?"

"She started accusing Grace and me of breaking in and being responsible for destroying the desserts and her life."

"Her life?"

"Yes, Jane said something to the effect that I ruin everything she tries to do. She got even angrier when I reminded her the seniors would be finishing at Southwind in the next few minutes. That seemed to throw Jane until she ordered Chef Bernardi to go across the street and announce today's event was canceled, but a special event with only Jane's Place would be scheduled. He left right before Officer Robinson arrived."

Harlan closed his pen. "And the rest, as they say, is history."

CHAPTER 31

Sarah was glad it was still Sunday, although almost time for Dr. Martin's memorial service. She couldn't help brooding over Harlan's assurance that her agreement to pay a token amount for the desserts was the best way of resolving today's mess. Sarah hated the idea of writing a check for something she didn't feel she should be blamed for. Then again, if Sarah was completely truthful with herself, she had to admit her startling Jane was the catalyst for today's disaster. Maybe Harlan's solution wasn't as bad as she originally thought.

Before Sarah left Harlan's office, he received a call from Chief Gerard that Jane was calmer, understood all the circumstances and possible outcomes, and would be glad to accept two hundred dollars for the ruined desserts. Harlan put Chief Gerard on hold, tendered the offer to Sarah, and advised her to accept it. Despite her misgivings, she agreed. Once she did, Harlan unmuted Chief Gerard and indicated her decision. The upshot was Harlan would write up something tomorrow explaining the terms of their agreement and Jane, upon executing the document, would receive a copy of the final paperwork and Sarah's check.

Sarah decided, except for writing the check, to put the earlier part of the day behind her. The one good thing, as Maybelle had shared with Harlan, was everyone who attended the Southwind stained-glass activity and luncheon had a wonderful time. Better yet, they left raving about Southwind and its two chefs.

Sarah quickly checked on RahRah and Fluffy before changing for the memorial service. As she walked toward the CJCC chapel, she heard her name called. Turning back, she saw it was Mandy. Sarah waited for her to catch up. "Hi, Mandy, where's Grace?"

"After spending part of today in the police station and still being at the top of everyone's suspect list for killing Dr. Martin, Grace couldn't face attending this service. I decided I should instead."

"Why? I thought you didn't know Dr. Martin."

"I didn't, except for what Grace told me about him. But in all the books they say the murderer usually comes to the service."

Sarah kept herself from smiling. She'd used the same line of reasoning when she attended the funeral service of banker Lance Knowlton, when Maybelle was accused of killing him. "It probably works better in books than real life."

"Maybe so, but I thought I'd see if I noticed anything that would help Grace. She didn't kill Dr. Martin, despite what people think."

"I know." Sarah reached for the other woman's arm and gave her a reassuring squeeze.

Together they walked up the steps and into the chapel.

On an easel on the altar was an eight-by-ten-inch photograph of Dr. Martin. The rest of the altar, with its lectern and religious symbols, was the same as it would be if anyone walked into the chapel any day of the week.

Sarah turned her attention to those in attendance. It wasn't a large group of mourners.

She was surprised to see Eloise sitting in the front row between Kait and a young woman Sarah didn't recognize. She assumed from the black suit the woman wore she was Dr. Martin's widow, Lynn. The remainder of the row was empty. Wanda and Franklin sat behind the threesome. Sarah didn't know if the other three young people sitting with Wanda were students or friends from outside CJCC, but they were obviously there to support Wanda.

The front pew on the other side of the chapel was empty. A distinguished couple was in the process of sitting in the second row. Sarah recognized the man as being Dr. Green, the president of the college. Because he was holding hands with the woman, she decided that was his wife and immediately dismissed her from being a suspect. Dr. Williams, Fern Runskill, Chef Bernardi, and Nancy Reynolds were already seated in the pew behind the one the president chose. Rather than joining the existing group of mourners, Mandy and Sarah sat in the last row of the chapel.

The service went quickly. The campus chaplain said a few kind words about Dr. Martin, followed by remarks from the president. Dr. Green commented about how much Doug enjoyed Carleton Junior Community College and had a vision for the growth of its culinary and hospitality program. Kait must have begun crying at that point because Eloise handed her a tissue and put an arm around her.

The final speaker was Dr. Martin's widow. A very attractive woman, Lynn Martin didn't appear to be much older than Wanda. "Doug and I weren't married long, but I will miss him every day for the rest of my life. He was meticulous about how he wanted things, but he was also loving and fun. I know he loved me, cared deeply for and respected his mother, Kait, and took great joy in working for the school his mother held dear. It would be a shame if his dreams and plans for the college end with his untimely death but, hopefully, because of others who share his vision, his dreams can be realized."

Mandy tensed next to Sarah. Sarah glanced sideways. Mandy's previously relaxed jaw was now clenched in a rigid line as she stared at Dr. Martin's wife. Sarah didn't think Dr. Martin's widow's remarks were so cutting as to evoke such a visceral response, even with the way Mandy felt about Grace. This reaction seemed personal—but was it personal enough for Mandy to have stabbed Dr. Martin? Was she the killer hidden amid the funeral guests?

Where, Sarah thought, had that idea come from? She stared at Mandy, realizing she knew little about her except she was older than Grace, worked as a paralegal for a plaintiff's law firm, and taught self-defense classes. Grace had met Mandy when she was a student in one of Mandy's self-defense classes, but Sarah wondered why Grace took the class and what motivated Mandy to teach self-defense classes. Had Mandy been abused? Was it the maturation of a childhood interest in some hands-on sport, like karate or jujitsu? Could Mandy have somehow been near the college and either overheard the discussion between Dr. Martin and Grace or walked in afterward and reacted to something he said directly to her? If any of this was feasible, would Mandy have used her bare hands or grabbed a knife and stabbed him in a moment of rage? To paraphrase some TV show she once saw, Mandy was in the right city, had a motive, and had the ability, but was she any more guilty than Grace might be?

Sarah's wild streak of thoughts was interrupted by the people around her standing up and Mandy talking to her. "What did you say?"

"I said I can't take any more of this, so I'm skipping out rather than going downstairs for refreshments and to pay my respects to the family. Are you staying or going?"

"Staying for a few minutes."

While Mandy exited through the back door of the chapel, Sarah followed the majority of the memorial service attendees down a set of stairs in a hallway behind the altar. When she reached the large room at the bottom of the stairs, a long table on the back wall had been set with tea sandwiches, mini-cakes, nuts, mints, and a bowl of punch. To the far side was a cluster of chairs for people who might want to sit.

The family members stood in the middle of the room. There was enough space between where Kait and Wanda stood and the spot occupied by Dr. Martin's widow for people to make two different lines to pay their respects.

Sarah made a beeline for Lynn, who smiled as Sarah approached her. As they shook hands, Sarah noted the simplicity of Lynn's makeup and lack of nail polish.

"I'm very sorry for your loss, Mrs. Martin."

"Thank you. And it's Lynn, please."

"Lynn. I'm Sarah Blair."

"Sarah, I appreciate you coming today. Did you know Doug well?"

"No, I only met him in passing, but I've heard a lot about him from some of his students and people who had more direct dealings with him. My sister is in the restaurant business."

Lynn's eyes widened. "Now I know who you are. You're the person who solved several murders in the past year."

"Well . . ."

"I wish you could solve Doug's. This isn't the time to talk—some people are finally coming this way—but would you mind meeting me, perhaps tomorrow?"

As much as Sarah wanted to learn more about Lynn Martin, she was equally surprised Lynn wanted to talk with her. Perfect. She agreed to meet Lynn at seven-thirty in the morning at the Coffee Bar. It might mean another morning without makeup and getting RahRah and Fluffy settled a bit early, but Sarah knew no good detective should avoid the obvious suspect: the newly minted widow.

Moving aside to let a couple share their condolences with Lynn, Sarah saw the line to Kait and Wanda was still long, but Franklin was standing by himself near the refreshment table. She opted to join him. "Hello, Franklin." She picked up a tea sandwich. "I'm a sucker for any white-bread sandwich with the crust cut off, especially when I haven't had dinner. Any idea what these are?"

"Yes. The one you're holding is pimento cheese and the other platter has pickle relish–based chicken salad sandwiches."

"I think I'll stick with the pimento."

"That's my favorite too."

She helped herself to a second tea sandwich. "These really are good. I better move away from this tray before I eat them all."

"I'm glad you like them." Franklin smiled.

Seeing his smile, Sarah was confused. If she remembered correctly, Franklin was a criminal justice major who was only taking Grace's knife skills class because of his interest in Wanda, but it sounded like he was taking credit for the sandwiches. "Franklin, did you make these?"

"I helped. Wanda and some of our classmates catered this memorial. It's being hosted by the college, so the culinary department gets called on to make the food."

"But I thought Wanda is into baking."

"She is. That's why she's been so excited to get to work with Chef Bernardi. Wanda needed to keep busy, so she made that tray of sweets. Because I was hanging around the kitchen, I helped out with the tea sandwiches."

"You cut them into these perfectly matched shapes?"

"No. My knife skills still leave a lot to be desired, but once they showed me how much and exactly how to do it, I proved to be quite accomplished using a spreader with pimento cheese." Franklin puffed out his chest and rubbed his hand down his sweater.

Sarah would have laughed, but, from an attempt or two doing something similar for Emily, she knew that spreading the same consistency in the same way on this many sandwiches without tearing the bread or leaving a finger impression wasn't as easy as it looked. Emily and she had chalked that up as another kitchen skill Sarah lacked.

"Satisfied about something, Franklin?" a male voice behind Sarah asked.

She turned to see Dr. Williams.

"Ah, yes, sir," Franklin said.

As Franklin fumbled, Sarah held her sandwich where Dr. Williams could see it. "Try one of those delicious pimento cheese sandwiches. Franklin was just telling me how he helped make those. In fact, he was explaining how the culinary program students catered today's event. I think letting them get practical experience is a good thing, don't you, Dr. Williams?"

"Most definitely. That's why we've been trying to come to an agreement with Jane's Place."

"Without considering Southwind's recent proposal?" Eloise had quietly walked up behind Dr. Williams.

Fern brushed her hand against Dr. Williams's sleeve, effectively moving him aside as she fielded Eloise's question. "Of course not. Dr. Williams didn't make himself clear. As you well know, CJCC, as well as Wheaton, was considering a proposal Jane made to use Jane's Place, but then some other options, including Southwind's, were put on the table."

Eloise jerked her head up and met Fern's gaze. "I'm not aware of any other proposals beyond the ones to use Southwind or Jane's Place. If the college is interested in a grant, is there some reason whatever else is being considered wasn't presented to the council?" Fern stood erect, but Eloise didn't back down. "Well?"

Fern looked around, as if making sure no one else was within earshot before responding in a voice so barely above a whisper Sarah had to strain to make out what she was saying. "Dr. Martin had a possible idea he was working on as a third alternative. Unfortunately, he was killed before it could become a reality. Dr. Williams and I are continuing to explore the possibility."

A third alternative? Sarah distinctly remembered Fern

telling her at Little Italy that Dr. Williams and she had no idea who Dr. Martin's donor was, nor whom else they might reach out to. Perhaps something had changed, or why would Fern raise the possibility of the existence of a third alternative?

"Eloise," Fern said, "there simply isn't anything to report or share. The opportunity probably died with Dr. Martin, but I promise, if something works out, I'll make sure your office is the first to know. Now I, for one, would like to try one of those pimento sandwiches."

She picked one up, bit into it, and swallowed. "This is delicious. Wasn't this meal catered by our culinary students?"

Franklin nodded. "Yes, ma'am."

Sarah pointed to Franklin. "Not only was it catered by the culinary students working together, Franklin here had a major role in putting the pimento cheese sandwiches together."

"Well, they should all be properly thanked," Dr. Williams said. "Franklin, can you remember the students who were involved in preparing this table?"

"Yes, sir."

"Very good. I've always praised my hospitality students who do a good job and now that I've assumed responsibility for the culinary program, I'd like to do the same for those students."

He pulled a small notebook out of his jacket pocket as he glanced around the room. "Tell you what—it would be easier to do this seated, and I see a few empty chairs on the other side of the room. Why don't we go sit over there, and you can tell me which students were responsible for what items on the table."

Franklin and Dr. Williams, already engaged in a conversation, walked away without saying goodbye.

Picking up another sandwich, but taking time to say goodbye and to remind Sarah that when she was on campus they needed to get together for coffee or lunch, Fern followed them.

"That," Eloise said, "was definitely the polite way to temporarily avoid a subject."

"Temporarily?"

"Do you think I'm going to let this go that easily? I wouldn't be doing due diligence for my constituents." Eloise grinned.

"What's so funny?"

"For some reason, I think this is one of those times Anne Hightower and I will be on the same side of a question. I'm looking forward to how Dr. Williams is going to answer the two of us when we start grilling him."

"If he's smart, he'll run for cover."

CHAPTER 32

Monday morning came too soon. Neither Sarah, Rah-Rah, nor Fluffy wanted to get up, but they did. Sarah wasn't going to pass up her chance to meet with Lynn Martin. She got to the Coffee Bar in plenty of time to buy a cup of coffee and find Lynn. Sarah couldn't believe how busy the place was. Apparently, it was a hangout for students, faculty, and what looked like a group of neighborhood runners.

Sarah glanced at the different tables, but didn't see Lynn. When she looked again at one of the joggers waving from a nearby table, she realized the woman was Lynn. She'd been jogging? Unlike yesterday's somber black attire, today Lynn wore a purple jogging suit, full makeup, and had her long hair pulled back in a ponytail. In this outfit, Sarah could see Lynn, unlike Sarah, didn't have a pound she needed to lose.

As Sarah joined Lynn at her table, Lynn said, with a smile, "Thank you for meeting me here. The CJCC running group runs from six to seven three mornings a week, and quite a few of us end up here at the Coffee Bar."

So much for being the grieving widow. "I wonder why everyone doesn't end up here." It was the best response she could come up with without being snarky.

"A lot of the runners have to get to work, so they either go home or use the locker rooms to shower. Have you toured this new student activities building?" Lynn didn't wait for Sarah to answer. "Not only does it have the Coffee Bar, indoor sports facilities, including weight and exercise rooms, a pool, and locker rooms, but it also has a floor of study carrels and mini–conference rooms."

"You sound very familiar with this building."

"It's been my home away from home since Doug and I moved here. Not only do I run three mornings a week and use the Coffee Bar afterward to socialize or get some work done, but I also teach a yoga class here two mornings a week."

Evaluating Lynn's activities, Sarah decided to play up the one, besides drinking coffee, that she could have a credible interest in. "I've always wanted to take a yoga class."

"If you remind me, I'll get you a pass so you can try my class for free. It meets on Tuesdays and Thursdays at eight."

Sarah arranged her features to look disappointed and even gave a wide sweep of her hand and arm in a gesture of dismay. "What a shame. I'm normally at the office by then."

When Sarah saw Lynn glance at her watch, she hastened to add, "I'm not due until nine, but I usually get there early so I can organize my desk, prep for the day, and enjoy a cup of coffee before things get harried. The stress of running from yoga to work would defeat any Zen moment I could capture." She held up her coffee cup. "At least, today, I'm getting to blend a visit with you with a better cup of coffee than I can make."

Lynn lifted her cup. "The reason the Coffee Bar's coffee is so good is the blend of roasted nuts they use. The length of time beans are roasted impacts their final flavor."

"You sound like you could be a barista," Sarah said.

"That's what I was doing when I met Doug. There weren't a lot of jobs for marketing majors when I graduated, and I didn't want to go back to school, so I took a job at a student-center coffee shop like this one. Doug came in the first morning I was there and then every morning after that at ten for a cold brew. His marriage was in trouble and . . . well, I was a good listener. It didn't take long for us to warm up to each other. Shortly after his divorce was finalized, we married."

Approximating some quick math, Sarah figured Lynn probably was only three or four years older than Wanda. Between his wooing Lynn while he was still married to Wanda's mother and Lynn's age making her more appropriate to be Wanda's slightly older sister than her stepmother, Sarah could understand Wanda's resentment of Lynn.

Again, trying to be empathetic to Lynn, Sarah leaned forward, putting her hands in an open position on the table rather than circling them around her coffee. "I'm sorry for your loss. I can't imagine how terrible it must be to lose your husband. You two were still practically newlyweds."

"Practically. Are you married?"

"Divorced, but we were married for ten years. That's a lot different than being married less than two years. Two years is still magic while ten is settled, the bloom is a little off the rose, and sometimes there's an itch." Sarah stopped talking. She didn't want to spend this conversation dumping on her dead rat or making this a pity party for herself.

Lynn laughed. "Sometimes it doesn't take seven or ten years for that itch to settle in, but that's not what I wanted to talk to you about. I want you to find out who really killed Doug and if I'm in danger too."

"What?" Why would Lynn think she might be in danger? Even though Sarah was doing everything she could to clear Grace, what was Lynn's true reason for seeking her out to find Dr. Martin's killer? If Lynn didn't think Grace was the murderer, shouldn't she be pushing Chief Gerard to investigate further? Plus, if Lynn felt she was in danger, wouldn't it be logical to have the police check out her claims and, if necessary, provide her with protection? Although she hoped Lynn would tell her something that might help clear Grace, Sarah knew the tense feeling in her stomach wasn't from the coffee, but from being reluctant to share too much with Lynn.

"You seem to have your information wrong. Chief Gerard and his officers are handling the investigation of your husband's murder."

"From what I've heard, Chief Gerard thinks he has an open-and-shut case. I don't see it, do you?"

"No."

"That's why I want you to find out who really killed Doug." She tapped a pink-colored nail against her coffee cup. Judging from the perfection of her manicure, she must have gone home after the memorial service and done her nails. It appeared Fern was right that Lynn was quite a merry widow.

"Look, it may have taken your husband ten years to decide to scratch his itch, but Doug didn't wait that long. Between his behavior and other telltale signs, like an occasional lipstick stain or perfume smell like you read about in books or see in the movies, I know my husband was seeing someone else. Because he spent most of his time in his office or on the culinary floor, she had to be someone he saw regularly, but I never caught him with anyone when I popped up periodically."

Sarah shrugged. "Maybe it was all in your mind?"

"No. Doug was on to me. I've mentally gone through the women he had the most contact with, and Grace doesn't fit the bill."

"Why not?"

"Oh, she's good-looking and tall, two things Doug went for, but Grace has that arm tattoo. Doug hated tattoos, so, for him, that would have been a nonstarter."

Sarah laughed. She couldn't help herself. "I don't think that would have been the only nonstarter for Grace to be the person he was seeing. Tell me, why do you think you're in danger?" Sarah leaned back and took a sip of her coffee. While waiting for Lynn, Sarah stared at her, trying to sort out what she believed.

If Lynn was frightened for her own safety, why was she out jogging with the neighborhood group? If she was grieving, why had she taken the time the day after her husband's memorial to give herself a perfect manicure and spruce herself up before she went running? More importantly, why wasn't she taking her concerns to Chief Gerard instead of Sarah?

"If you think you know who or why Dr. Martin was killed and fear you might be in danger, you probably should talk to Chief Gerard or Officer Robinson, not me."

"I spoke with Chief Gerard."

Sarah had a feeling what was being unsaid was like the reaction Emily and she had to him in the past. "And?"

"He was polite, but I could tell he thought everything I told him didn't fit his theory of the case or was merely coincidental. That's why I wanted to talk to you. I've heard you were doing some investigating into this matter."

"Not really."

The fact Chief Gerard had apparently given Lynn lip service but discounted what she told him didn't surprise Sarah. She could picture him writing Lynn off as a grieving widow who was imagining things. Although Sarah knew she should stay out of whatever it was Lynn wanted to bring her into, her curiosity was piqued. She wouldn't be satisfied until she'd had a chance to evaluate everything for herself. "What things make you feel like you might be in someone's sights?"

"The evening Doug was killed, I needed some time to process everything, so I went on a run. A car almost hit me."

"That doesn't sound too suspicious. There are always accidents being reported because drivers don't see joggers until it's too late."

"This was different. I'm sure it was intentional. The sound of the car revving into a different gear and coming up behind me too quickly subconsciously registered, so I turned around. When I saw the car veer into the runner-bicycle lane, I instinctively jumped into the grassy area. If I hadn't reacted, I might have been killed."

Sarah leaned forward. Grace had gone for a drive the evening Dr. Martin died. Was it possible?

"Did you see the driver?"

"No. After I jumped into the grass, I rolled down a hill. By the time I stood up, the car was gone."

"Chief Gerard could be right—it was simply a car out of control. Is there anything else that makes you suspect you're being targeted?

"Just an occasional funny feeling like someone is behind me, but when I turn, there's no one there. That could also be my own paranoia, because everyone seems to want something from me now."

Sarah clucked her tongue in what she hoped sounded like an expression of sympathy. "That's horrible. I mean, you just lost your husband and all. What could anyone want from you, except to offer their sympathy?"

"The president of the college and Dr. Williams want a building. Somehow they think I should give them one in memory of Doug."

Although Lynn was put together, neither her jogging suit nor what she'd worn to the funeral the day before yelled high-end fashion designer of the expensive nature that underwrote buildings. Besides, considering her age, where would she have the money for a campus building—Doug's life insurance? "What makes them think you can donate a building on campus?"

"Apparently, Doug told them about the windfall we made on some property I inherited from my parents. When I sold it, it produced enough money I could pay for two buildings and have a lifetime of luxury left over."

"Wow!" was all Sarah could say while making a mental note that Dr. Martin apparently liked women with money.

"It's funny. When Doug and I met, I didn't have anything except what I earned as a barista and the undeveloped land my parents left me near the college where Doug was teaching."

"When he married you, did he know about the property?"

"Not that I was aware of. That's probably the time we were the happiest. Once the school came after the property, about six months after we were married, Doug started negotiating the price with them on my behalf and . . . well, he didn't give in easily. We made a killing."

Lynn clapped her hand over her mouth. "That's probably not a word I should be using now."

From the little Sarah knew about Dr. Martin having his finger in different pots, she bet he knew of the college's interest in the land and pulled the wool over his star-in-her-eyes barista. "Why did you come to Wheaton instead of staying where you were or going somewhere else?"

"Dr. Green offered Doug the culinary position with the understanding that when the programs merged, Doug would be the man to lead them. Even though this is a small college in a small town, Doug decided it was a perfect stepping-stone for his future. If, for the time being, he was going to be happy being a big fish in a little pond, it was fine with me."

"How did the move work out for you?"

"In the beginning, fine. I found it easy to make friends in Wheaton through my yoga, running, and doing some marketing for the annual charity race sponsored by my running club and the Wheaton Wildcats. A few months ago, things changed. Even though Doug occasionally did something nice or apologized, he was short-tempered and mean. I don't know if it was something at work or the fact his mother and his ex-wife's daughter were both here in town, or . . ."

Having an idea why Lynn was hesitating, but still wanting her to verbalize it, Sarah prompted her. "Or?"

"Or because of the lack of trust I had after I accused him of seeing someone else. He denied it, but it never felt genuine. For months, our marriage was on the rocks, but, in the last week or so of his life, we'd reached a point of no going back. In your investigation, I want you to find out who he was cheating on me with, because that might be the person who tried to kill me."

Thinking about what Fern had said in Little Italy and Nancy had intimated in the hallway to Chief Gerard, Sarah couldn't help but question whether Lynn or Dr. Martin was the reason their marriage was on the rocks. Part of her worried if Grace had been driving the car, but she was more inclined to agree with Chief Gerard it was a flight of fancy. Maybe Lynn was planting the seed of feeling endangered in the minds of Chief Gerard and Sarah to take suspicion off herself? After all, according to two eyewitnesses, she was on the culinary floor around the time he was killed. Sarah couldn't rule out that Lynn reversed the nursery rhyme and killed her husband in a fit of passion.

The other possibility of the story Lynn was feeding her was she wanted Sarah to use her investigative skills to find out who the other woman was. She might not have killed her husband, but Sarah got the distinct feeling she might want to stop just short of murder if she found the woman who destroyed her marriage.

Today's meeting had raised questions, but there were two things of which Sarah was certain. The first was Lynn was anything but a grieving widow, despite how she spun her concern about Dr. Martin's killing, so the CJCC better start looking for another donor. No matter how much sweet-talking the college president did, Lynn wasn't giving the school a penny.

The other thing about which Sarah was positive was she had another suspect to add to her growing list. She only hoped Lynn didn't realize Sarah suspected Lynn could be the murderer—because then Sarah might be the next victim.

CHAPTER 33

Leaving Lynn, Sarah was more confused than ever as to who killed Dr. Martin. As she walked to her car, she tried to clear her mind, but there was too much running through it. Realizing she was in front of the building that housed the culinary arts program, she decided to take a few extra minutes to sit on the uncomfortable bench—the one where she had waited for Grace, in what now seemed like a lifetime ago—and try to sort things out. Once seated, Sarah pulled a pen and pad out of her pocketbook and opened it to a clean page.

Under the heading of *Facts*, she wrote:

1. Dr. Doug Martin: head of culinary program—about to be in charge of culinary and hospitality department. Blocked Jane's Place from becoming the home of the program. Possibility of him

getting his own building underwritten (was he planning on using family money???). Not nice—cheating on his wife, or was she cheating on him? Homophobic or simply baiting Grace for an unknown reason? DEAD

Under the heading of *Suspects*, Sarah wrote:

1. Grace Winston: No way! Excellent knowledge of knives—and there was a valid reason for her to have crossed the line. Out driving when Lynn allegedly was run off the road. Blood on her apron.
2. Mandy: Grace's partner—would go the extra mile for her but probably wouldn't kill for her. Not sure how much she knows about knives. Has self-defense training and could have used a nearby object to defend herself if she happened to come to the college and Dr. Martin and she got into it. Note: she came to the memorial service!
3. Dr. Zach Williams: He hoped to gain from Dr. Martin's death when the culinary and hospitality merged. Head of the hospitality program but trained in culinary knife skills. Considered making overtures to Lynn and/or Kait for a new building but now pursuing a new donor. In front of Eloise, he verbalized an interest in Jane's Place without consideration of Southwind's offer. Even if not the killer, clarification needed on his relationship with Jane. Is he on the take? Is he telling the truth about seeking a new donor? Where exactly was he at the time of the murder?

4. Jane Clark: Desperate to save Jane's Place. Dr. Martin stood between her and her restaurant being saved—impulsive—could she kill?—Yes.
5. Chef Robert Bernardi: Expert pastry chef who lost his own business because of gambling (addiction?). Taught pastry courses and recently associated himself with Jane's Place as its official pastry chef. What did Jane have over him that he took orders from her and was willing to help sabotage Southwind's Jell-O outing for the retirement home's residents? What was his relationship with Dr. Martin to be hired as an adjunct? Definite knife knowledge—even gave lecture on it. Observed on the floor after the murder, but where was he when it happened?
6. Fern Runskill: Worked in admissions last year but now in CJCC's fund development department. Was on the floor shortly before and after the murder. Witnessed Dr. Martin and his wife being together and the tension between them. Overheard Dr. Martin and Grace's altercation. Interested in getting donors for the school but pragmatic, despite brainstorming with Dr. Williams and Chef Bernardi. Worked herself up through different departments at the college and admitted making nice to Dr. Martin because she knew he was in line to be head of the combined culinary and hospitality program. Attended knife lecture and indicated cooking and knife knowledge.
7. Nancy Reynolds: Culinary arts teacher. Up for tenure? Taught different courses beyond the elementary or beginner course, so definite knife

skills involved in what she taught. Office next to Dr. Martin—overheard plenty. Did any of it apply to her? Was she in Dr. Martin's sights, like Dr. Williams was in hers when he tried to leave the floor before the police arrived?

8. Wanda: Stepdaughter of Dr. Martin. Hated him for what he did to her mother and for his remarriage to Lynn (his bimbo?). Not thrilled with how he treated his own mother. Wants to be a pastry chef and is interning or helping Chef Bernardi. Although taking the introductory knives skills course, must have more extensive skills to work with Chef Bernardi. Kind to Kait. Not overly upset at Dr. Martin's death, which was especially weird since she was one of the two people who found the body. Other person was her boyfriend, who Dr. Martin humiliated and put in danger shortly before Dr. Martin's murder.
9. Franklin: Adores Wanda. Eloise's nephew—how could he be involved? Gung ho on criminal justice program. Taking knife skills course to be near Wanda but has the strength to use the small knife on Dr. Martin. Good observer. One of the first to find Dr. Martin but not overly upset about it. Excellent compartmentalizer or would he do anything for Wanda? Was student Dr. Martin embarrassed and endangered.
10. Kait Martin: Dr. Martin was her son. Was he a good one? What was their true relationship? How did her money and memory play into his plans? What was the real reason she was on the floor in the kitchen at Jane's Place? Did it relate

to Wanda or did her emotions and memories get in the way of her remaining ability to reason? Could she have been at the school Friday morning?

11. Lynn Martin: a real conundrum. Former barista (demonstrated ability to work quickly with spoons and knives). Only a few years older than Wanda and came into the picture before Dr. Martin was divorced from Wanda's mother. Did Lynn learn Dr. Martin knew the college he worked at was going to make an offer for her land before he romanced her? Admits her marriage had gone sour but who was to blame? (She says him, but others felt she was the one who strayed.) Why did she reach out to talk to me? Does she have a relationship with any of the other faculty members? Was she still in the building at the time of the murder? Does Lynn's attitude and lack of sorrow raise the possibility she flipped the nursery rhyme or simply go to her credibility?

Sarah stared at her pad. She underlined the only thing standing out to her—the very last word: *credibility*. Who was credible? When she added in the things her mother, Mr. Rogers, Harlan, and Eloise had told her, it complicated things even more. She was going to have to find out where everyone was at the time of the murder. Maybe talking things over with Harlan would help clarify the something she was missing.

CHAPTER 34

Back at the office, Sarah was glad to see Harlan not only had already made coffee, but he wasn't tied up with anyone. She poured herself a cup and knocked on his open door.

He looked up from where he was making notes on a legal pad from a book open on his desk. "Since when did you start knocking?"

"When I need to confer with you."

Harlan waved Sarah toward one of the chairs in front of his desk. "What's on your mind?"

"Grace."

His brow furrowed, but he didn't change his tone. "Sarah, have you been investigating again?"

"Not intentionally. After Dr. Martin's funeral, his widow, Lynn, asked to meet with me this morning. I think you should know some of the things she said."

Although Harlan raised an eyebrow, he didn't say anything. Sarah assumed he was too busy gritting his teeth to talk, so she launched into telling him about her meeting with Lynn and the inconsistencies she saw comparing Lynn's comments to what she'd heard from many of the faculty members.

Because Harlan didn't cut her off or admonish her, Sarah repeated the various allegations people made about Dr. Martin's quid pro quo use of his influence on everything from tenure to whether the culinary and hospitality program would partner with Jane's Place. "In the end, I don't know who to believe."

"But, that's not what's bothering you, is it?" Harlan peered over his glasses.

Sarah couldn't meet his gaze. She looked toward the floor as she answered. "No."

"That's why you really came in here, isn't it?"

Sarah shifted in her chair. She continued looking at the floor for a few seconds before she met Harlan's gaze. "I hate to even admit it to myself, let alone say it aloud, but what's bothering me is I can make as strong a case against Grace as I can against any of the other suspects. In the past, when I investigated, it was because I absolutely knew Emily, Maybelle, or Jacob couldn't have been"—she raised her fingers to make quotation marks—" 'the perpetrator.' "

She lowered her hands and rested them on the arms of her chair. "Intellectually and emotionally, I know Grace is innocent, but then this devil's advocate raises its head."

Harlan leaned back. "Go on."

Sarah frowned. "One side of my brain says Grace wouldn't hurt a fly, but the other side knows Grace is a survivor who's fought for everything she has. She doesn't get angry easily, but you've seen how loyal she's been to Emily and Marcus. Yet, as important as they are to her, there's no question in my mind that her relationship with Mandy takes precedence over anything else. We've got at least two witnesses who overheard Dr. Martin and Grace's confrontation, plus Grace told us about it. Let's say Dr. Martin pushed that emotional button, the one none of us can control. Well, maybe Grace lost it for that moment."

"Think about how many times Jane has pushed you to that point, but you've never killed her. What makes you so worried Grace went a step further than you would have in a similar situation?"

Sarah bent her elbow and rested it on the chair's arm. Tilting her head, she leaned the side of her face against her thumb and the first three upraised fingers of her left hand. "Gut feeling or fear. Harlan, I've tried attributing a motive for killing Dr. Martin to everyone else, even his mother, but I keep coming back to it being a murder committed in a moment of passion. A lot of people wanted things from him, but I can't believe topics like tenure, Jane's Place, or rejection of a request for a donation rose to the level where one would lose control."

"So you think Grace is guilty?"

"Absolutely not! The problem is, I don't know who is."

"Well, much as this goes against my better judgment, let's put our heads together and go over everything again. Let's start with where you think the biggest inconsistency is."

"That would be the information I got out of my meeting with Lynn this morning. If what she told me is true, several people, either intentionally or, by repeating erroneous information, deliberately misled us."

"Who?"

"Fern, Dr. Williams, Nancy, and Chef Bernardi indicated there was trouble in the Martins' marriage, but their inference was Lynn was the one having an affair. Lynn said Dr. Martin was. Also, a property Lynn inherited from her parents was sold for a fortune to the last school Dr. Martin taught at. She claimed he knew nothing about the value of the property or the school's interest until six months after they were married, but she's smart. After their honeymoon period ended and her suspicions about him were raised, I bet, although she didn't tell me, Lynn questioned the reason he married her."

"Another money connection?"

"Exactly. In addition, if Lynn's account of her current relationship with Dr. Martin is credible, it opens up numerous questions about everyone's motives."

"What's your gut feeling about Lynn?"

"That her asking to meet with me was a way to set me up, but I haven't figured out how. She asked me to find who her husband cheated on her with because that might be the person trying to kill her."

"Her?"

"Yes, she turned the discussion to why she was afraid someone was trying to harm her. What bothered me was nothing about her fears seemed genuine."

Harlan took off his glasses and examined the lens. "Why?"

Sarah stood, her eyes opened wide. "Because she alleged a car almost hit her and that she saved herself by jumping into the grass and rolling down a hill. If that was the case, she should have gotten bruised or scratched, but when she put her hands around her coffee cup, not only was her manicure perfect, but I couldn't see any signs of trauma on her hands or exposed arms. None of the other examples she alluded to had any substance. If you ask me, she was trying to set me up like a nursery rhyme from when I was a girl."

"Now you're not computing at all. Earth to Sarah, or maybe it's Mars to Sarah."

"Stop that. You're being silly. When Emily and I were children, we jumped rope to the rhyme: *Went upstairs to get my knife. Made a mistake and stabbed my wife.* What if Lynn was afraid Dr. Martin was leaving her and, rather than being the one stabbed, she turned the tables. It could have been a planned or unplanned reaction."

"It's a possibility, but you said she indicated their marriage was over."

Sarah slumped in her chair. "True." She stayed quiet for a moment, thinking. "What if she was embarrassed or gave him an ultimatum and things went sour?"

"Again, what you're saying about Dr. Martin's death being a murder of passion has merit, but, from the divorce cases I've handled, there are a few elements that may be missing for me to believe Lynn is the killer."

"Like what?"

"Lynn wasn't financially dependent on Dr. Martin for her existence. She'll still be able to teach yoga, run with the neighborhood runners, and treat herself in any way she desires. Even her age, which may have been a detriment in some of the snotty circles of academia society Dr. Martin was in, will work in her favor for starting over. I'm more inclined to look for an academic motive because the murder took place in Grace's classroom."

"You think the physical location of Dr. Martin's death is significant?"

"Yes. You mentioned tenure. How does that play into this?"

"Grace said from the start of the program until now the college used very few full-time hires. They avoided having to offer benefits by hiring individuals for a class or two as an adjunct. A few years ago, CJCC converted some of the adjuncts to full-time. Many of those faculty members are under consideration for tenure, but I'm not sure which ones they are."

Harlan lay down his pen. "Or whether the present adjuncts, like Chef Bernardi, were going to have their contracts renewed. We know Chef Bernardi accepted employment with Jane's Place. Does that count as he needed a new job, a conflict of interest, or is he jumping the gun on the college and Jane's Place working together? And what about Dr. Williams? Have things changed for him too?"

"Possibly. Dr. Green named him as the interim covering Dr. Martin's program, and he doesn't seem to be hiding his interest in heading any future merged department."

Harlan glanced at his watch. "I hate to cut this off, but I'm due at the courthouse in forty-five minutes, and I still have something I need to review. It seems to me, though, we've brainstormed enough other possibilities that you can feel comfortable having your devil's advocate give Grace a pass. More importantly, now that you feel better about Grace, you can leave the sleuthing to the professionals."

CHAPTER 35

At her own desk, Sarah tried to reconcile her discussion with Harlan with some of the things Lynn and others had said and done during the past few days. There were too many discrepancies that needed to be resolved. The more she thought about them, the more she doubted Chief Gerard or Harlan would address them in time to keep someone else from being hurt because of the proposed merger of the culinary and hospitality programs and the subsequent desire to move the faculty, students, offices, and classrooms to a new building.

If Sarah was right, Dr. Martin's refusal to accept Jane's proposal tied directly to his belief he could obtain funding for a named building. If successful, not only would he have scored a big career win at Carleton, but it could have been a springboard for a job at a more prestigious college in the near future. That tied back to what Lynn told her about Dr. Martin's reason for accepting the college's job offer.

But from whom did he plan to get the endowment? Although Wheaton and Birmingham had plenty of wealthy people with ties to the college, if Dr. Martin was wooing one of them, it didn't make sense that Dr. Williams, Chef Bernardi, and Fern didn't think the individual could be pursued. On the other hand, what about Dr. Williams's seemingly overeager stance to partner with Jane?

Sarah wracked her brain, trying to remember what else Fern had said while they stood in the restaurant's alcove. The only people Sarah remembered her mentioning by name were Lynn and Kait, members of Dr. Martin's family. Could Dr. Martin have thought he could wrangle the money out of one or both through some backhanded means? Fern had mentioned Kait's mental state and Lynn's feelings about her late husband. Both were reasons the present faculty doubted any money could be obtained from either.

Considering Dr. Williams's hope for the job, Sarah understood why it made sense for him to put Jane's proposal back on the table. Once the degree program was established, its success rested on attracting students. That success would directly reflect on whoever became head of the merged program. From a practical sense, until the entire program could be housed in a new building, using Jane's Place allowed potential culinary majors to see they would be working in Jane's top-of-the-line kitchen, while hospitality students could be given a taste of the practical place available for them to learn their trade. Still, couldn't Southwind's proposal be implemented equally quickly? Was there a payback or something else Dr. Williams was getting from Jane?

Having practical, rather than only classroom, experience on their résumés would help with placement of many of the existing students. One of those students, Sarah realized, was Wanda. Obviously, she was getting exposure to the pastry chef world when she helped Chef Bernardi set up the desserts at Jane's Place. Being able to claim an internship or participate in a program that included making a variety of high-end desserts under actual conditions, while supervised by a known pastry chef, would give her a leg up on other job applicants.

Sarah hadn't considered Wanda as a possible suspect, but, coming at it from this way, she could very well be the killer. Wanda hated Dr. Martin, so it wouldn't be hard for him to have pushed her over the edge between anger and action. She obviously was familiar with knives. If Wanda heard Dr. Martin planned to loot Kait's funds, like he'd done her mother's, her feelings for Kait might have come into play. Wanda was bright and, although she claimed to have been upset finding Dr. Martin's body, it didn't seem Franklin needed to do much to calm her down.

Maybe that was because Franklin was in on the murder with her. Perhaps it had been premeditated? Sarah certainly hoped not. Eloise adored her nephew. It would be a giant blow to find out he was involved with a killer or was an accessory to a murder. Then again, he was so gung ho about the criminal justice program, it seemed doubtful he would cross the line of the law, but Sarah well knew that sometimes the biggest advocates of law and order were the ones who best knew how to get around it.

Another thing about Wanda was she knew Grace. Being in her class and seeing her around the culinary floor, Wanda might have learned some of Grace's habits or seen Grace leave Dr. Martin in her classroom when she left to find Sarah. To Sarah's chagrin, there was only one person who could clarify Wanda's behavior at Jane's Place: Jane.

Coming face-to-face with Jane was the last thing Sarah wanted to do, but understanding, from Jane's perspective, what occurred during the dessert fiasco might clarify some of the thoughts whirling in her head. She glanced at her watch. Lunchtime. Harlan couldn't fault her for taking her lunch hour.

Sarah switched on the office's answering machine and drove to Jane's Place. Although it was open for lunch, the few cars parked in the lot belied its lack of business. Rather than going in through the back entrance, Sarah walked around to the front door as she tried to gather her thoughts as to what was the best way to pose her questions to Jane—if Jane didn't throw her out of the restaurant first.

Jane was standing at the hostess stand. She picked up a menu and flashed a smile. "Table for . . ." The smile disappeared as she dropped the menu back on the stand. She lowered her voice so the seated customers couldn't hear her. "What are you doing here?"

Sarah held her hands up in front of her. "I'm not here to make trouble for you."

"Are you here for lunch?"

The thought of a lunch served to her by Jane was frightening. Sarah had no idea what Jane might do to it. "Not for lunch. I just to need to ask you a few questions."

"Investigating again?" Jane tossed her flaming red hair. "Ask away. Nothing I say will help Grace. Chief Gerard may have convinced me not to press charges, but, after all the times I've tried to help Grace by offering her better jobs than she has at Southwind, her breaking in here was the last straw."

Sarah ignored the jab at Grace. It was more important she stay calm and ask her few questions and get out of the restaurant with the answers. "I know Chef Bernardi is working for you as your pastry chef. Yesterday, did he bring Wanda with him as his assistant?"

Jane took a moment to answer. "No, not exactly. Wanda was here the day before for Chef Bernardi's lecture. After it, she asked if I could use an assistant pastry chef. I told her I couldn't hire anyone else. She raised the possibility of an internship for college credit, if she could get it approved with a faculty sponsor. I replied that would work for me, and I hoped there would be many instances of such internships if my proposal for CJCC to use Jane's Place was accepted."

If Wanda broached the subject of an internship with Jane on Saturday, it wasn't logical to Sarah that anyone would have reviewed it at the college over the weekend. "But, the internship couldn't have been approved by Sunday."

"Wanda showed up at the same time as Chef Bernardi. They immediately began working together, so I assumed he agreed to sponsor her for the internship and I would get the proper notification during the school week."

"Have you?"

"Not yet."

Two people came into the restaurant. Sarah stepped aside so Jane could seat them.

When Jane returned to the hostess stand, she said, "Is that it? I need to check on some things in the kitchen."

"Only two more questions, please." When Jane didn't bolt from behind the stand, Sarah continued. "Did you or anyone else, to your knowledge, see Kait come in the back way?"

"I didn't, and I don't think Chef Bernardi did either. What's your other question?"

"Jane, I know you were looking for an angle to get Dr. Martin to accept your proposal. Did you ever figure out why you couldn't find one?"

Jane grasped the top of the hostess stand and held it tightly. Sarah was afraid she wasn't going to answer her question.

"I couldn't find one because there wasn't one. Dr. Martin only wanted a new building, and he was going to get it by hook or by crook. Apparently, he forgot to look behind him for a moment."

Sarah opened her mouth to ask a follow-up question, but she could tell from Jane's face she'd worn out her welcome. Instead of asking her a question, Sarah merely said, "Thank you" and hurried out of the restaurant.

CHAPTER 36

After stopping home to take care of RahRah and Fluffy, Sarah hurried back to the office. Settled in front of her computer screen with a fresh cup of coffee on her desk, she heard Harlan coming in the back door of the building. He waved at her as he carried his briefcase into his private office.

"How did it go?"

Harlan came back outside into the waiting room and stood on the other side of the counter that separated Sarah's desk from the waiting area. "Pretrial went fine. We've got a trial date in six months. How did your lunch hour go?"

"Same old, same old."

"Not out investigating after our discussion?"

Sarah stared at him. Had Harlan had a change of mind

regarding her sleuthing? From the twinkle of his eye behind the glasses and the smile he was trying ever so hard to contain, there was no doubt he knew she'd left the office.

"How did you know?"

"Elementary, my dear Dr. Blair."

Exasperated, she stuck her tongue out at him.

"Now, now. Let's keep this on an adult level. I had another idea after our discussion. When I called the office before my pretrial, the answering machine picked up. Usually, you don't go to lunch to take care of RahRah and Fluffy until later than when I called. Consequently, I decided you were out investigating. I gather I was correct?"

"Yes. I went to see Jane."

He raised his eyebrows and licked his lips. "Ah, the plot thickens. What did you learn from Jane?"

"That she still blames me for everything that has ever gone wrong in her life. And that Grace also is now on her list of no-good people."

"Anything else?"

"The most important thing was she believes there was no way Dr. Martin would ever have agreed to using Jane's Place because he was committed to having a new building. Other than that, Jane thought Wanda was helping Chef Bernardi on Sunday as part of an internship and that neither she, nor anyone else, to her knowledge, saw Kait come in the restaurant's back door. What was it you called about?"

"I was still hung up on the tenure question. I think we need to find out who might have been up for tenure and if there was anyone Dr. Martin was going to oppose."

Sarah thought it was interesting their investigation

now shared a royal "we." Apparently, Harlan no longer was satisfied with letting Chief Gerard handle all aspects of the investigation. "This is a change of position for you. Are you into investigating now?"

"Not exactly." Harlan was no longer smiling. "I ran into Chief Gerard at the courthouse. He was going to act, but decided to give me a heads-up. The jacket, as he suspected, came back with Dr. Martin's blood on it. Between Grace's fight with Dr. Martin, no one else being in the classroom with him, the knife being one she had out for the demonstration, and the blood on her apron, he feels he has enough evidence to arrest Grace."

"But he can't!"

"Chief Gerard was going to do it this afternoon, but he agreed to let me have her turn herself in tomorrow morning. That leaves us a few more hours to develop motives I can use to convince Chief Gerard someone else might have committed the murder. As effective as you were during your lunch hour, it seems to me it would be a good use of your time if you went over to the campus and tried to tie down the tenure issue."

She pointed at her computer and her desk. "But what about my work here today for you?"

"Consider this as being another duty as assigned. Besides, the only thing going on here this afternoon is Cliff and Carole coming by to discuss some of the zoning regulations for modifying the shelter. Presently, we don't have enough space to guarantee we can keep everything separate in terms of animal types, ages, and sizes, as well as nursing mothers and their babies and having enough isolation areas to quarantine new arrivals. From my research, I think we can convert one of the preexisting structures for our use, but we'll need some new construction, which will require applying for building permits."

Much as Sarah was interested in what needed to be done to modify the shelter, Sarah knew her fundraising role, even with organizing the talent show, was months away. Grace's need for her help was now. Consequently, as Harlan spoke, she powered down her computer.

Chapter 37

Driving to campus, Sarah considered what order would be best to catch everyone she wanted to talk to. She hoped she could find them either in their offices or at the Coffee Bar. She decided to start with Dr. Williams and any of the other culinary faculty members she could find before trying to confirm what they told her with Fern.

In the building, Sarah weighed whether to take the steps, like she'd done with Grace, or the elevator. She justified the elevator because it would bring her out closer to the culinary offices. Before she had the chance to push the elevator button, Fern's clicking heels, followed by her calling Sarah's name, foiled Sarah's plan. Judging by the coffee cup in Fern's hand, she probably was coming from a stop at the Coffee Bar.

"Here to finally drop off an application for next term?"

Sarah shook her head. "No. I need to do a little more research."

Fern glanced at her watch. "I've got some time before I'm meeting with a possible donor. Want to come up to my office? Maybe I can answer some of your questions."

Although Sarah would have preferred finding Dr. Williams first, she didn't want to pass up an opportunity to meet with Fern. She was sure Fern knew the scoop on everyone and could clarify the college's tenure policy. "Sure. That would be great."

"Perfect." Fern went straight toward the stairwell, slowing only to toss her coffee cup into the trash can just outside the door to the stairs. "It's only one floor, but I go up and down these steps so much I count it as part of my exercise routine."

Running up the stairs behind Fern, Sarah wondered what else Fern included in her exercise routine. There was no way going up and down one floor, no matter how many times a day Fern did so, could possibly burn enough calories to maintain Fern's trim figure.

When they reached the second floor, Sarah paused to get her bearings. In the past, the only office she'd ever visited on this floor was the admissions office, which was across from the elevator. The development suite of offices was located directly below the culinary classrooms.

Fern led Sarah past a conference room to three small offices clustered together. Fern pointed toward the middle office. "Being the newbie, my office is the inner sanctum of the department."

Sarah wasn't sure what Fern's *inner sanctum* reference meant until, sitting across from Fern, it dawned on her the room didn't have a window. Instead, Fern had hung a large painting of an outdoor scene being viewed through the framework of a window behind her desk. Fern's effort to bring the outside into the office felt a little eerie to Sarah. Rather than reveal her true feelings, Sarah said, "I like your painting."

Fern glanced at the painting and then met Sarah's gaze. "I do too. It reminds me of how far I've come and how far I still need to go."

Sarah stared at the picture again. To her it was odd and artificial, but wasn't art supposed to be interpreted through the eye of the beholder? "Sort of a motivational piece of art?"

"Exactly. I'm a big believer in setting goals. Whether earning my associate's degree, working full-time in restaurants while I finished the two more years needed for my bachelor's in business, or taking jobs in admissions and now fund development, I've always looked ahead. Now, my goal is a window."

"That's like my sister, Emily. From the time we were kids, she always knew she wanted to be a chef. Em never let anything get in her way of becoming one."

"Good for her. It takes that kind of dedication. And it isn't always fun. I'm sure she's found moving forward sometimes means making hard choices."

"She has." Sarah stared at the picture again. "I envy the two of you being so driven and decisive. In comparison, I feel like I've spent the past decade floundering. Even now, trying to go back to school, I'm not sure what to study."

"It's hard to pick the right discipline, but don't worry, you don't have to at this point. We tell students all the time to be flexible. Take the basics—math, English, and the other core courses. Once you finish those and a few electives, they'll lead you to a major. And after that, who knows? I started here as a culinary student. Who would have thought I would end up in financial development and administration? I'm not the only one. Did you know Dr. Green's undergraduate major was art history?"

"You're kidding. I thought he was a numbers man."

"He's got an MBA and his PhD, but his love is art. Visiting galleries and exhibits is what he does whenever he gets time off. Let's look at this from another angle. What do you most enjoy?"

"Well, I can assure you it isn't cooking or anything having to do with a kitchen."

They both laughed.

"Okay, we can rule out the culinary courses. How about hotel management or something related to hospitality?"

Sarah shook her head. "Too close to food. I enjoy dealing with the people who come into Harlan's office, but I can't see myself bossing a staff to keep the public happy, nor can I picture myself cheerfully dealing with guest complaints."

"Perhaps criminal justice? You've had some success in that area."

"Too much accidental success." Much as she wanted to go into the details of her possible fields of study, Sarah needed to change the subject. Time was getting short before Grace had to turn herself in. Sarah could come back and talk with Fern about classes later. Now her mission was prying information out of Fern's brain. "Fern, I'm trying to help Grace, but there's a lot about the college world I simply don't know. I was hoping you could explain a few things for me."

"I don't know if I can help, but I'll try."

"Were you involved with Dr. Martin's merger plans?"

Fern blanched. "Yes. Here in the fund development office, we each have different schools or areas we work with. The culinary and hospitality programs fall under my portfolio of disciplines. Consequently, I was working with him on different aspects of the new department."

Sarah leaned forward. "Several people claim Dr. Martin opposed the use of Jane's Place because he wanted to make his own mark by bringing a new building to campus."

Without meeting Sarah's gaze, Fern took her time answering. "I guess, now that he's gone, I can admit that was true. He felt it would benefit his career in the long run if he could show leadership of the combined department and the ability to fundraise a building in a community he hadn't lived in long."

"Would it have?"

"Definitely. And to be honest, it would have been as much a boon to me as to Dr. Martin." She waved her hand toward the windowless wall in her office. "I think it's safe to say, it would have gotten me a window—maybe two. Now . . ." Fern frowned.

Sarah focused on the plaques and award certificates hanging on Fern's other walls. They were a mixture of academic, culinary, admission goal achievements, and outstanding admission-department member awards. Looking at them, she couldn't understand Fern's negative attitude. "Considering all of your honors, surely you'll get a window before you know it."

"Around here, things take time." Using the same hand, Fern gestured at one of her award walls. "Plus, these don't matter much. People evaluate you on what you've done most recently. That's why Dr. Williams and I have made finding another donor a priority. We're trying to think outside the box for a possible contributor." Fern smiled. "I want my window and his heart is set on being named head of the new department and receiving tenure."

"I didn't realize Dr. Williams isn't tenured." Sarah remembered Grace explaining there were a lot of people being considered for tenure. "Do you know who else besides Dr. Williams is up for tenure?"

"No, but there are several. Dr. Martin was evaluating the current faculty and what he might do with them. He had to get his recommendations to Dr. Green by the end of this week."

"Did he have any problem children?"

"What program doesn't have prima donnas or annoying faculty members? There were a lot, like Nancy Reynolds, who were thorns in Dr. Martin's side."

Thinking of how Nancy prevented Dr. Williams leaving the floor before the police arrived, Sarah could imagine she might verbally clash with a boss. "What bothered him about her?"

"He called her a busybody. She constantly watched the comings and goings of everyone from his office. He swore she knew who was in the hallway from the minute a person got off the elevator. Their biggest blowup, though, was over her teaching load. She lost it when he took away one of her classes. Still, Nancy wasn't his only problem."

"There were more?"

"Definitely. Nancy was only one of many. That's why deciding who to recommend for tenure and which adjunct contracts to renew was Dr. Martin's immediate concern. He didn't want to get stuck with anyone he didn't want on his new team. He was so busy working on the personnel issues that we put anything to do with the new building on the back burner until he submitted his recommendations."

"What do you think Dr. Martin planned to do with Dr. Williams?"

Fern brought her fingers together in the prayer tent position. "I'm not sure. From things he said, I know Dr. Martin didn't think much of him, but I never saw what Dr. Martin was preparing for the president. The only thing I can assure you is that making his personnel decisions was Dr. Martin's highest priority during the past week."

If whittling down his staff was on his mind, there was a good chance Dr. Martin discussed some of his decisions with different faculty members. Perhaps one had felt so wronged by the Malevolent Monster that, in a fit of passion, the person grabbed a knife and stabbed him. The logic worked, but who had the skill to place the knife so the wound was fatal and the blood drained downward? Or had someone simply gotten lucky?

"While Dr. Martin was tied up with his tenure recommendations, were you still working on finding a community donor for the building?"

"No." Fern hesitated. "I didn't have to. He'd figured out how to fund the building. Dr. Martin was planning to have his wife pony up the money."

Although Sarah knew from her recent discussion with Lynn the alleged source and span of her wealth, Sarah was curious how much information Dr. Martin had shared with Fern—and if it confirmed what Lynn had told her at the Coffee Bar. "She has that kind of money?"

"Yes. Apparently, Lynn made a fortune on a land deal."

It sounded like Dr. Martin had left out his role in negotiating the sale or that his wife might not want to go along with another business transaction with him. "Did Dr. Martin have a backup, if Lynn refused?"

Fern slipped her hands from the prayer position to using one hand to hold the forefinger of the other. Pulling her hands closer to her chest, she glared at Sarah. "Are you friends with Lynn?"

Sarah was surprised by Fern's reaction. She decided it wouldn't be a good idea to tell her about the details of her meeting with Lynn at the Coffee Bar. "Not really. As you probably saw, I paid my respects to her after the service for Dr. Martin and I ran into her again at the Coffee Bar the next day. It's just that from what you told me at Little Italy, I didn't realize she had the money or the willingness to underwrite a building for him. That's why I'm curious if Dr. Martin was reaching out to the community, who he had in mind as a backup donor."

Fern released her finger and stared at the nails on her right hand. "Between you and me, I think he planned to manipulate his mother into being the donor if Lynn wouldn't do it. During our last campaign, Kait pledged a substantial bequest to the school. I believe that if he needed to, Dr. Martin, as her financial guardian, was going to advance the money for the new building from Kait's funds while she was still alive."

"That sounds dishonest."

Fern conceded it might be a little shady, but noted it hadn't happened and now wouldn't. She reiterated what she said at Little Italy about Kait's mental state. "It may sound a little macabre, but she's off the table until she dies."

"Let's hope that isn't soon."

"I'm not sure everyone shares your sentiments." Fern snorted. "As you saw at the memorial service, for as long as it takes, Dr. Green wants to make sure Carleton College stays close to her heart. He's instructed Dr. Williams and me to make nice to her on a regular basis so that, no matter who assumes control of her financial affairs, Kait doesn't let them change her will."

"I guess fund development takes a lot of tact."

Fern put her hands together and glanced upward before grinning as she looked back at Sarah. "Prayer, luck, tact, hand-holding, the stars to align just right, and who knows what. Mainly, it takes patience and relationship building. With Dr. Martin's personal motivation and funding source for a new culinary building, I thought I was going to get a chance to get my window without going through all the hurdles."

Sarah again pointed toward Fern's award wall. "It may take a little longer, but I have no doubt you'll get that window or even two sooner than later."

"I hope so. It's always nice to know what's going on outside."

CHAPTER 38

Sarah was glad fate had intervened for her to talk to Fern. Now she not only knew Lynn or Kait were his planned targets for the new building, but that probably, somewhere, there was a draft memorandum or were notes detailing Dr. Martin's determination of the fate of each culinary and hospitality faculty member.

From talking to Fern, Sarah felt even more certain there was a money trail for Chief Gerard to follow. For Grace's sake, Sarah needed to find Dr. Martin's recommendations, if they still existed, to clarify the trail for the chief. Consequently, she decided her first stop had to be Dr. Williams's office. In his acting capacity, he had to have access to all of Dr. Martin's papers. She hoped he was in.

His door was open, but Dr. Williams wasn't there. In fact, his office appeared to have been abandoned. The few folders that had been on his credenza were gone and the wastebasket, now empty, was sitting upside down on his desk. Sarah looked down the hall to see who else might be in their offices. A light on at the end of the hall in Dr. Martin's office caught her eye.

Sarah walked toward the light, glancing at the other offices on the way. The doors of most were closed. Some, like the one with Chef Bernardi's name, had office hours posted for Tuesday and Thursday. Nancy's office had a message taped to the door indicating she'd be back at four. The door to Dr. Martin's office was open. Although there was no one in it, she recognized Dr. Williams's black suit jacket hanging on the back of the chair behind the desk.

The desk and credenza were covered with stacks of folders. There was an open but empty drawer in one of the three filing cabinets in the office. Considering how much paper she could see, she doubted there was anything in the drawers. She glanced at her watch. It was only three-forty. Nancy wouldn't be back until four. Sarah had no idea when Dr. Williams would return.

She stared at the folders on the desk. Occasionally, she snooped through the papers on Harlan's desk when he wasn't there. Surely, if she didn't disrupt the order of Dr. Williams's folders and papers, there wouldn't be anything wrong with taking a quick peek. After all, time was of the essence to help Grace.

Slipping inside the office, she closed the door, except for a crack, so she could hear if someone was coming. Going behind the desk, she evaluated the folders. While the ones on the left seemed haphazardly stacked, she noticed the ones on the right were divided into more precise piles, as if they'd been reviewed and sorted.

She opened the folder on the top of the first pile. It was filled with vendor procurement forms. The file below it also related to requisitions. Taking a step back to get an overview of the piles, she noticed the third stack was hidden by the ones around it because, with only two folders, it was much shorter than the others.

Sarah picked up the top folder from the pile. It was thinner than almost any other file on the desk. Opening it, she saw only two sheets of paper. Skimming them quickly, she realized she'd hit pay dirt. One, marked *draft*, was the proposed tenure recommendation letter, while the other was a typed listing of the culinary and hospitality employees' names with annotated, handwritten notes.

Fearful Dr. Williams might come back before she finished reading them or that they'd be destroyed before she could share them with Harlan and Chief Gerard, Sarah whipped her phone out of her pocket. She snapped pictures of the two pages. Putting her phone back in her pocket, Sarah was about to read the rest of the first page when she heard a rustling sound outside the door. She slipped the sheets back into the folder, closed it, and returned the folder to its place on the desk.

As the door opened, Sarah grabbed a pen from the fancy desk set sitting in the middle of the desk.

"What do you think you're doing?" Nancy asked.

"Trying to leave Dr. Williams a note. You'd think with all these folders and pieces of paper he'd have a blank pad or sheet of paper on his desk."

Sarah held the pen up so Nancy could see it. "I was hoping to see both of you, but neither of you were in your offices. Because the sign on your door said you'd be back at four, I decided to wait. When I saw the door was open, but his jacket was here, I came in to leave him a message to call me about Southwind. Do you have a piece of paper I can use?"

Without another word, Nancy left.

Sarah hoped the combination of the heat in her cheeks and how she was sweating didn't give her away.

Nancy returned with a small white pad. She handed it to Sarah.

"Thank you." Sarah quickly scribbled a note, pulled the sheet from the pad, and, after returning the pen to the holder, laid the paper on the center stack of folders. She walked around the desk and handed the pad back to Nancy. "I'm Sarah Blair. We met briefly in the hall the day Dr. Martin was found in Grace's classroom. I was wondering if I could speak to you for a few minutes."

Nancy raised an eyebrow. "Let's go back to my office."

Sarah slowly followed Nancy out of the office—just delaying enough to grab the note and shove it into her pocket.

While Nancy seated herself behind her desk, Sarah remained in the doorway. Nancy pushed a stack of lined cards with writing that lay on her desk away from her and then sat back. She crossed her arms and stared intently at Sarah. "You do a wonderful coughing spell."

Laughing, Sarah instantly appreciated the sharp-tongued woman as much as she had when Nancy prevented Dr. Williams from taking the elevator off the culinary floor before the campus police arrived.

Uncrossing her arms, Nancy waved her hand at her guest chair. "Come on in and take a load off your feet. Rumor had it you might come a-visitin'."

From the phrasing of Nancy's words and the slightly different twang than most Wheatonites had, Sarah pegged her as a Texas transplant.

"I heard you were doing some investigating."

Sarah started to deny what Nancy said.

"Your reputation precedes you, but I think you're barking up the wrong tree coming to see me, because my answer is easy. I didn't have any kind of relationship with Dr. Martin."

"Excuse me?"

Nancy pushed back a strand of hair escaping from her gray ponytail. "Look, even though it hasn't been officially announced, Dr. Martin was hired to clean things up and create a merged culinary-hospitality department. Although Dr. Martin was still in the process of looking things over before he made wholesale changes, my office being next to his gave me the opportunity, without even trying, to hear and see a number of things."

This tied in with what Fern had said about Nancy, but, somehow, Sarah didn't agree Nancy was a busybody. Rather, Sarah pegged her as someone who, being in good physical proximity to business gossip, wasn't going to ignore it. Sarah knew if she was in the same position as Nancy, she wouldn't. "I gather his door was open a lot of the time?"

"Almost always. And if it wasn't, it meant Dr. Martin was mad about something and was either ranting into the telephone or shouting at someone in person." She smiled. "You can safely conclude I heard quite a bit."

It was obvious to Sarah she wasn't going to have to spend a lot of time sweet-talking Nancy to learn what she wanted. She leaned forward, placing a hand on Nancy's desk. "What kind of plans did Dr. Martin have for your department?"

"He wanted to enhance his new program by gutting the status quo."

"Gutting sounds like overkill. How could he do that?"

"By using the rules of academic life in a way none of us could fight."

"I don't know academia. Would you explain what you mean?"

Nancy held up the lined cards. "See these? I was preparing them for my students. Like me, there are a lot of people working here who care about the young people we teach. We don't make a fortune, especially when you consider how much time we put in. We're not showy, but at CJCC we can teach. We never have to worry about publish or perish or doing any of the things that translate into money for our schools."

"Isn't teaching what it's all about?"

"Not at most schools. Dr. Martin's plan was to build up more of a publish-or-perish type faculty. Consequently, he was going to make sure full-time and adjunct faculty who simply taught were gone by not giving them tenure or renewing their contracts. No tenure, no job. No contract, same result. You have to move on."

"But how could he get away with refusing tenure to everyone?"

"Oh, he wouldn't have. You can bet the one or two who kowtowed to him would still be around."

"Would Dr. Williams, who I understand is up for tenure, be one of those people?"

"I think so. Even though Dr. Martin couldn't stand him, he probably would have held his nose and signed the paperwork. Dr. Williams is an expert at groveling, and he's been around long enough he knows where the bodies are buried."

"Are there a lot of bodies?"

"A fair amount. But denying tenure wasn't the only way Dr. Martin planned to clear the ranks. He could force someone out by taking away responsibilities, like removing Dr. Williams from overseeing the hospitality program."

"But if he gave him tenure?"

"In a situation like that, Dr. Williams would either accept being tenured, but marginalized, or leave on his own accord. For adjuncts, like Chef Bernardi or me, no amount of groveling would ever have been enough. Although we keep the college's costs down by working for no benefits and a set amount of money per class we teach, Dr. Martin planned to get rid of us."

Sarah processed what Nancy was saying. "I thought you were a full-time faculty member."

"Most people do, because I've been here longer than almost anyone. My ex-husband is Wheaton High's football coach. When we moved here, our kids were young and I only wanted a part-time job, so I took an adjunct position. My marriage ended, from what I understand, in the same manner yours did."

"I'm sorry." Sarah wondered if the coach was now with the bimbo who'd broken up Nancy's marriage like Jane destroyed Sarah's.

"Don't be. I could have acted with the fury of a woman scorned, but, after our divorce, it was simply easier to take my pittance of alimony and child support and raise my kids working as an adjunct rather than looking for a full-time position. Although adjuncts rarely get moved into full-time roles, I hoped, with Dr. Martin's planned reorganization, I might beat the odds, since I usually teach four classes a term and have several other departmental responsibilities."

Nancy dropped the recipe cards on her desk and met Sarah's gaze. "Unfortunately, Dr. Martin didn't even want me around part-time. The Malevolent Monster got it in his head I was a busybody who disapproved of his behavior."

"That's horrible."

"No more than ignoring what I've accomplished for this program. Do you have any idea how many run-of-the-mill chefs who graduated from here have the ability to look like master chefs because of the knife skills I taught them?"

Sarah wrinkled her brow. "I thought Grace was the knife skills instructor."

Nancy threw her hands up in the air. "Grace's course is an introduction to knives. In that class, the finesse of the knife cut is incidental. I taught that until this term, but my advanced courses are the ones where students learn and perfect the hand skills necessary for each type of cut. I also instruct them on the various ways they can use their newly acquired skills to create signature dishes."

"I guess a chef can never have too many cuts in his or her repertoire."

"That's right. The ability to make beauty from a knife cut is what distinguishes master chefs from cooks. That's one of the reasons the culinary school, when it presents its annual awards, gives a special Knife Skills Award to a member of the graduating class. There is a plaque hung near the classrooms listing all the winners."

It was apparent Nancy had missed the low-level sarcasm in Sarah's remark. Rather than insult her by admitting she hadn't read the plaque, Sarah adopted Nancy's tone. "I saw it when I was up here the other day. It must take a lot to earn the award."

"It does. For people who know our program, like those in the Birmingham culinary world, winning the award carries a lot of weight. Throughout the years, our award winners, who opted to pursue culinary careers, all secured excellent positions. Unfortunately . . ."

"Unfortunately what?"

"Unfortunately for some, vices like gambling or drinking caused a few to squander their opportunities."

"I gather Chef Bernardi's loss of his pastry shop because of gambling is an example of what you're talking about?"

Once again, Nancy nodded. "And, it looks like he's blown the second chance here that Fern helped get him."

Sarah was perplexed. Chef Bernardi was still teaching, had office hours, and when he spoke at Jane's Place, offered his attending students extra credit. "But he's still working."

"For now. Dr. Martin put him on notice last week that his contract wasn't being renewed." Nancy met Sarah's gaze. "I heard him do it."

Sarah believed Nancy, but if what Nancy was saying was true, it seemed funny Dr. Martin, who didn't tolerate fools lightly, hadn't fired Chef Bernardi immediately. Maybe it had something to do with Chef Bernardi's contract or his connection to Jane's Place, but neither seemed like things that would have stopped Dr. Martin from acting swiftly. "I saw Chef Bernardi doesn't have office hours until tomorrow. Do you know how I can get in touch with him?"

"Check Jane's Place. I think he's living and working there. But that's not what you want to know, is it?"

Sarah didn't answer. Even though she tried not to change her expression, Nancy's amused reaction made her realize she'd probably screwed up her face at being caught.

"It's okay. You can ask me outright. Based upon our discussion, you want to know if this time being the scorned woman was enough for me to murder Dr. Martin? The answer is simple. I empathized with Lynn and hated Dr. Martin, but I didn't kill him. I can make a knife cut in the exact manner he was stabbed—so the blood drains down instead of spurting—but I lack the one thing necessary for me to be the murderer: the guts to do it."

Chapter 39

Sarah wasn't sure if the photos on her phone that were burning a hole in her pocket or Nancy's adamant denial of the ability to commit murder were the basis for the conflicting thoughts racing through her brain. Talking with Nancy had, if anything, added more for her to think about.

Personally, Sarah liked Nancy, but some of what she said simply didn't ring true. Remembering how Nancy stood up to Dr. Williams in the hall when he tried to sneak off before the campus police arrived and imagining what it took to survive four classes of students each term, Sarah questioned Nancy's assertion that she lacked the nerve to use a knife effectively against Dr. Martin in a fit of passion. After all, wasn't the saying something about "even hell hath no fury like a woman scorned."

Not wanting to check her phone from a location where

Nancy or a returning Dr. Williams could see what she was doing, but not wanting to wait any longer, either, Sarah walked to the classroom side of the hallway. She ducked into a classroom door alcove. It seemed like an eternity, rather than three days, since she'd done the same thing in order to call Harlan to come help Grace.

She opened her phone and brought up the pictures she'd taken. Nancy had been right. If the one marked *draft* was the recommendation Dr. Martin submitted, the present faculty would have been gutted. Although there were question marks next to some names on the list of people, Dr. Williams's name wasn't one of the ones included in the draft recommendation letter. The same notation next to Nancy and Chef Bernardi's names—*don't renew*—confirmed what Nancy had said.

Feeling she'd once again hit a dead end in her investigation because multiple suspects had the same motivation, Sarah put her phone in her pocket and stepped out of the doorway. She decided she needed a cup of coffee to try to figure things out. As she walked by the award plaque, Sarah stopped to examine it more closely.

On Friday, she'd been too far away to notice its crisscrossed knives. Moving closer, she read the *KNIFE-CUT ACHIEVEMENT AWARD* lettering above the knives and the various names engraved on little plates for each year the award had been given. Perhaps the killer had received the knife award? She began reading from the most current date of the award.

The last winner was Grace. Sarah was glad no one else was in the hall to hear her sharp intake of breath. She quickly scanned the other names. Only two others, who'd won the award in successive years, were familiar to her: Fern Runskill and Robert Bernardi. Seeing three of her possible suspects on the list confirmed the excellence of their knife skills but didn't provide her with any ammunition Harlan could use to convince Chief Gerard that Grace wasn't guilty. If anything, it might give Chief Gerard more of a reason to believe Grace was the murderer if he insisted on following his stupid blood trail.

Sarah pushed the elevator call button. Its slow arrival gave her more time to think about all the suspects. Each of them had some type of knife skills and some reason for hating Dr. Martin. While she could establish motivation for any of them to want to murder Dr. Martin, what was the reason or trigger to go off the deep end and actually kill him?

At this point, had an autopsy showed multiple stab wounds, Sarah might have concluded that everyone who was related by blood or marriage to Dr. Martin, worked at the college, or was employed at Jane's Place, joined together to do him in. Unfortunately, while that might be the solution in an Agatha Christie book, here there was only one stab wound, so only one killer.

There was no question Grace had Dr. Martin's blood on her, but many of the suspects were skilled enough to have placed the knife without causing a blood spatter. What distinguished them from each other? Who was telling the truth? Who was lying? Was Dr. Martin cheating on Lynn or did Lynn cheat on him? With whom? Maybe someone in the running club or a faculty member? And, did someone really try to hit Lynn with a car? Were professional worries or personal issues, like Chef Bernardi's gambling or Wanda's pent-up anger about Dr. Martin's treatment of her mother and Kait, the basis for his murder?

For every question Sarah raised, there seemed to be two conflicting answers. Thinking about whodunit wasn't going to help Grace. During the short time remaining before Grace turned herself in, Sarah needed to find out whodunit.

Nothing occurred to her during the elevator ride or her walk across the street to the Coffee Bar.

CHAPTER 40

After buying a white chocolate mocha, Sarah looked around for a place to sit. Every table was full. She scoured the room, trying to find someone she might invite herself to sit with.

Across the room, near an exposed brick wall, Sarah noticed Franklin sitting alone at a table for two. He seemed engrossed in a book.

Sarah walked over to where he sat. "Franklin, may I join you?"

He jerked his head up from his book. Sarah repeated her request.

"Of course." He closed his book and started to jump up to pull her chair out for her.

Sarah motioned him to stay put. As she sat, she read—upside down—the title of his book. It was a nonfiction book about a now-famous crime fighter. She pointed at it.

"Are you reading that book for pleasure or for one of your criminal justice classes?"

"Pleasure. Though what I'm reading now fits in perfectly with some of the things I'm studying this term."

"Like the knives course?"

"Oh, no. This chapter is the story of a Southern cop's first year on his beat in New York City. He ran into a lot of funny things, like people not understanding his accent. In one instance, in a Laundromat, he said *gone* and his partner mistook it for *gun*. You can imagine how people tried to take cover when his partner pulled his gun out."

It didn't seem like a book Sarah would put at the top of her to-be-read list, but she didn't want to insult Franklin. "Sounds like an interesting memoir."

"It is, especially because I graduate this year, and I'm hoping to be hired by a police force."

She pointed at the book. "In New York?"

"Oh, no. My roots are here. I'd like to work for Chief Gerard, but the Wheaton force is at full capacity. That's why I'll apply for a position in Birmingham and some of the nearby smaller cities."

"You don't have a desire to change schools and get a four-year degree first?"

He shook his head. "I might go back later, but right now I want to obtain some practical experience."

Considering how much she now valued the idea of getting a degree, Sarah was surprised at how adamant he seemed. She also was sure Eloise couldn't be pleased with his decision not to continue his education.

Sarah glanced around the Coffee Bar, looking for Wanda. She didn't see her. "Does Wanda agree with your plan?"

He frowned. "That's a touchy subject for us. She doesn't

mind me earning money interning with the campus police, but she thinks I should immediately pursue the other two years of my degree. Wanda is afraid if I don't get my degree now, I never will."

"It is a lot tougher and more intimidating to go back later." Sarah sipped her coffee. "Believe me, I know."

"But that's not what I want to do now."

There was a finality in his voice that made Sarah stop. The last thing she wanted to do was antagonize him. "Well, I hope Wanda and you can work through this. You seem perfect for each other." She feigned looking around again for Wanda. "I'm surprised not to see her here with you. From something your aunt Eloise said, I thought the two of you were inseparable."

The lines of his face relaxed. "She's helping Chef Bernardi over at Jane's Place."

Sarah drank more of her coffee, waiting to see if Franklin would say anything else. He didn't, but he also didn't open the book in front of him.

"Good," Sarah said. "That makes me feel like the world is normal again. Speaking of normal, how is Wanda doing with all of this hullabaloo?"

"She's still pretty upset. Not so much about Dr. Martin's death, but about what's going to happen to Kait now."

"Can't she stay at the retirement home?"

"Sure. She's got plenty of money, but Wanda is afraid someone's going to take advantage of her."

"How?"

"Well, Kait's always been a supporter of Carleton. Since she moved back to Wheaton, the college has regularly reached out to her to have lunch in the faculty dining room or to attend a lecture or concert. Wanda thought it was partially because of Dr. Martin, but now, with him gone, the college seems to have increased its outreach. Wanda's afraid someone will woo Kait to donate, above and beyond, a bequest she's left for the college."

"Kait has that much money?"

Franklin motioned for her to be a little quieter. As he looked around to see if anyone was listening, Sarah modulated her voice.

"Sorry, I didn't mean to shout that out. It just surprised me."

"It surprised Wanda too. People take the presence of students for granted and talk as if we're not there. Based upon things she saw and overheard during the past year, Wanda concluded Dr. Martin planned on getting his new building funded either by his wife or Kait. When his marriage went on the rocks, Wanda figured that, because he controlled Kait's money, he'd authorize the building's donation from Kait's account."

"That must have gotten Wanda upset."

His fingers curled around the corner of the book in front of him. "Of course it did. She felt it was bad enough he'd used up her mother's money, but now she thought he was violating her second mother. They had a big row about it last week."

Sarah could imagine some of the things Wanda might have said to Dr. Martin. She doubted Wanda had minced words. "At least, from what I understand, before his death, Dr. Martin never siphoned off Kait's money for his new building, so Wanda doesn't have to worry about that."

"True, but you know what's ironic?"

Sarah raised an eyebrow.

"Wanda's fears weren't put to rest with Dr. Martin's

death. Maybe it's because of the amount they know Kait's planned as a legacy gift, but, between holding the service and inviting her to an afternoon tea today, Wanda is afraid the college is going to press Kait for another donation."

There might be some basis to Wanda's fears. Considering Kait's son just died, it seemed odd to Sarah that anyone from the college would have invited Kait to anything this soon, but, then again, she'd been at Chef Bernardi's lecture. Maybe this tea already was scheduled and someone, thinking of Kait's short-term memory loss, didn't cancel it, thinking Kait wouldn't be that upset by today.

Still, if Wanda had known about this tea, why would she have obligated herself to work with Chef Bernardi at the same time? What if Franklin hadn't been free to bring Kait to campus? "Franklin, when were today's plans made?"

"Ms. Runskill called Wanda this morning. She said after seeing Kait upset last night, after the service, Dr. Williams and she thought Kait might enjoy getting out today. Because Wanda was busy with Chef Bernardi today, she asked me to bring Kait to campus for her to have afternoon tea with them."

He pointed to his phone, which lay on the table. "Ms. Runskill is supposed to call me when they're done. I came here to get some reading done."

Sarah took that as a signal it was time for her to leave him alone. She held up her now-empty cup. "Thanks for letting me join you. I need to be moving along. Say hi to Kait and Wanda for me."

"I will."

As Sarah started to leave the Coffee Bar, she saw Dr.

Williams standing in line to pay for coffee and a sandwich. She knew he looked like he enjoyed his meals, but something didn't add up if he'd just had afternoon tea, with its little sandwiches and scones. "Dr. Williams?"

He turned toward her. "Yes?"

"I'm Sarah Blair. We met—"

"I remember. You were the one who came upstairs Friday with that murderer, Grace."

Sarah wasn't going to get into it with him. What she needed to know was too important. "Dr. Williams, did you just have afternoon tea with Kait Martin and Fern Runskill?"

He waved the sandwich so she could see it clearly. "If I'd had tea with them, would I be buying a sandwich now?"

"Of course not." She tried to push down the feeling of anxiety overcoming her. "This is important. Did you see Kait and Fern today?"

Apparently preoccupied with moving up in the line and paying for his sandwich, he didn't answer. As he turned away from the cashier, Sarah repeated her question.

"Ms. Blair, I don't see why Kait or Fern should concern you."

"Please . . ."

Dr. Williams frowned in exasperation. "I've been trying to go through Dr. Martin's papers most of the day, but I did run into them coming out of the elevator on the culinary floor a few minutes ago. Now, if you'll excuse me."

As he began walking away, Sarah grabbed his sleeve. He jerked it away from her. "Ms. Blair!"

He shook his arm as if she was still holding it.

"I'm sorry, Dr. Williams. It's just that Fern's office is

on the second floor. Do you know what they were doing on your floor?"

Sarah leaned forward to hear his muttered answer. "Fern said something about the two of them using one of the prep kitchens to make a new signature dish she'd created just for Kait."

Chapter 41

Petrified at what she was thinking, Sarah wildly looked around the Coffee Bar for help.

Franklin was still reading. She hurried to his table. "Franklin, I need you to call the campus police. I think Kait may be in trouble in one of the culinary classrooms."

"What?" He started to move from the table.

Sarah stopped him from jumping up from the table. "Wait—I may be wrong, but please, before you do anything else, call them."

Leaving him dialing his phone, she ran out of the Coffee Bar, across the street, and up the stairs to the third floor. Fern and Kait weren't in the first classroom she came to, but she could hear voices coming from Grace's classroom. Without thinking, she opened the door and went in.

Kait was perched on a stool at the same prep table her son had died at. There was an array of knives and vegetables lying in front of her. Some of the vegetables were cut into the different styles and shapes Emily and Grace had shown her. Fern's hand was encircling Kait's. A small knife was in Kait's hand.

It took Sarah a moment to realize Fern was guiding the knife in Kait's hand toward Kait's other wrist. Although Kait squirmed, trying to free her hand or drop the knife, Fern overpowered her. As Fern slashed the knife across Kait's wrist, Sarah yelled, "Stop!"

Fern turned her head in Sarah's direction, relaxing her hold enough that Kait wrested her hand from Fern's grip. The knife clattered to the ground. Sarah and Fern both went after it. Fern won. Getting to her feet, she held the knife above Sarah.

"Stand up. And don't try anything."

Slowly, Sarah complied, but, partially ignoring Fern, she used her body to shield Kait, who sat cowered on her stool. Sarah glanced at Kait's wrist. There was a trickle of blood on it, but Sarah didn't think the cut looked deep.

Sarah felt the prick of the point of the knife in her back. She took a step forward. When the knife didn't seem to follow, Sarah turned around, keeping herself between Fern and Kait. "Fern, you don't want to do this."

"Do what? I was showing Kait different knife cuts when you jumped me, causing Kait to cut herself. Maybe you should tell me what's come over you?"

For a moment, Sarah thought she'd misunderstood the situation, but then she remembered how Fern had been firmly guiding the knife over Kait's wrist. "This isn't the way to get your window. You don't need Kait's bequest. Dr. Williams and you will find another donor."

The laugh that welled out of Fern's throat chilled Sarah. "Nobody wants to invest in a culinary building. I know. I tried hard to find a donor, but couldn't."

Sarah prayed Franklin had done what she asked. In the meantime, she had to keep Fern talking. "I thought using a knife effectively for various cuts separates cooks from master chefs."

"That's Nancy-speak. She thinks there's nothing more important to a chef than knife skills."

"Nancy told me the culinary program put a lot of emphasis on learning knife cuts—even to the point that there's an annual award recognizing a graduate for knife-cut excellence. I read on the plaque that you won it the year you graduated."

Fern tilted the knife, but kept it pointed at Sarah. "Another paper award for the wall. I guess Nancy forgot to mention she underwrites the plaque and its small monetary award. Dr. Martin told her she could continue sponsoring the award, but he wouldn't permit her to personally present it."

"Why?"

"Because she wouldn't be on staff. He wasn't renewing her contract."

"Ooh, that must have hurt."

"It did. That was the breaking straw in their relationship. From that point on, with her office right next to his, that busybody was always in his or his guests' business. She had a habit of popping out of her office at just the right moment to annoy him."

And, apparently you. Maybe spying was one of the reasons Nancy kept her door open. "You don't sound like a Nancy fan."

"That's an understatement. I don't know what she told you, but you can't trust anything she says. She leaves things out, like not mentioning she funds the knife award. And I bet she didn't tell you she's friends with Lynn. Consequently, she shares and encourages Lynn's delusions, like someone is out to get her. Why, I bet Nancy told you I was involved with Doug rather than confirming what everyone knows—Lynn was two-timing him."

Sarah caught Fern's slip in calling him Doug instead of Dr. Martin. Now, it was obvious to Sarah what Nancy had deduced from her constant monitoring of everyone coming and going tied in with her friendship with Lynn. "But Nancy was right, wasn't she? You were the one seeing Dr. Martin, weren't you?"

"Yes. That busybody seemed to know I was on the floor from the very first step I took in the hall."

Sarah bet Nancy recognized, just as she did, the clack of Fern's heels. "For some reason, I was under the mistaken impression from when you talked to Chief Gerard that you were rarely on the culinary floor."

"I never said that. I can't help what Chief Gerard or you inferred. I was honest about that day. I told him I was up there when Lynn showed up and I came back later because Nancy wanted to see me."

Sarah tried to remember the sequence of events she'd seen and heard on the day Dr. Martin was killed. Something didn't add up, but she wasn't sure what it was. "Was that when you overheard the argument between Grace and Dr. Martin?"

"Yes. That's why I hurried to Nancy's office. When I'd seen Dr. Martin earlier, with his wife, he was already on the warpath. Both times, I was glad to stay out of his way."

That was what didn't add up. Something had caused

Dr. Martin to leave Grace's classroom in the middle of his first tirade and then he'd come back again. Sarah tried moving, but Fern's brandishing of the knife in her direction stopped her.

Sarah's mind was whirling. Fern had to have been the reason Dr. Martin stepped out of the classroom, wasn't she? "Too bad finding out about your relationship deterred Lynn from making the donation. Tell me, who was madder, Dr. Martin or you?"

"What did you say?" Fern met Sarah's gaze.

Sarah felt as if her eyeballs might be scorched by the look Fern was giving her as the two faced each other. Sarah took a deep breath. "Whether Nancy told or Lynn found out you were the one having an affair with Dr. Martin and she nixed underwriting the building, I'm sure, from everything I've heard, Dr. Martin wouldn't have accepted the blame for losing Lynn's sponsorship. He probably would have put the fault on you and been nasty about it. And you, hurt at his words, might have responded out of passion."

Fern shifted her weight in place. It wasn't enough for Sarah to get by her. "Interesting; you do put odd facts together well. What else is going on in your mind, Sarah?"

"Nothing. Except that you're going to let Kait and me leave. Right now, you have the stain of one death on your hands, but it wasn't premeditated. Things won't go as easily for you if you kill one of us. We can stop this now, and I'm sure Harlan will help you."

"I think we've gone too far for that. Thanks to Kait, you're going to meet with an untimely culinary accident."

As upset as she was, Sarah found the idea of meeting

her maker in a kitchen ludicrous. "Nobody will ever believe that. They know I avoid kitchens. If anything happens to me in a kitchen, that will only raise everyone's suspicion of foul play. From what you've said, have I put together the way things happened?"

"Pretty much. When I was in Doug's office the first time, he told me Lynn had found out about us and there would be no building. Lynn arrived, so I left. I went down the hall and waited by the far classroom as they had a heated exchange. Once Lynn left, Doug marched into Grace's classroom. I waited, hoping to intercept him when he left so we could finish our discussion. Apparently, that's when Grace cut herself and some students were helping her while Doug yelled at everyone. Dr. Williams wandered down the hall, and I guess Doug caught sight of him, because he came out of the classroom and said something to him I couldn't hear before the two went into Dr. Williams's office."

"And you didn't leave then?"

"No. I stayed by the second classroom as everyone, except Grace, left the classroom. At that point, Doug left Dr. Williams's office, slamming the door behind him, and went back into Grace's classroom. When they started arguing, I moved closer to the elevators to hear better. Both were hot and then Grace stormed out and down the steps without noticing me."

"Dr. Martin was still alive?"

"Obviously. I went into the classroom. He picked up attacking me where he'd left off. I tried to comfort him by saying even though he'd lost Lynn's deep pocket, we'd find another way to fund the building but, at least now, we could make our relationship public. That's when he laughed and said we were done."

"Why?"

"Because even if he couldn't get a new building, he could control Jane and Jane's Place and make it a win for himself without any help from me. He swept the different cuts of cheese and knives from the table to the floor and compared me to them. Doug told me he'd had enough of my spiked hair and tongue. Then he picked up a white jacket, made a motion of wiping his hands of me on it, dropped it on the floor, and turned his back away from me."

"He pushed you over the edge, so you stabbed him?"

Fern spoke quickly, her words almost taking on a staccato sound. "Without thinking, I picked up the jacket and held it around the deboning knife. He wouldn't turn back to face me. Instead, he made another crack. I saw red and stabbed him in the neck. He was gone before he knew what hit him. I got scared and left."

"But you took the white jacket with you?"

"In case any of my DNA was on it, I rolled the jacket up, stuffed it into my tote bag, and took it with me. I figured I'd take it back to my office and later throw it in one of the college's big garbage cans."

Trying to take advantage of what she thought was a lapse in Fern's attention, Sarah kept talking. "But you ran into Nancy on your floor before you got to your office and she wanted you to come back upstairs?"

"Yes, I thought it was a perfect alibi. No one would suspect me when I was down the hall with a witness, to boot. I told her I needed to do something in my office for a moment and then would be right up. After she took the elevator up, I ran down the stairs, dumped the jacket in the trash can near the stairwell, and used the stairs to get back to the third floor. Unfortunately, that young eager-beaver campus policeman found the jacket before it could be taken away."

As the door behind Fern opened, a person shrieked and flew at Fern. Sarah ducked and used her body to envelop Kait. The campus police chief came through the doorway a step behind the flying Franklin.

Chapter 42

A few nights later, sitting on the carriage house's living room floor, Sarah nuzzled RahRah. Across the room, Mr. Rogers leaned over one of Sarah's overstuffed barrel chairs, explaining to Kait exactly how Fluffy preferred to be held. From Sarah's vantage point, she didn't think it mattered. Fluffy was in a state of ecstasy with the attention she was getting.

From the looks of it, everyone in the room was in the same state, except their mood was directly attributable to the tiramisu Emily and Grace had just served everyone. As people ate and paid Emily compliments, Grace joined Sarah on the floor. "Thank you. Without you, I might not be enjoying this moment."

"Don't be silly. I didn't do anything."

"Except ferreting out the real killer."

"Let's not go there. My mother and sister have been

giving me grief for putting myself in harm's way. If I hear 'you should have left it to the professionals' one more time, I don't know if I'll be able to contain myself."

"You didn't mention Harlan."

"That's because he came around to realizing the information people told me in answer to my questions was the only objective investigation going on. The problem was my deductive reasoning and *aha* moment came together at the wrong time." She shuddered.

"To my benefit." Grace pointed to Wanda and Franklin sitting near the fireplace, holding hands. "And, I think theirs too."

Sarah nodded. "I think he's going to make a great police officer. His instincts are spot-on, and he does a great job tackling."

"In some ways, the one I feel sorry for is Fern. What's going to happen to her now?"

"She did the crime and will have to do the time, but Harlan interceded and got her a good criminal lawyer. At least in terms of Dr. Martin, I think the murder charge will be reduced to reflect it was a crime of passion rather than premeditated murder. I'm betting that eventually she'll end up using some of her talents for the benefit of other inmates."

"I can see that. You know, Harlan's good people."

Sarah stroked RahRah under his chin. He responded with a purr.

"I know that, Grace. Not only did he help Fern, but he's also arranging, with her blessing, to be Kait's guardian as she continues on her journey."

"He could be more if—"

"No, he's my boss." Besides Sarah didn't know if it would work out, so she didn't want to say anything to anyone, even Grace, but she'd had a call a few hours ago asking if she'd like to claim her rain check for Little Italy with Glenn on Saturday night. The tingly feeling she'd again felt when she said *yes* was, she hoped, the beginning of something special.

"What are your plans, Grace? You're going to leave Southwind, aren't you?"

Grace nodded.

"Jane's Place?"

"No. I'm not sure there still is going to be a Jane's Place. The college hasn't taken either Jane or Southwind up on their respective proposals because Dr. Williams thinks he may have hooked a donor for a new building."

"But what does that mean for you?"

"I'm leaving for a dream come true. Dr. Williams made me an offer I can't turn down. He's still the interim, but he's making plans. He offered me an instructor position. The job comes with insurance."

"Have you told Emily and Marcus?"

"The minute the offer came in. Knowing how much teaching at my own college meant to me and the benefits I'd have, they urged me to accept the position. Of course, I offered to help them when they're in a pinch or at least provide them with a steady stream of well-trained culinary student interns. What about you?"

"Well, I'm not leaving my job, but I did sign up to take a night class."

"Going to major in criminal justice?"

"I don't think so, but I really don't know. It's kind of funny, even with everything Fern did trying to get her window, she set me on the right course. I'm going to follow her advice and concentrate on the basics. Hopefully, by the time I finish the core courses, I'll figure things out.

In the meantime, I've got a lot of things to juggle planning the two fundraisers for the animal shelter."

"Don't worry. Things have a way of falling into place."

"That's what I'm hoping."

Grace pointed at Sarah's mother and Mr. Rogers. "They're cute together."

"Oil and vinegar, but it seems to be working."

"The same can be said for your cat and dog. They shouldn't get along as well as they do."

"True, but I'm not going to tell them. I'm simply going to love them." With that, she snuggled closer to RahRah.

RECIPES:

Emily's Egg Salad

6 large hard-boiled eggs
4 tablespoons mayonnaise
1 teaspoon white vinegar
1 teaspoon yellow mustard
½ teaspoon salt
½ teaspoon finely grated Vidalia onion

Peel the eggs and place them in the food processor. Pulse a few times, stopping when the eggs are finely chopped. In a medium bowl, mix the other ingredients. Once they're mixed well, add the chopped eggs and mix until just combined. Can be garnished with a touch of paprika. Makes 3–4 servings.

Sal and Laurie's Tiramisu

3 egg yolks
7 tablespoons powdered sugar
2 tablespoons rum
Brew 4 cups strong coffee
500 gm mascarpone
2 packs ladyfingers
½ of a large container of Cool Whip
Cocoa for sprinkling as topping/garnish

Add 2 tablespoons of the sugar to the egg yolks and mix until the color of the mixture becomes whiteish. Add the mascarpone and mix for five minutes. Add the rum, remaining 5 tablespoons of powdered sugar, and the Cool Whip. Mix thoroughly.

Using the coffee completely cooled, dip the ladyfingers in the coffee quickly, without soaking them. Layer them in a dish and cover them with the above cream mixture.

Dip more ladyfingers into the coffee and layer them over the cream mixture. Apply another layer of cream. Sprinkle with cocoa and cool in the refrigerator.

Stained-Glass Jell-O

This can be made with up to four different colors of Jell-O or store brand gelatin.

4 small boxes (3 oz. each) or 2 large boxes (6 oz. each—if only using two flavors) of Jell-O or store brand gelatin.
1 (14 oz) can sweetened condensed milk (Don't use evaporated milk!)
2 envelopes unflavored gelatin
Water

Dissolve each small box of Jell-O in one cup boiling water (keep flavors separate). If only using two flavors, prepare the two flavors from the large boxes separately. Chill at least three hours, until firm. (Overnight works well.)

After chilling the flavors, cut them into small blocks. Carefully mix the small blocks or cubes of Jell-O in a 9-by-13-inch pan, using your hands to gently toss the colors.

In a separate bowl, measure ½ cup cold water. Sprinkle the 2 envelopes of unflavored gelatin on top. Let the gelatin thicken for a few minutes. Once thickened, add 1½ cups of boiling water. This will dissolve the gelatin. Add the can of condensed milk. Stir and allow to cool to room temperature.

Make sure the milk gelatin is cooled to room temperature and then pour it over the colored Jell-O cubes. NOTE: If the milk gelatin mixture isn't cooled enough, it will cause the colors to run.

Chill overnight. Cut into blocks and serve.

Visit us online at
KensingtonBooks.com
to read more from your favorite authors, see books by series, view reading group guides, and more.

Join us on social media
for sneak peeks, chances to win books and prize packs, and to share your thoughts with other readers.

facebook.com/kensingtonpublishing
twitter.com/kensingtonbooks

Tell us what you think!

To share your thoughts, submit a review, or sign up for our eNewsletters, please visit:
KensingtonBooks.com/TellUs.